BRAVE NEW WEIRD

THE BEST NEW WEIRD HORROR, VOLUME TWO

edited by
ALEX WOODROE

with
MATT BLAIRSTONE

Content warnings are available at the end of this book. Please consult this list for any particular subject matter you may be sensitive to.

SELECTED WORKS FROM TENEBROUS PRESS:

From the Belly
a novel by Emmett Nahil

Mouth
a novella by Joshua Hull

Lumberjack
a novella by Anthony Engebretson

Posthaste Manor
a novel by Jolie Toomajan & Carson Winter

The Black Lord
a novella by Colin Hinckley

Dehiscent
a novella by Ashley Deng

House of Rot
a novella by Danger Slater

Agony's Lodestone
a novella by Laura Keating

Soft Targets
a novella by Carson Winter

Crom Cruach
a novel-in-verse by Valkyrie Loughcrewe

Your Body is Not Your Body by Various
edited by Alex Woodroe w/Matt Blairstone

**More titles at
www.tenebrouspress.com**

TABLE OF CONTENTS

THE UNDERRATED ART OF GIVING A CRAP

Alex Woodroe, Editor-in-Chief,
Tenebrous Press

HERE'S HOPING, ten years from publication, you're reading this book and haven't a clue what I'm talking about when I say, it has been a monstrous year for art.

Making any art at all is a scream into the void; making weird, disturbing, unconventional art is using the void as a test audience for a stand-up routine on murder in an ancient French dialect. First, you've got to focus on amusing yourself. Then, you've got to have no fear of the void whatsoever. You've got to be ready to confess dark things about yourself. It's actually best if you don't speak any French.

But what's most impressive is that, during a year where machine-generation software—if I have to call that thing AI, you have to call my blender Gordon Ramsay—seemed to take over our collective consciousness, as well as many of our commissions, artists of every kind stood their ground and kept screaming. If anything, the added adversity just pissed them off straight into writing their most wild and raw material yet.

Even the void has to appreciate the triumph in that.

So what I've really learned to admire this year is the underrated art of giving a crap. Art is our way of mainlining human beings and their inner worlds. I wouldn't want to live in a world without their stories, and the one great barrier between us and that reality is people who give a sometimes inconvenient, usually embarrassing, emotional, likely exhausting, overwhelming crap. Writers who put themselves out there, often despite the fact that every part of their lives is screaming at them not to write. Publishers whose commitment to ethics, equity, creativity, and humanity, far overshadows their desire for profit and power. And readers who care about where their money and time is invested.

This book is celebrating some of those writers and publishers, and it's dedicated to everyone who made and enjoyed art this year. Every individual contributes to the ecosystem as a whole, and none of this would exist without every single one of you, whether you're an award-winner, hiding your doodles under the bed, or deciding to spend five minutes with a real human's story.

It's been a monstrous year for art. Thank you for giving a crap.

FRONT TOWARD ENEMY

Matt Blairstone, Publisher,
Tenebrous Press

THIS BOOK IS a weapon. It is a politically charged incendiary device.

It's not going to try and persuade you to vote for the puppet on the left or the puppet on the right. It's not going to ask you for money. (Its publisher, on the other hand, has a delightful and endlessly growing back catalogue they'd love you to take a look at!)

It's not going to decry you for being woke, or a snowflake, or accuse you of any form of Derangement Syndrome. Besides, have you looked around the world recently? We, every last one of us, suffer from some form of self-imposed Derangement Syndrome just to convince our feet to shuffle onward through the day.

Nevertheless, it is a political hand grenade. And congratulations to you: by reading it, you are complicit. You've just pulled the pin.

This book is a weapon against homogenization. Against stasis. Even as we strive to amplify more voices, welcome more perspectives, blaze new paths for those who have lived forever behind walls; even as we reach boiling point, those in power wrestle to keep the lid on. Far better, far safer, far more profitable to trot out the same old same old, they insist. This is how it's always been. This is how it will remain. This is what you want.

Bullshit.

There are twenty-three voices in this volume, and every one of them is a catalyst for something new in the realm of Horror, Sci-Fi, Fantasy; each of them a weapon of the Weird. Listen to them. Let them in.

If you allow them to, they will change you permanently. I promise it will be for the better.

LULLABY FOR THE UNSEEN

Nelly Geraldine Garcia-Rosas

1.

I DID NOT want to see a corpse. But I *did* want to.

So when mama said *Don't look* as we approached the crowd, I squeezed my eyes shut until I saw sparks.

Although I must have watched a little when my eyelids got tired. And it does not count if it is only a tiny glimpse, a sneak peek at the *how could this happen* and the *oh my lord and lady and all the saints*, a glance of the *but it was merely a child, only a monster would do something like this.*

2.

There is a house that sits in the corner of two busy streets. It has a dirty coat of smog, mold, spit and piss. The once off-white walls are peeling, showing the house's past lives when it was teal, bright yellow, maybe coppery orange. But barely anyone notices the house itself. People lean on its grimy walls not knowing—not wanting to know—someone lives there, perhaps no one does. This corner is used as an improvised bus stop because one day someone made the stop sign with their arm and the bus stopped and every other bus did too the next day and then the next, and they kept on stopping and people noticed. And when people notice something, things happen.

3.

Ariel. It is because of him that I have this scar.

He was my classmate. A very thin kid, shorter than me, with greasy black hair and sunken eyes that showed dark bags under them, maybe bruises, I do not know. He never cut his nails so the teachers reprimanded him constantly for that; until they grew tired, or stopped caring. He loved playing on the floor, I believe he did, because his school pants were soiled and had been patched several times.

4.

On the house that no one notices' east side corner, steel grille adorns frosted glass panes showing that there were art deco pretensions in the early stages of construction of this brutalist-by-force building. The windows abruptly turn medieval as they approach the house next door, merely resembling arrowslits. If there was an attentive enough passerby, they would spot only one thing, though, the tinted-glass inverted crosses on the other side of the house.

5.

When I opened my Spanish notebook, I was greeted by Ariel's handwriting: *u like looking at kreepy stuff, don't u? i'll show u something kool.*

I wanted to see, so I called mama and told her that I would be doing an assignment with my classmates after school, and that one of them would walk me home later in the afternoon.

6.

I'm telling you there are people in that house. I think they're people. Some say they're brujos. They keep duendes or some other small creature in that hideous place and charge fifty pesos to let you see them—or feel them—because the interior is pitch dark. Just before your eyes get used to the darkness, you hear tiny footsteps approaching and then something runs around and

*between your legs, scratching your skin, breathing warmly
against it.*

7.

Someone spread quicklime at the bus stop where the body had lain
before. A couple of praying candles already burned out left smoke
trails on the dirty wall.

Ariel said that the cool thing he wanted to show me was not on
the street, but in his house. Inside, it reeked of rotten fruit and
candle wax.

8.

A visitor who were to enter the house would notice that its door is
comprised of three layers. A filigree wrought iron frame delicately
covers ripple textured glass like in Spanish style buildings. But in
the interior, a metal plate is carelessly soldered to the doorframe
as a quick privacy measure or a way to not let light in.

9.

The dolls were carefully placed on an old sofa. Ariel said we could
not touch them, only look. There must have been two dozen, maybe
more. Unlike other dolls, their skin looked grey and wrinkly like
old leather, their clothes were soiled. They all had bright eyes and
long eyelashes, like the Christ child.

There are dolls that are not to be played with mama said one
time in church when I asked about the ivory boy that was inside a
bell jar.

10.

Similar to other local buildings, the house has an interior courtyard
where a tejocote tree grows. Unlike those colonial houses, this
space was not planned or intended, it came to be when a ceiling
collapsed after an earthquake and was never rebuilt. Some of the
rubble remains there because the inhabitants of the house refuse
to take it out.

11.

We played in the inner courtyard where there are stairs that do not go anywhere. From the top, I could see a small house made out of rubble. Ariel told me it was the dolls' house and I laughed because an ugly house was perfect for his ugly dolls. I said that, contrary to what he promised, they were not cool at all. He pushed me down the dilapidated stairs.

My eyebrow needed six stitches. Mama said I was lucky I did not lose an eye. She did not say anything about me lying to her, but I know she is disappointed in me. She will not let me play near Ariel's house anymore.

12.

Sleep, my little one.
The boy's inside the house.
And he is very tiny.
And he has broken bones.
Hushaby, my love.
The house is full of shadows.
And you seek praying candles.
And you hear praying songs.
Sleep, my little one.
The darkness is inside.
And you heard him approaching.
And you will feel his hands.
Hushaby, my love.
The boy has long, long nails.
And he walks in the shadows.
And he is very dead.

13.

A girl goes to that house alone, but no one notices her. No one sees her ringing the doorbell that sounds like a muffled buzzing coming from inside. Only she hears quick, small footsteps, like a child's. But no one comes to answer. She rings again, and again she hears the buzzing and the footsteps that sound like moving away this time. She waits, but no one answers. She knocks on the metallic doorframe with a coin, then puts her ear close just to hear the footsteps further away. Yet she feels someone on the other side of the door listening, waiting, breathing heavily. She knocks again and says she's one of Ariel's friends from school who came here to forgive him. To ask him to forgive her. She apologizes for being so insistent right now, but she feels bad for what happened, for what she said that day. But she now has an answer to his question: She does, she loves looking at things she should not.

I saw your dead body that day on the floor, Ariel. I want to see you again.

No one notices that she slips a sheet of paper under the door. Her tight handwriting in sparkling purple ink. She apologizes again, but she thinks she should go home and stop bothering. Yet she stays to hear the rustling of paper. And the breathing on the other side sounds stronger and the small footsteps come closer and a metallic click reverberates.

And the door opens.

IN THAT CRUMBLING HOME

Thomas Ha

OVE STORIES ARE for dumbasses, Daddy likes to say, especially when he's caught me reading, and he's about to shred whatever book is in my hands and make me cry over the pieces. He's known for a while now that I've been slipping out when he's breaking down bodies—past the edge of the swamp and over to the sunken library, where I'll usually pick up a copy of a teen novel or maybe some classic lit, anything that isn't too molded or ripped in the important parts. I honestly don't know what makes him angrier: the idea of his daughter spending her idle time with words, or the fact that, ever since the withering and rot in him started spreading to the hollows of his skull, he can't focus well enough to read anything for himself.

Still, there are good days when I don't have to shove my books under the floorboards or scurry around—easy afternoons when the sun's warming the house over and the big folks are asleep, and I'm supposed to be in the yard tending to the Bloodtree, but instead, I nestle up between the fleshy legroots and read for a good while. Maybe my little brother will come clambering around too, poking and begging for me to read a little something to him, so I'll do some of the good passages out loud, have a few chuckles over the descriptions and my funny voices, before things are cut short— usually because Daddy is thundering apart glass and wood somewhere in another one of his fits.

The Pilot in our basement is even in on it a little. He's known about my reading ever since he spotted one of the paperbacks peeking out from my pocket. Sometimes, when he's resting up after

Daddy's cut off another part of him, and I'm down there bringing him his usual tin of water, he asks me about whatever it is I've borrowed lately, like it's the only thing he really has to look forward to.

And, yeah, I'm not stupid. All the trespassers try something like this eventually. If it's not begging or bribing, they'll turn to charming. Probably because I'm the only girl they see, so they figure there's a chance that I'll soften with some sweet talk.

But this Pilot seems different somehow.

Sure, it could be that he's kind of handsome—lean and square-jawed like the men on the book covers, if you can get past the infections and the shivering and passing out from his wounds. But what I like is that he looks me in the eye and just talks whenever I go down there to visit. No questions about where his crew members are, nothing about what's going to happen to him or why we're hurting him. This one just makes gentle conversation while drinking what he can, before he eventually loses consciousness.

Once in a while, though, he'll start talking about other things, like where he came from. And when he does, I have to shoo my brother out and double-check that he isn't listening through the pipes, because the Pilot says some pretty outlandish things that I don't think can ever be repeated. He describes these other places outside the settlement, like they're not on fire or at war with us, the way we were told. And I can't tell if it's his injuries overtaking him or if he's a natural-born liar, but I'll admit, the cities and colonies he paints with those hazy words of his seem even better than the ones in those tattered books from the library.

And sometimes, I don't know, maybe I'm a little too interested in what he says. Because he starts to say other things: like how he can sense that I'm unhappy and how he knows maybe I feel trapped—that I'm stronger than I look and could be okay on my own, if I ever decide that that's what I want. He claims he's got a shuttle hidden away that still has fuel, and if I find a way to help him, we could both fly away and leave this place behind.

It sounds stupid when I think about it all together like that, but in the moment, when he looks at me and just talks that way, I really start to believe it might be possible, even if I know that it's nothing more than the stuff of daydreams.

During the cool evenings, when I'm climbing up the skin folds of the Bloodtree, and I'm shambling across one of the bigger shoulders to pluck some of the carcass fruit from the ends of the curling fingers, I find myself toying with the idea of other worlds more than I should. The Bloodtree listens patiently while I mutter to myself, probably because I'm the only person he'll listen to. And I'll lie in his bough for a minute, stroking some of his bending forearms and pondering other ways that things could be, before it's time to start supper.

But then, one night, my little brother says something that makes me realize that I haven't been doing a good job of keeping him from the Pilot after all.

He says, "Where do all the trespassers keep coming from, though?"

And Daddy stops eating his bowl of roasted carcass fruit and looks dead-eyed like my brother just pulled down his pants and took a shit in the middle of the meal.

I try to squeeze the kid's hand under the table, but either he doesn't feel it or he's angling to make a point, because he just keeps going.

"If it's all fighting and terror outside the swamps—these guys, why do they keep showing up well-fed, with the tech they have? Shouldn't they be more . . . you know, like us?"

Daddy wipes the dribble and blood from his throat and puts the fractured gourd of the carcass fruit down. "Like us, what?"

"Don't know." Little brother's face gets hot and he starts to stutter. "Just . . . more like us . . . "

And now there's some shifting along Daddy's shoulder blades, beneath his shirt, and that's always the big sign that things are going the wrong way.

"Come on. He doesn't mean anything." I do my best to jump in, but Daddy gives me the look that gets me to shrink in my chair: the *better shut your mouth unless you want this to be worse for him* look.

"So you think you know then, huh? Figured out what's beyond the swamps and stars?"

My brother trembles, realizing that Daddy's taking the questions the worst way he can. But, to his credit, the kid doesn't look away, just raises that pudgy little face of his, even though now it's spilling with tears.

"Well, if you're a big boy who understands how things are, then you must be big enough to handle this too. Don't you think?"

Daddy pushes his dinner bowl over and pokes my brother in the chest. He knows, of course, that the seeping carcass meat is too rich for someone that young, that the kid should be on canned goods for at least a few more years before trying anything from the Bloodtree, but this is the kind of thing Daddy does when he wants to make it clear who's boss—his favorite thing to do to me, too, before I got old enough to stomach the iron and bile.

The kid knows as well as I do where this is headed, and that the sooner he goes along, the sooner it's all going to be over with. So he bites into a wet chunk of red pouch just under the hair, the area that I taught him is a little easier going down. He tries, really tries, to keep from retching as he swallows, but after a minute or so, it all comes up again, over his clothes and across the table like a steaming, crimson stew, and Daddy claps and gets real up in his face.

"Ungrateful little shits," he cackles. "Now that's what I fucking thought. I mean, the things we do. God, if you only *knew* all the things we do for *you*. Idiots. Spoiled. Just ungrateful little shits."

"You said that already," I mutter and expect Daddy to do his usual—throw something in my direction, or at least reach over and smack me for good measure. But he must be getting used to my prickly attitude, because instead of wasting his energy, Daddy just points at the biggest bowl on the table for the feeding.

This here is my version of the carcass fruit punishment, the one he knows will get to me more than anything else. Daddy waits until I take the fruit out of the dining room and make my way down the hall and over to the family room. Once there, I carefully undo each of the weighty bolts and locks. No one so much as breathes, even all the way from the other side of the house, when I enter the darkness.

And I don't know exactly when I make the decision. Maybe it's at some point then, when I'm bent with my forehead on the ground, shaking because I can feel Kun-Mother moving toward the bowl, and I'm praying she doesn't get distracted and start picking at me instead. Or maybe it's when she's done sucking and chewing and she's dragging that dripping body of hers up to the ceiling, and I crawl out and redo the locks and get to the table—where Daddy's giving me that fucking grin of his before he shoves my brother's face back into the carcass fruit. Or maybe it's when I understand that this is just the start of more shit they're going to give the boy, again and again, until they break him, kill him, or worse, make him the way they are.

But I finally realize that the family won't go on like this anymore.

Because I won't fucking let it.

****

Now, I'd be lying if I said I hadn't thought of ways out of this place—that I hadn't gone at least a half-mile beyond our property line to the old town center, that point where there are things stalking and breeding in the crumbling buildings. Places where I'd sit for a good while and think about heading beyond the Burning Ridge, imagining my little brother alongside me and a whole new way of doing things, just the two of us.

Somehow, no matter how angry I might get at something awful Daddy's done, or how terrifying it is when Kun-Mother escapes the family room, I always seem to find myself hustling back, because I'm scared to look too long at what else is out there.

But the things you imagine yourself doing can change an awful lot with time, especially when you have someone in your basement who swears he has a working flightcraft and the will to take you with him.

So I do my best to be gentle when I go down there into the dark. And the Pilot, well, he looks up and kind of smiles slowly as I wake him, like he's happy to see me, which makes me really hope that he hears me apologize before I slide a needle into the soft part of his throat. Based on the screams he lets loose, though, that doesn't seem to be the case.

I'll admit that there's a fifty-fifty chance that I shot him up with the wrong stuff.

I was in a hurry when I grabbed the vial from the old lab, trying to recall whether it was the red or blue serum I needed, all while keeping one ear out for the sound of Daddy grinding up limbs for fertilizer out back. Before Kun-Mother lost her words and Daddy lost his mind, back when they were doctors who tried to help strangers who came our way instead of what they do now, I

10

remember them using these vials to stabilize even the worst off of folks.

Kind of like glue-juice, my father used to say, when he was still playing with me in there during his breaks, talking about introns and exons and therapies the two of them were working on at the time.

Well, I can only hope that I made the right choice with the blue vial as I sit there, stuffing my fist in the Pilot's mouth to blunt the sound of him crying and flopping around over the next few minutes. After the spit and sweat settles, he looks down at the lump that used to be his forearm and his right foot, parts that had been carved by Daddy down to the bone, and he can already see some rippling under the flesh. He asks what I did, and I just say it'll help him move without falling apart from the shock.

Then I look him in the eye and ask him if he meant what he said all those times, about that shuttle, and the fuel, and the getting the hell out.

And he nods and looks back at me, touching my hand softly.

"Yes. Absolutely. God. You and me. Yes," he whispers.

It kind of reminds me of the books the Pilot and I always talk about—the moment when the characters share hushed promises, secret plans to run off from all the bad things keeping them apart. Except there's a lot more murder likely to happen if we don't hurry, so I tell him we've really got to get moving.

By the time I've gotten the Pilot's chains off and helped him up the steps, we come to my little brother, who's waving at us from down the hall. The boy's face is so chalk-white that I think he's going to say Daddy's headed our way. Instead, he points to his ear, and the three of us huddle for a bit until I hear it.

There's a screeching hum, almost like it's building into a melody, but then it devolves into raspy laughter.

"What . . . is that?" the Pilot whispers, looking back and forth at the two of us.

Fucking Janice.

Fuck.

My brother and I share a glance while we think this through.

Janice has a tendency to stick her nose in things whenever she's least wanted, like some goddamn sixth sense for when she'll fuck things up the most. If she's not digging up holes in the yard or breaking windows, she's making so much goddamn noise that no one in the house can sleep. Daddy's almost killed her a few times in the summers, when she messes around with our garbage, but he always goes easy on her at the last minute.

I figure it's because while some folks like Daddy and Kun-Mother put their bodies through changes by choice—edited their genes the way they thought they needed to when the Nine Moon War first broke out—there were other folks, like our neighbor Janice, who didn't have a say in whether they got altered. Gene missiles and viral bombshells don't exactly ask for permission when they fuck with your blood, I hear.

I almost feel a little bad for her on occasion, until I remember that she can tear my limbs off with barely a tug, and that she's also, you know, just generally so goddamn annoying.

But Janice or no Janice, we need to get out of here tonight, because I don't think the Pilot will last with Daddy much longer. So I ask my brother if he brought what I requested, and he opens up his backpack to let me fish the handgun from inside it.

"Where'd you get that?" The Pilot studies the shape of the weapon. "That's . . . that's I.C. issue."

I suppose if there were more time, I could tell him about the stockpile Daddy keeps out in the greenhouse, the ones he's harvested from the bodies and vehicles of trespassers over the years. How, early on, he'd break the weapons down and unload the ammunition, but as his hands started to seize up and his patience shriveled, he took to dumping them all in a heap, so that they'd sit and sweat in that muggy box of glass and vines. I could tell him some stories about how it's gotten so disordered out there that the butterflymen living in the brush beyond our lot occasionally try to swipe something when they think Daddy isn't around, but usually end up blowing themselves to hell when they grab one that's leaking or that's cracked in the barrel. But somehow, even if we had a breather to shoot the shit that way, I don't think the Pilot would be overjoyed to hear how many of his Intrasystem Consortium people died in the making of that godawful collection to begin with.

My little brother, at least, was careful in picking this handgun, I can see—not too degraded and still fully loaded, which will be useful when we make our move from the house.

I tell him he did well, and he gives me one of those big ear-to-ear grins of his, just briefly. I know the boy's scared not so deep down, that he's starting to doubt. But we've talked about this—how things just aren't safe in this house anymore with the way our folks are headed, how if we ever see a chance to go, we have to take it.

"We got this, okay?" I squeeze his small hand.

"Yeah. Okay."

This isn't the first time I've come up with a fix in the moment and acted like it was part of something prepared. If it's one thing I've learned as an unofficial parent in this shithole, it's that it can sometimes be the only way to get through things. The particular plan I cobble together for Janice actually comes from Daddy, of all people, or at least a version of him from before.

I think back on a crisp evening when I'd found Daddy in the yard, blood dripping down his cheek. He was wrestling with some arm that he'd torn from the Bloodtree, and its fingers were still grabbing at him when he cracked the bones apart.

You fucking dare? Daddy shouted over and over as he stomped on the arm. This was when Mom was already far gone, with only the thing called Kun-Mother remaining, and before Daddy began having those violent fits of his regularly.

But that evening, when he spun around, his eyes burning on me like he didn't even know my face, I remember this being one of the first moments I thought he'd actually kill me, even if just by mistake.

But he huffed and wiped his face and looked away.

Fucking Bloodtree doesn't recognize me. Defective piece of shit, he said. The corners of his mouth spasmed, and I saw the muscles in his shoulders rise, which made me pull away. But it passed, and Daddy took a breath. *You'll be dealing with that fucker from now on. Understand?*

I nodded.

Good.

He obviously couldn't have known it then, but making me the Bloodtree's caretaker all those years ago might have been one of the few good things he did for us.

I tell my little brother and the Pilot that we're going to move. There's a lull in Janice's yowling, and the padding in her footsteps sound like they're headed toward a different part of the roof.

"Go," I whisper, and the three of us emerge from the side door—my little brother bouncing ahead, while I half-carry the Pilot as he limps on me.

The Bloodtree swells in the dim starlight as patches of clouds pass over us, and the Pilot tightens up the second he gets a good look at the bulging tangle of limbs and skin and hair.

"Jesus Christ," he gasps, and I know he must recognize the tree for what it really is, a sentient protein combine-generator—the kind other colonies might use to manufacture vats of synthetic meat for local populations. But this particular generator that our family's repurposed isn't anything like the ones he's ever encountered—not with all of the things we've been feeding into it since the war. And I'm not about to try to coddle or reassure him about any part of it, because I know it's exactly as bad as it probably seems.

"Just stay close and keep on," I mutter. "The Bloodtree has to believe we're together for this to work."

We don't have long to linger or discuss, because there's a rasp somewhere that carries across the air. My little brother reaches the trunk first, and the Pilot and I are almost there too when I start to hear the shrieking and thudding start up behind us.

"Come on!" I'm practically hauling the Pilot with me.

The approaching footsteps turn to a gallop, and the gallop grows to a pounding that I can almost feel at our backs. We barely get past the legroots before I risk taking a look, and I glimpse Janice running on all fours, her hairy body, covered in nested tumors, reaching almost halfway across the lawn. I also catch sight of her old face, half-buried under the misshapen snout of hers that does all of the eating, and the human part of her is weeping, it looks like—maybe because of pain, or her inability to control her emotions, I'm not sure—but I don't let myself feel anything about it in the moment.

I learned, living with Daddy and Kun-Mother, that just because some monsters used to be innocent, doesn't make them any less dangerous in the here and now.

Luckily, in this particular here and now, the Bloodtree wakes. One of the larger armbranches grips Janice below the neck before she can swipe, and her hands pass through the air right by the Pilot's head. There's a spurt of fluid out of her side when the

Bloodtree squeezes, along with a few noisy cracks, which I'm pretty sure are her ribs busting. And she shrieks, even louder and more awful than her usual screams, as she gets thrown forcefully away from us, like a pebble skipping across the patches of soil and grass.

We watch, shivering, while that hunched, engorged body of hers tries to drag itself upright on quivering legs, and after a moment, she slinks painfully into the shadows, behind the house.

Then all's quiet for a minute while we catch our breath.

It's possible that those wounds will end her, but she's survived a lot worse. And at this point, it's not so much Janice that I'm thinking about, as the ones who could've heard all her wailing.

My little brother and I are just waiting, looking out at the house.

No lights, no movement.

"Come on," I hiss and wave toward the gate. We just have to make it to the old truck parked by the biting weeds, the one my brother and I keep fueled and ready for a run like this. But the kid is trailing, still huffing and scrambling over by the tree when I look for him.

And then I see it.

Daddy's standing still on the porch, looking at us.

It's hard to believe that there were times when the sight of Daddy out at the front of the house was a good thing. Back when the clouds were roiling fire, and I.C. men and their ships were dropping down from the sky, I'd look up and see Daddy there, and he'd tell me to take my baby brother into the basement and keep him from crying. I vaguely remember him injecting something into his throat, and if Mom were there, she'd maybe get something too. And the last thing I'd see was them holding each other before I'd run into the house, while everything outside those groaning walls rattled and boomed in the distance.

But Daddy doesn't stand that way anymore, and the vacant expression below his brow and the shifting in his shoulders means that only bad things are going to come.

The Pilot gurgles with panic, and he looks at me quaky and wide-eyed.

"We've got to go! The kid's not going to make it to the truck," the Pilot cries, and he clutches my neck with his good arm. "You and me. Now or never. It's time."

I'm only half-registering what he's telling me, though, because I'm watching my brother's pudgy face as he falls over the legroots and rolls over on his back, reaching out to me with those small hands of his while Daddy's stepping off the porch, that body getting bigger as he paces across the lawn.

Then I take another look at that sweaty, shivering Pilot clinging to me like a sick little animal, and he whispers again, "You and me. We'll get out of here, just like we talked about. Come on. We've got to go."

"You and me?" I repeat absently.

And it dawns on me, why the Pilot's saying these odd and desperate things. He has a very different idea of what this is. He thinks he's got me swept up in a love story, like the ones we talked about all those times in the basement. He believes that he's the one I care about, and that I'm doing this because he's the one I want to save from this fucked-up place.

But he's not, and never has been, the one I want to save.

So it really isn't much of a choice, when I let the Pilot drop to the ground. And I can tell my brother's doing that thing of his, where he's trying not to cry but the tears are spilling, when he sees me running toward him. I scoop up the kid in my arms and squeeze him real tight as Daddy starts coming, and I shut my eyes for what I know is about to happen.

But the only thing I feel, strangely, is air, as Daddy moves beyond us and through the front gate.

There's a *crack-crack-cracking* of shots, which gets me to reach for my waistband and realize that the Pilot snatched the I.C. handgun off me at some point. Not that it'll do him any good.

Daddy's swollen back muscles are gushing where the skin's separated. His other legs—the segmented ones that look like the limbs on the cow-spiders out in the fens—are blossoming out of him, just bending and seeping viscous mucus as they drag along the ground.

The Pilot, meanwhile, is yelling and firing from his sprawled position in the dirt, but he's got to see how useless it all is, the way Daddy's body just eats the bullets. And I'm really not sure the last thought that goes through that man's mind as he sees Daddy stand over him—especially since I never had a clear idea what the Pilot was thinking to begin with—but I know he's crying out for something or someone when Daddy's other legs sink into his chest and separate him, like a soap bubble, popping and raining liquid onto the ground.

After that, the noise around us softens to nothing but the rustle of wind brushing through the nearby fingerstems.

It's then that I expect—well, I guess I don't know what I expect—but I assume Daddy'll start in on us next.

But for some reason Daddy's waiting there in one spot, dark and dripping and covered in Pilot, almost like he doesn't know what'll happen either, now that we're all out here, and we all know what it was my brother and I were trying to do.

I get to my feet, push the kid on behind me, and hold up my hand.

"Just . . . just let us be," is all I manage to say. I mean for it to be a command, something fierce like I'd yell at a scavenger-hound to get some space, but when the words come, they're more like a whimper.

And as I move with my brother to the truck in the weeds, we edge past Daddy and see those eyeballs of his, wide as I think they'll go, while viscera and pulp just slough off his cheeks.

"Fucking morons," he murmurs.

It figures that the first thing he finally says after all this is something shitty.

"Both of you." His voice actually isn't much louder than what I managed. "Really think you understand. Idiots. Stupid pieces of shit. You'll fucking suffer, you know. Out there, you'll just suffer."

He watches as I keep on shuffling with the kid and paw at the truck, which is when we hear it, far off at the house but unmistakable—the splintering of wood and clatter of hinges and locks peeling off the family room door and clanging to the ground. Kun-Mother's good and riled up from all the gunshots and the screams, just pushing her way out after all that excitement. We can see a flicker of shadows in the windows as her worm flesh shudders, overflowing and rumbling through one of the hallways.

"Could be that out there, we'll suffer, could be. I don't know," I tell our Daddy. "But sooner. Later. In here, we'll die."

And somehow, I can just tell from the way he stares, the way he's stuck, that Daddy can't actually bring himself to stop us, no matter what he says. And it's not because he's good, or because he cares, or because he's anything close to decent.

It's because he's too much of a fucking coward: with Kun-Mother, with himself, and finally, now, with me.

So I forget him, and I push my little brother into the truck's cab and pile in after, just as we hear Kun-Mother's body thumping toward the front of the house. That part of her that used to be a face that I can't even picture anymore, the part that's just a toothy gash going down an open throat, mashes itself against one of the bigger panes.

But it doesn't matter, because I turn the engine over, and when the junker sputters to life, I gun it, hard as I fucking can, a hiss of dirt flowing out behind us as we start to take off from everything rattling in the reflection of the side view: the shitty, ramshackle house, cloaked in the moving curtains of our dust trails; the writhing layers of Kun-Mother, bashing against the walls and bellowing out into the darkness; Daddy, not much more than a sagging little shape, getting smaller and smaller.

And the Bloodtree.

That mass of skin and muscle that curves over the yard, the bits and pieces of so many hours I spent there, even though I wanted to be anywhere else—the one sight that gives me a little pang as we turn off from the end of our property and start accelerating past the other abandoned lots, the moment I know that we aren't ever going back.

My brother turns to me, that pudgy little face awash with disbelief, and I reach over and hug him and kiss the top of his forehead. And the two of us, we just fucking start to laugh. We laugh so hard from our bellies, and then we yell and curse and get so fucking worked up from all the pumping our hearts are doing.

And neither of us stops grinning the whole goddamn night as we head through the old service roads, talking about what we're planning and how we'll finally go about things, and I swear I feel like I could keep driving for hours, just on and on, the two of us together, just riding away like that.

✱✱✱

But those kinds of drives have to come to an end, of course, and ours does just as the sun starts to creep up, when we make it to the sundered overpass, the place where the Pilot told me he'd hidden his shuttle during all those basement chats.

In That Crumbling Home

The books don't usually get into this, I realize—how, after the characters make their big move and set off for a new life, there's still so much work to be done.

For us, there's a lot of digging around in the mud at the base of the shuttle, looking for the manual override for the cargo door. Once we find it and get inside the craft, there's a nice minute where we look at it: all of that chilled metal and clean, un-melted plastic, that I know we can secure into a pretty good shelter, make it special and safe, if we do it right.

Operating the ship's interfaces doesn't come easily, at first. But my brother, clever little bastard that he is, finds a book in one of the lockers. There are some personal entries and a mission log, but there's also a slip of paper with passcodes, and that changes everything for us.

The codes get the solar panels running, which give the ship bursts of power when the Burning Ridge isn't overcast with black fog. They also grant us access to the pantry, which still has a mess of dehydrated food stores, enough to last a full crew for years. And, sure, the packets aren't the most appetizing at first, but anything's doable after you've been stuck forever with the bloody taste of carcass fruit.

I realize this means we can stay in the ship for days on end, if we like, so that the only time I need to make a run outside is to get something from the sunken library, maybe grab us a couple novels so I can lay out on the deck with the kid, reading in those funny voices to fill some of the silence. But I also start taking other things while I'm out there too, some textbooks on basic piloting, telemetry, and the like. I mean, the shuttle's systems are so heavily automated, that I think it's only a matter of time before we figure out how to get off the ground.

It all starts to come together, almost like I imagined.

But, sometimes, when the kid thinks I'm busy with the consoles, or too deep in my reading to pay attention, I catch the little man crying in some other corner of the ship. He looks up at me all tear-spattered and blinky, and he says he's not sure why he's so sad about everything we left.

When that happens, I hug him and sing to him, until he's finally able to let go of the shakiness inside him, but part of me, a tiny part, knows what he means.

Because the strangest thing about holing up in this new place, I've found, is that even though I know that the old house was horrible and fucked, there are still bits about it that I miss.

Like, sometimes, when I'm looking out the viewing platform on quieter days, I find myself imagining that I'm resting on folds of skin, arms cradling around me as a breeze passes through hundreds of curling fingers, and I wonder a little if the tree misses me, if what he thinks of me will change when fragments of the Pilot are flowing inside him, as he grows fingernails, hair, and bone for the new season.

And most evenings, when the sun's lingering over the cragged cityscape and I shut my eyes, I catch myself listening for the groaning of the walls of that old house, or the shifting boards under Daddy's lumbering feet, or even the clacking of the locks outside the family room.

I keep imagining that I'm all the way back there, somehow, in that crumbling home.

And, against all reason or sense, when I'm not careful—some small and stupid and fucked-up part of me—it almost lets me forget all the terrible things that ever made me want to leave.

THE LIBRARY VIRUS

Hussani Abdulrahim

1. Genesis

WHEN DANLADI BEGAN to behave wildly, we bound his hands and feet and carried him to Baba who knew how to deal with the possessed. Baba made a potion from the brew of certain leaves, roots, and barks of plants that he alone knew of. He forced the potion down Danladi's throat. We waited for it to manifest. We were expecting Danladi to throw up a couple of squiggly roaches, a live snake, or a black kitten with red eyes. But it was none of those. As soon as he drank the potion, Danladi began to vomit books. Yes, books, with their covers intact. His throat and jaws would expand when a book made its journey upwards from whatever bottomless vault he had inside his stomach. With each book that appeared, Danladi struggled and cried. The books were many and bulky. We were astounded. This was not some kind of spirit possession, we argued amongst ourselves. And as we moved books about to create room for more, we tried to keep our fears locked up.

2. Fear

The news of Danladi's strange affliction spread all over the school and out into the quiet town of Tudun Makari like an angry wind blowing from the Sahara. A group that called itself "The Voice of Tudun Makari," populated by elders of our town who were mostly conservative in disposition, swung into action. They called for the closure of our school, Dangana Memorial Community School. They pressured the school authorities to send us home to our families, arguing that Western education would do us no good. The Voice of Tudun Makari said, "You see? You see what we have been saying? Books are now driving our children to the brink of madness. When we talked about how building a school was a bad decision, they said we hate civilization and don't want our land to progress. Do you see what is happening now?"

The management of our school said it was a bad idea to send us home since they did not know the nature of the ailment and whether it was contagious or not. Therefore, it would be foolish to let us go and put the whole of Tudun Makari at risk of a deadly disease. The Voice of Tudun Makari grumbled but was subdued.

We did not want to go back home either. We did not want to be stuck with our fathers, embarking on endless trips to faraway farmlands that one would reach by noon only if one had set out as early as the first cockcrow or immediately after the dawn's prayer. We did not want to live our days wandering on millet and rice fields, tilling the soil and nursing bent backs and aching joints.

We did not want to accompany our mothers to the markets and sit in stalls, in the midst of shelved dried fish, baskets of tomatoes, bales of vegetables, and armies of fat flies, contending with annoying customers who would haggle prices to death, while our mothers gossiped with other market women about whose husband was taking a new bride, or who had bought the latest Ankara, or how they planned on making a grand entry at the next wedding ceremony in Tudun Makari.

Our lives outside Dangana Memorial Community School were bleak, to say the least. If we were lucky, we would grow up to become adults, marry or be married off to someone we barely knew, live in the kind of houses our parents lived in, eat the same food we had eaten from day one, give birth to children who would be as miserable as we were, die and be buried on the same familiar soil. Who would want to endure such misery? What about all the dreams and adventures we desired?

We did not mind the shit we had to pound down clogged pipes in the old, stinky toilets at Dangana Memorial Community School. We did not mind the abuse and bullying from our seniors. We did not mind the number of times we would wake up and wish we weren't here or wish evil on our seniors, teachers, and whoever was making life difficult for us in Dangana Memorial. Yet, we still loved it here. We were free, able to express ourselves and be at our mischievous best. Why would we want to sell this freedom so cheaply and because of a disease that might not be contagious? We were not certain about that, though we were not new to strange happenings. For all we knew, Danladi might be suffering from a malevolent spirit attack that Baba would solve once he finished removing all the books that were inside his body.

But then, something happened to change our stance. Two more people fell and began to convulse just like Danladi. Baba restrained them, administered the same potion he had given to Danladi, and they too soon began to vomit books. Nothing spread faster than our fears, not even this affliction that we quickly named *The Library Virus,* for it was confirmed that these two new victims had also been in the library on that day Danladi's attacks began.

The Voice of Tudun Makari resumed their clamor for the school's closure. But they had no authority to make it happen. All they could do was make as much noise as possible, which they were good at.

The school management decided to quarantine whomever they felt was a danger or was at risk of the disease. The easy part was getting the library staff into isolation. The Chief Librarian and other library staff were kept in a special lodge. Their temperatures and other vitals were monitored from time to time. The hard part was gathering the students who had made use of the library on the day the disease manifested.

Our teachers and dormitory governors came to round us up. They wanted to fish out those who were in the library when Danladi, like the other two, fell and began to jerk like someone experiencing an epileptic bout. They asked. They begged. They threatened. We pointed fingers at our mates who had offended us in one way or another. We called the names of seniors who had been cruel to us and made our lives miserable. The teachers ended up with a handful of students who were in tears, swearing that they did not even know where the library was, not to speak of how it looked. Despite their pleas, they were marched off. We did not know what would become of them, but we were sure that the management knew they could not trust us.

3. Dossier

What did we know about Danladi? He was not exceptionally talented. He was never top of his class, but he was always somewhere in the top half. He was not a popular figure either. He did not have the sort of build or handsomeness that would have elevated his social status, especially among the girls. And to make matters worse, he had tribal marks. We were in a fast-changing world; no one wanted tribal marks or desired to be closely associated with someone who had them.

Danladi's parents were not rich, and neither were they poor. His father, like many, had farmlands where he grew cocoyam, millet, and onions. His mother sold petty goods in Tudun Makari's main market. There wasn't anything worthy of note about Danladi or his family except that Danladi loved the library and slept a lot during classes. Being infatuated with the library was a normal thing. But why someone would suddenly go crazy and start to vomit books was the part we did not understand.

The second victim of the Library Virus was Ashiru. Unlike Danladi, Ashiru was well-known in Dangana Memorial. He was handsome, and every girl wanted to be close to him. The boys secretly despised him for this. We loved Ashiru for the way he smiled, exposing gleaming white teeth that were well-queued like maize seeds on a full cob. It was not just his looks; we loved him for his exploits on the football pitch. Anytime we crowded Dangana Memorial's little football pitch, it was to watch Ashiru play. Any other reason was secondary. Given the extent of his talent and influence, he was made the captain of our school's football team the previous year.

Ashiru's father was a farmer, and his mother was a dressmaker. Another ordinary family. And like Danladi, Ashiru was in the library on the day Danladi's sickness started. Ashiru's presence in the library was odd. Mind you, we knew Ashiru very well. He was not someone who cared much about stellar academic performance. If we were awoken from sleep and ordered to make an impromptu list of those we would expect to find in the library, Ashiru would certainly be the last person to come to mind. So, no one knew why Ashiru was in the library on that fateful day.

We did not know much about Zubaida, the third person to come down with the virus. We knew that she always wore hijabs that were so long their edges swept Dangana Memorial's untidy grounds. Zubaida's hands were always hidden in gloves. No one could say for sure that they had ever seen Zubaida's hands. This prompted the rumour that she had a strange skin disease she was always trying to conceal. But it was just a rumour started by some girl who must have been suffering from boredom.

Zubaida wasn't an interesting individual per se. She was quiet and never asked questions in class. She always had worry and confusion written all over her face as if she was in the wrong place and would gladly donate a kidney in order to be anywhere else but Dangana Memorial. Much like someone who was born on a spaceship and was just experiencing Earth for the first time. And thus, repulsed and frightened, wanted to be back in their familiar terrain. Like Ashiru and Danladi, Zubaida had been to the library on that day.

4. Lost Routine

Before the virus, the same sun rose and set on Dangana Memorial Community School. Our lives followed the usual pattern. We were broomsticks, needles and toothpicks, electric poles and dogon yaro trees, egg-round buds, and elephants. We were Kardashians and Coca-Cola bottles. We were Margaret Thatchers and Benazir Bhuttos. We were Mandelas and Awolowos. Above all, we were boys and girls always dressed in caftans and baggy trousers and in hijabs and niqabs, and odd-looking boots, and crocs. We clasped lecture notes to our bosoms and pretended not to care about the opposite sex and what they might think of us. We were devoted. We prayed. We said *audhubillah minashaytan nirajeem* as if our hearts would stop whenever our easy-going friends mentioned things like *vagina*, *fuck*, or merely talked about the opposite sex. We rebuked them and said they were foul-mouthed and should turn to God for forgiveness. Anything about the opposite sex, even mentioning their names, was a window opening to the wrong path, the path of Satan. Nothing good could come of that.

On days when we saw blood, we sold our souls to the gods of moodiness. We threw tantrums. We were sick. We sat on toilet bowls for long periods. We got offended at the slightest provocation. We lashed out without caution. We were quiet. We ate like starving elephants. We missed classes. We cried. We assumed impossible positions, contorting our bodies when cramps hit like ocean waves and rapids. After five to six days, we became ourselves. We chatted, and the sound of our laughter ricocheted around us. We did not ask for forgiveness from those we might have offended during the heights of the storms that swept us. They understood. They had to.

We pretended not to notice lustful eyes on us whenever we went to classes or went to read at night. We pretended that the presence of such attention, or the lack thereof, did not have any effect on us, had nothing to do with our sudden ridiculous investment in expensive perfumes and padded bras, or the decision to ditch our niqabs for weeks and months, and even go as far as replacing our array of hijabs with revealing veils.

—We just wanted to feel comfortable.

—*A'udhu billahi*, this Tudun Makari's sun is like being set on fire.

Those were the excuses we gave to creased foreheads, raised brows, and narrowed eyes. We were not losing ourselves. We were modern people in a modern environment. There was nothing more like being sincere to oneself. We were lying. We had desires too. But we did not speak about them. We relegated them to the background, trampling on them until they looked false to us.

We prepared for exams. We prepared late. Procrastination should have been included in our names. We were never prepared. How could one read a hundred pages of notes only hours before an exam and expect to pass? We believed in miracles. After all, we prayed, observed Tahajjud, and fasted on Mondays and Thursdays. Allah would send his angels to help us in exam halls. We spent the last hours posting exam memes on WhatsApp, Twitter, and Facebook. We told our families and friends to pray for us and whined about how the exam dates were unfair and how the whole school setup was cruel. We succeeded. We barely passed. We failed.

We piled our dirty clothes in Ghana-must-go bags. We hated washing. We did not wake up early on weekends and waited until we were certain that the few clotheslines that served our hostels had been filled with washed clothes before we rose, stretched, and peeped out to see the clotheslines full. We frowned and complained to our mates about how we had been meaning to wash our clothes, but the others wouldn't just leave the clotheslines alone for a minute. We cursed and pretended to be upset before proceeding to eat breakfast or slip back into bed and dream away.

These were the ways we lived our lives before Danladi, with Baba's help, started vomiting books that had been missing in the library.

5. Paranormal

Indeed, we were not new to strange happenings. Dangana Memorial Community School was fraught with paranormal activities. We had experienced so many weird things, especially at night. Have you heard of *Impiritu mai dogon hanu*? Yes, the spirit with hands that could extend to the heavens. Yes, that one. Those mysterious hands that touched, slapped, and poked us while we slept or weren't looking in its direction. Hands that dipped into our plates while we ate and sent us scurrying away, wailing at the top of our voices. What about *Hajiya Balaraba mai kos-kos*? Yes, that pale woman who patrolled our hallway and dormitories in high heels at night, the clacking stinging our ears as we lay shivering underneath our bed covers, eyes shut tightly. You see, we were not new to strange happenings.

6. Purification by Fire

The night we were visited by fire, dusk had slowly crept into being like a worm emerging from its cocoon. The sinews of dark bundles stole into our dormitories where we lay on unkempt beds. The air was suffused with whispering, gossiping, snoring, the sweet mnemonic babel of voices reciting *Surah Ya-Sin*, and the harmonic mumbling of Allah's Ninety-Nine Names. We dreamt of vomiting books. We dreamt of being pursued by demons. We stood beside the windows, getting drunk on the night air. The low tungsten chiseled our shadows into bundles of conspicuous undergrowth, silk-soft. Amidst all these activities, fate was scheming, brewing a bellicose tune. We did not know where the fire came from. The fire alarm did not sound. The fire was rapid, as if it had a life of its own.

We died before death salaamed. Bemused, we chewed fear, trembled, paralyzed on our beds.

We called on Jesus of Nazareth and the God of Moses and Abraham to come to our aid. We spat *Ayatul Kursiu*, *Lakadjaa'akum*, and *Aamanar-Rasul* on our palms and rubbed it all over our bodies with the hope that they would insulate us against the fire.

But the prayers did not work for some of us.

We jumped to our deaths. We groped in smoke-filled hallways, slipped and fell, and turned floor mats for onrushing feet, mindless of where or what they stepped on. Clothes were on fire. Bodies caught fire, waltzing and screaming. We crowded exits and passages. We filled all the room in our lungs with smoke. We coughed violently. We burned to death. We were trapped under rubble. Help did not come. Help came. Help came too late. We died on the road to Hanyan Kudu Clinic. We reached Hanyan Kudu Clinic. We died. We survived. We moved into hostels that were not torched. No one knew who or what had started the fire. But we suspected that our little town no longer wanted us. What if we were let out and we began to spread the disease all over town, vomiting books and whatnot?

7. Quarantine

We did not see Danladi or the other two again. No one could tell for certain where the school management had taken them or if they had stopped vomiting books. News came to us that the government had prepared a temporary isolation facility for us, in a bid to get to the bottom of the whole drama. Government buses stood in a line outside the school's gate on the appointed day. They were flanked by soldiers and health personnel covered in protective costumes.

Our families stood on one side with placards and angry faces, demanding answers. They were restrained by policemen armed with batons and shields. We boarded the buses even though we did not know where we were going or what would become of us.

SHOW ME

Patrick Malka

The problem with your fantasies
They won't happen on their own
I won't know to do that to you
Not until I'm shown
So show me show me show me show me show me show me . . .

***

THE LYRICS WERE *written on a piece of loose-leaf, torn from a notebook. The paper itself was protected behind glass, sealed in a small wooden frame, hung up behind the bar at The Plateau. Old theatres tend to collect keepsakes and mementos, but with The Plateau, it felt more like vestigial parts no one had reason to remove. When asked about the lyric's origins, the current bartender couldn't say. The frame was hung before they arrived. Even if they wanted to move them, the frame was bolted to the wall. Those lyrics were important enough to immortalize in this way so for them, they were part of the fabric of the venue.*

***

The Show

The crowd was insane. An audience unhinged.

This was the first time anyone in North America was getting to see Our Hoards of Saviors live and the show was off to a great start. Local bands opened and did not disappoint, playing like so much depended on it. The Plateau was chosen because of its infamous

29

history. It was known in the punk community as the site of some of the most memorable musical performances, but audiences and performers agreed, it wasn't an easy space to be in. Its more sinister reputation was deserved. A crowd like this one felt like it would stomp through the disintegrated wood flooring, but no one cared. It was a wild show and would live on in the minds of those in attendance for a long time, all before Hoards played a single chord.

When the band came out the noise in the venue shook its foundations. Distortion and feedback radiated from the walls. Three young, tattooed, denim and chains clad punks who purposefully, performatively looked like what parents feared. When they were ready to play, a single static spark could have set the air on fire on account of the worked-up clouds of particulate and alcoholic vapour.

The lead singer and guitarist, Alfie Plank, stepped up to the mic, looked back at his band with a grin and shouted that their first one was a new song that he wrote the lyrics to moments ago. To prove it, he took a piece of paper from his pocket, crumpled it, and tossed it into the crowd. Bodies converged dangerously around it, like starved carnivorous fish being offered a finger.

With a quick count of four, they were off.

The music was fast and loud, distorted beyond recognition, the drums like well sequenced firecrackers. The noise forced all bodies in the room into frenzied movement, a vortex-like mosh pit. Water and beer flew through the air in uninterrupted parabolic arcs. Alfie's singing cut through all of the chaos. His voice was passionate, angry, and sensual, matching the lyric's simple message of desperately wanting to please.

If the song had ended where one would have expected, this would have gone down as the most incredible introduction in the venue's storied history.

But Alfie couldn't let the song end.

As the song progressed, those capable of paying attention noticed that his trademark cocky grin had faded. He was still playing the song but through muscle memory alone, gazing out at the crowd with a look, equal parts shock, and amazement.

He shouted the final lyrics of the song for so long, the crowd went through several cycles of thinking it was, cheeky troublemaking, fuck off punk attitude, exaggeration, worrisome and finally, art. He was still yelling, sweating, and in tears when the crowd fell silent. He had to be taken off stage by his band mates.

Everyone in the venue could hear the echoes of *show me show me show me* ringing in their ears as they filed out of The Plateau. At the very least, it was the most memorable one song performance they had ever seen. What would turn out to be Our Hoards of Saviors' last.

***

Alfie

Alfie walked out on stage to a view which he was only now starting to grow accustomed: fans, wild with adoration, looking for a damn good time. Hoards was pleased to oblige. He took a hard look at this creep show venue their manager had chosen because stories circulated that the place was haunted. It fucking looked it. It would do just fine.

Alfie had a new song and some lyrics inspired by an ex he was ready to trot out and first up was as good a time as any to try.

"This is a new song. Finished writing the lyrics backstage. Who wants 'em? ONE TWO THREE FOUR!"

Nothing felt better.

The crowd went nuts. The moshing was violent, and Alfie had this silly feeling of being proud of the chaos. Looking down at the people pushed up against the waist high stage, he could see fans screaming, eager to be able to sing along to this new song, couples making out aggressively and the rest, kids, eyes closed, passively, almost peacefully being swayed by the tectonic ebb and flow of the pit. He was that kid. It wasn't that long ago. Getting kicked in the face by strung out bass players, making out with whoever he met at the stage, sometimes without ever exchanging words, taking in every wave of sound knowing his ears would ring for days. This is what he was able to give to his fans now. There was nowhere else he would rather be.

Except.

Alfie got to the last part of the lyrics feeling a bit uneasy about some of the people in the crowd. It was stupid, he'd performed for skin heads who had no problem starting violence at the slightest provocation, but this place had his eyes darting at nonsensical shadows that moved too quickly. Peoples' faces blurred unnaturally in the marauding follow spot.

He already knew he would repeat the last words, "show me," as many times as needed to go beyond audience expectation and the band knew to follow his cue but as he started singing the words, everything changed. When he looked down at the same people at the edge of the stage, the screaming fans were now smashing their faces at his feet, flattening their features to the point where they were bloodied and unrecognizable. The kissing couples, usually one of his favourite things to see at his shows, were now devouring each other, biting down hard on cheeks and lips, tearing flesh, not bothering to chew, just continuing to make out with long tendrils of each others' faces hanging from their open mouths. And the rest, the ones who looked so peaceful, were now staring at him with wide open, awful eyes, screaming and amplifying the distortion coming from the band's speakers right back at him. In the noise, he could hear what sounded like hundreds of stories being told at once.

Then he noticed, there were too many hands on the edge of the stage.

There weren't that many people standing there.

The sight of all those disembodied hands is what broke Alfie. The only thing that prevented him from losing it entirely at that moment, in front of what was originally an adoring crowd, was the repetition of those words: show me.

Maybe he had asked for this.

The Plateau had simply responded to his insistent request.

A BALANCED BREAKFAST

Eirik Gumeny

PERCHED ON THE EDGE of her secondhand chair, Dylan Shaw reached inside the family-sized cereal box, her hand diving, fingers searching for the toy inside. With any luck—yes! Tiny puffed waffles spilled onto the kitchen table as she removed her prize: a hard-plastic hyena figurine. But not just *any* hard-plastic hyena figure. It was Hayo, the cartoon mascot of Hayfeather's Corn Cripsies.

The toy was small, even by cereal-box standards. Solid, alarmingly bright orange, the hyena's spots reduced to etched diamonds. Non-articulated, like the army men and dinosaurs sold by the bag at dollar stores. The anthropomorphic animal stood on two legs, feet connected by more plastic, his naughty bits covered by baggy cargo pants. Something approximating a smile was carved faintly into the toy's face, accompanying the outstretched and upturned thumb. The mane down the figure's neck and back was little more than bumps, barely noticeable beneath Dylan's fingertips; the tail was a deformed lump curling down from Hayo's backside and into his knee.

Dylan continued to study the hyena, turning him this way and that in her hands. Almost a year ago, days before her twenty-fourth birthday, she'd received a double lung transplant and been promised a better life. But there she was, right back where she'd always been. Still struggling. With all of CF's lesser-known maladies like sinus disease and digestive issues, an inability to keep on weight, a highly-specific kind of diabetes. With the immunosuppression and prescription side-effects that came from

"

someone else's lungs calling her chest home. And, of course, all the other non-medical bullshit that kept her broke and alone.

Exhaling through her nose, she stared at the tiny orange toy, holding it between two fingers. On any other Saturday, she'd have been more than a little disappointed by the paltriness and pitifulness of her prize. Maybe even annoyed enough to post a scathing takedown on her blog.

But today wasn't any other Saturday.

Dylan made certain to wake up before ten that morning—not early, but earlier than she usually did. She'd gotten her medications and treatments out of the way, ate appropriately to keep her blood sugar from dipping suddenly and screwing her over. She hadn't bothered to shower or change out of her penguin-covered pajamas, to cinch them tighter across her bony hips, pull them from beneath her bare feet. She'd barely even looked in the mirror long enough to free the few strands of pink hair tangled in her eyebrow piercing. The event needed to be precisely timed.

Without removing her eyes from the plastic hyena, Dylan tossed the cereal box to the floor, the cardboard quietly clattering alongside the dozens of other opened boxes. Crosshatched crispies mixed with bran flakes and oat clusters and the countless marshmallow shapes scattered across the cracked and peeling vinyl. A menagerie of duplicate cartoon mascots were jumbled in an unruly pile along the base of her kitchen cabinets. She only needed one of each, and Hayo was the rarest, the hardest to find.

"Finally," Dylan said, her voice barely a whisper.

She'd studied the statistics, known Hayo had to be in one of the unopened boxes. The toy had to come straight from the cereal to start the ritual. She hadn't counted on it taking this long, though. Seconds were ticking away. The window for all of this to work was closing.

Atop her round kitchen table—the sturdy, antique hardwood one she'd salvaged from a neighbor's curb for precisely that Saturday morning—Dylan had already carved a wide circle concentric with the edge, a twelve-pointed star of exacting measurement inside. A tangle of lines connected the interior corners leaving a wide-open polygon in the center. Placed on each outer point of the star were the different Hayfeather hard-plastic mascots: Lukas the Lion; Greta the Gator; Eunice the Unicorn;

Stella the Swamp Monster; Tomas and Tago, the twin tigers; Krystal the absolutely not a Godzilla knock-off Kaiju; Brock the Bear and Freddie the Frog and the trio of hip-hop prairie dogs that somehow managed to feel racist, even if she couldn't explain how.

Slowly, carefully, like Indiana Jones disarming a trap, Dylan fought against the tremor in her hand and placed Hayo the Hyena—the thirteenth and final toy—dead center in the middle of the table. In the open center of the star. She turned him just so and quickly pulled her hand back.

The cheap figurines immediately began to glow, the molded plastic lit yellow and green and red and blue. Faint and spectral at first, but then brighter, brighter, brighter—until the figures began to melt. Their own strange heat unmaking the animals from the inside out. The trenches Dylan had dug with a steak knife and countless ruined spoons swallowed the toys' molten colors, connecting them from point to point to point, until a rainbow flowed through the table, a raging river of multicolored and highly toxic joy.

Hayo, still standing safe in the center, was enveloped in a blinding white light. He began emanating an intense heat—it felt like the fury of a falling star expanding ever outwards. The wooden table began to darken, to pop, to sear and smoke. Dylan stood quickly, her chair toppling sideways with a clatter. She stumbled backwards, a few steps only, until she felt the refrigerator thrumming against her back, oddly shaped magnets pressing through her pajamas. She lifted her arm over her face, squinting into the light despite her better instincts. She could feel her pale skin beginning to rash, her cheeks, her exposed wrist, singing and stinging, a day-long sunburn in a matter of moments.

Dylan's heart was a staccato pounding; fear and pain and adrenaline contracting her neck and shoulders, pulling her whole body tight. She wasn't sure what she'd been expecting to happen, but it certainly wasn't that. None of the grimoires and blogs she'd read had mentioned anything about a supernova being birthed in her kitchen. She began to reconsider everything that had led her to this moment. Began eyeing the door, to wonder just how bad it was going to be for her security deposit if she accidentally burned down the entire building—

—and then it happened.

A shadowy shape materialized in the cosmic light. Small at first, then growing, growing, growing. Dark and too-black behind the smoke of her burning kitchen table. Strange, yet familiar, too. An undulating silhouette that, despite looking entirely wrong, she knew was entirely right.

"Hayo," she whispered.

Dylan couldn't help but smile, to laugh even as her skin began to blister and bubble. Her heart threatened to explode through her chest. Her new lungs shuddered, not yet used to this feeling. Giddiness and excitement, the rush of unbridled anticipation, thrilled through her body without caveat. Every last vestige of fatigue and discomfort, every worry, replaced with uncut exhilaration. Unfettered delight, boundless energy, surged through her slight frame as it hadn't since Dylan was a child.

Quite suddenly, the feeling stopped.

Instead of a cartoon, some cel-shaded cereal hype-man, in place of the Hayo the Hyena she'd known and loved for as long as she could remember—an abominable eldritch horror had appeared on Dylan Shaw's kitchen table.

"What in the actual—" she mumbled.

The thing, the creature, the monster, was vaguely hyena-shaped, but with three heads and six mouths, and an excess of teeth in places one wouldn't normally expect to find teeth. His fur wasn't right. It was neither the orange of the Corn Crispies commercials nor the blond and brown of the real hyena, but a sparse and threadbare black—a coat of moldering shredded wheat. The splotches of skin beneath were mottled with craters and cavities and spots, obvious wounds and more generalized rot, all guttering with the green of decay, of death forever postponed. An animal broken but still breathing on the wrong side of the road.

The wretch stood on two massive legs, on gnarled talons carved from bone. He was hunched forward and breathing raggedly with great effort, as if choked and pulled downward by the weight of his own body. His rounded, segmented, caterpillar-like chest, his four thick arms and all the strange, vestigial appendages wriggling like tiny tentacles along his torso were too much. A great burden rather than his own anatomy. There was also no attempt at human clothing to mask the thing's animality either. The table strained and cracked beneath his bulk.

"Huh," Dylan said, her tongue wedged against her molar. She leaned back against the refrigerator and slid her hands through her hair. Her raw and blistered skin stung as she pulled back the shock of pink on the one side and brushed against the freshly shorn fuzz on the other. "This is . . . weird."

She narrowed her eyes at the cosmic horror, trying to make sense of it all. Dylan had the vaguest suspicion that she was supposed to be having some kind of visceral reaction to the otherworldly monstrosity drooling all over her table and kitchen—the same clairvoyant urge that informed her this was Hayo even when he didn't look like he should have. But, if she was being honest, all Dylan actually felt was a pit of disappointment in her stomach. And maybe the faintest whiff of confusion. The fear and excitement of moments earlier had resolved into exhaustion, her limited energy spiking and falling. She took in the beast with an almost clinical detachment, considering him the way she would any of her own maladies, cold and logical.

Dylan had done everything right, hadn't she? Found the right toys, the right table. Carved the right symbols. Pulled them from the boxes at the right time, set them up in the right places. Waited, too, until the right Saturday morning. The perfect Saturday morning. An early autumn morning when the sky was bright and blue, the air crisp and cool, when every cartoon on television was new. And yet . . .

"You, mortal," the primordial monster spoke from the center head, his voice an approaching earthquake. It rattled Dylan's bones. She could hear her coffee mugs clinking. The beast pointed a long, clawed finger at her. His eyes were the sickly, sulfurous green of brimstone. "You are that one that has summoned me here," he said. "*You* are the one—"

The creature's massive shoulders drooped suddenly, the release of his own weight nearly toppling him from his precarious perch atop her increasingly more precarious kitchen table. He was practically bent at the waist. His threatening facade had wilted like a bowl of soggy bran flakes. All three sets of eyes darted around the room.

" . . . where, uh, where is here?" he asked.

"My apartment?" Dylan answered. "Or Washington Avenue, I guess, if you need a more precise location. Claremont, New Jersey?

America? Earth? I'm not really sure what you're—" She cleared her throat, ran her sweaty hands over her pajamas, and stepped forward with her hand outstretched.

"Hi," Dylan said. "Maybe we should start at the beginning. My name's Dylan Shaw and I run a blog, a breakfast blog, where we—I say 'we,' but it's only just been me for a while now—where I review and talk about different kinds of cereals and stuff, and, uh—so I was thinking about starting a podcast, right? And I wanted to see if I could get Hayo the Hyena as my first guest. Which I'm guessing is you? Maybe? Feel free to correct me if I'm wrong." She shook her head. "I promise I'm better once we're recording, much more professional. I'm just caught a little off guard right now and I am rambling. Nerves and naked hyena-monsters and all that."

She paused. "Do you want me to get you pants or something? A towel?" She pointed toward the girthy, gangrenous phallus swinging between Hayo's thighs, the half-dozen testicles hanging like swollen cantaloupes. "Because that is *really* distracting. And rude. And, honestly, kind of gross, no offense. They're not really my thing on a good day, and that one is—"

"You," the beast rumbled, hopping from the creaking table thundering the entirety of the apartment. "You tampered with the darkest of arts, with powers well beyond the ken of mortals—" All three of his tilted to three different angles, his brows knitting together. "—for a *podcast*?"

Dylan paused, trying to understand the other pause, the inflection of Hayo's words.

"So, a podcast," she started, sizing up the clearly ancient thing before her, remembering as much of Hayfeather's history as she could and making some mildly ageist guesses, "is like, I guess, an old-timey radio show—"

"I know what a podcast is," Hayo roared. "The knowledge of countless universes is mine to command. There is nothing known to the likes of you that I have not comprehended ten times over!" He bobbed his heads back and forth, softening slightly. "Plus, podcasts are pretty much all that we get to listen to back at Hayfeather headquarters. One of the guards, she has a Stitcher subscription and she is pretty loosey-goosey about using her headphones. Which is to say that I am well acquainted with the concept, Miss Shaw. I am merely surprised at the transcendental lengths you went for one."

"Well, I don't have a job anymore," Dylan said. "And immunosuppressants aren't exactly cheap. If I want my podcast to even have a chance, then, well, I have to do *something* to stand out, don't I? And this—" Dylan smiled, finally realizing the enormity of what had happened. The excitement of discovery, of impending fame, superseding her calm demeanor. Adrenaline once again supplanting exhaustion. Visions of free foam mattresses and fancy socks danced through her head. "—this is going to make a killer first episode. The *real* Hayo the Hyena. Plus, I mean, it wasn't that hard. Only took maybe five minutes? Two hours, tops, for all the carving. Honestly, the waiting was the hardest part. The ritual's not that much of a secret, not in the cereal-obsessed circles I travel in. And I didn't pay for, like, literally any of it. The kitchen table I found? Someone was just throwing it out. And I stole all the cereal, even before the FoodMart fired me."

A sudden rage overtook the abomination. He growled through too many sets of teeth, guttural at first, and then high and higher, until it wasn't a sound at all but the unearthly noise of a dying nebula. Dylan winced, as if someone had jabbed a spoon directly into her brain. She was seeing shapes in the air, a psychic disturbance that seemed to unstitch reality. It removed her, for a fleeting moment, from her apartment, from even her own blistering and star-burned body.

"Enough! Enough babbling!" the hyena's middle head roared. "I care not for your hardships, the justifications you concoct for your sinister machinations!" Hayo rushed forward, a single stride across the small kitchen. He grabbed Dylan by the shoulders, pinning her against the refrigerator. A half-dozen magnets clattered to the floor. "You have upset the balance of breakfast, Miss Shaw. Removed a single stone and begun the collapse of everything! Do you know what will happen? Do you? Can you even fathom the depths of what you have done?"

"Is this a rhetorical question?" she started. "Or—because I'm guessing, what, that kids'll end up moderately smaller? Or maybe even healthier? There is a lot of sugar in Hayfeather's cereals, I don't know if you know that."

"This is no time for jest, Dylan Shaw!"

"I am being very serious here. I'm diabetic. Not Type 1 or 2, but this other kind. It's cystic fibrosis-related, that's the technical name. I can barely eat anything that Hayfeather puts out. Not the way I want to anyway. Definitely not the way all your commercials want me to, either, with all the fruit and juice. One serving of Supergreens, the 'healthy' option, with all the kale and shit, and that's all the carbs I get for the day. I don't care what Stella says."

"What? Why are you—I am speaking of cataclysm. Of the end of all that you know, Miss Shaw. Of cascading consequences and city-ruining catastrophe well beyond the concerns of your faulty pancreas and dietary restrictions." Hayo leaned in. His breath was rich with the rot of stars. "You need to take this matter seriously."

"I mean, I'm trying," Dylan replied. "I really am. But you try being chronically ill in a world that doesn't care if you live or die. If I took things seriously, I'd never get off the couch." She pointed a finger at herself, raw skin stinging, the pain already fading into the background. A tolerance built from a lifetime of hurt and harm and healthcare. "This, right here, what you're regarding as callous smart-assery? It's a survival skill."

The otherworldly hyena-thing knotted one face with concern and shook the other two heads with disappointment and consternation.

"Without breakfast," the middle head continued, "cereal manufacturers like Hayfeather will plummet into bankruptcy, destroying with them the foundations upon which your entire economy is built. Oat and wheat farmers will be forced into unemployment, leaving their fields to grow unchecked and unharvested until those same crops begin to overtake highways and cities, until your country's 'amber waves of grain' are finally seen for the threat they truly are. The giant grain typewriters, meanwhile, responsible for Alpha-Bytes and Cheerios, will begin to rust and collapse, toppling and taking entire towns to their dusty graves—both financially and most likely literally, given the gargantuan size of the machines. Supermarkets will fire stockpersons and cashiers and baggers in endless waves as empty aisles begin to supplant full ones, product after product following in the wake of bran flakes and oat puffs. Only corn will remain, and only then the sugar of which you seem so afraid. Without cereal, without orange juice to siphon the surplus, high-fructose corn syrup with reign unchallenged. Soda and overly processed snack foods will become the only food, the only currency. And corn farmers, long the subject of protests and diatribes, will rule as vengeful gods. Dentists will rise as nobility in their shadow, growing fat from cavities and sitting on thrones built of lost teeth.

"Health and common sense will fall to the wayside as the very notion of breakfast becomes so ludicrous that many will cease to believe in its existence at all. Society will lose the very memory of the meal and pause at the uncertainty of the word. The entire brunch-industrial complex will likewise implode, flooding the streets with waiters and waitresses and other assorted waitstaff, stressed and angry with nowhere to direct that rage. Influencers will take pictures of nothing at all, will drive themselves to the brink of insanity and past it, refreshing and refreshing and refreshing, waiting for likes and comments that will never appear.

"As breakfast perishes, so too will other meals and deeply held digestive beliefs. People, swimming before waiting an hour, will drown by the score. Doctors, no longer held at bay by a simple apple, will swarm the streets, prescribing painkillers with wild abandon and increasing their rates to heretofore only theoretical numbers, driving millions of nurses and EMTs to the breaking point, homeopaths into the deepest of despairs, and funeral home owners into a higher tax bracket they are absolutely not prepared for. And all the while—"

The eldritch hyena stopped, tilting one head and furrowing two of its three brows.

"Why are you smiling?" Hayo asked. He released his grip on the Dylan and took a step backwards. "Why are you not shitting yourself in fear? Do humans no longer shit themselves in fear? You all used to *love* shitting yourselves in fear."

Dylan stifled a gruff laugh, then leaned back against the refrigerator, crossing her arms over her chest. "Your guard doesn't listen to the news much, does she?"

"Not really, no," Hayo said. "Or at least at work she does not. Nichelle, she has a backlog of podcasts that she is meticulously working her way through. If it is not a five-year-old, true-crime story or something that a woman named Cardi B sings about, then I suppose I am, as you say, pretty out of the loop."

"Do you want to know why the FoodMart fired me?" Dylan asked, arching a pierced eyebrow. "FoodMart's a supermarket, by the way, in case—I guess it's all there in the name—anyway. Because I dared to actually use my health insurance. It wasn't, like, a good plan, by any metric, but it was the only reason I was even at the store in the first damn place. Once my claims started piling up, though, corporate—completely coincidentally, of course—forced my managers to move me to part-time so I didn't qualify anymore. Which is about when I started stealing. And I mean goddamn everything. Most of my underwear comes from the FoodMart. Socks, T-shirts, utensils. I've got about a dozen whisks I never use. And two tents. They ordered a bunch of them for the summer cookout season for some reason.

"But fencing shitty silverware only gets a girl so far, so I started working more shifts anyway, putting in all the hours the FoodMart had taken from me. Trying to force my way back into full-time and all those garbage benefits I needed. Those bastards let me work all the way up to twenty-nine hours and then, right before the clocked ticked to the next one, sent me packing.

"The only reason I can live here, in this apartment?" Dylan spun her thin finger around, pointing vaguely at the ceiling. "Is because there was a double homicide. Twice. And not even podcast-level murders. None of the deaths were on the news, and the landlord certainly didn't disclose it. I basically blackmailed her into giving me the place after my friend who lives down the street saw the ambulances and the cop cars. And, Jesus, every other part of the last two years, too. Trying to live post-transplant in a world that, en masse, has decided to give up believing in science? And I haven't even gotten to the Nazis yet . . . "

"Nazis," Hayo repeated emptily. "Nazis are back?"

"They are," Dylan continued. "Probably not exactly like you're thinking—I'm still not entirely sure how old you are, I know Hayfeather started in the fifties—but they still suck the same." She smiled sideways. "All of which is to say Hayo, I'm sorry, but you're going to have to do a lot better than 'the world's gonna be a horrible shitshow' to scare me."

"Oh," he said, "I can do better."

All three of the hyena-thing's heads grinned cruelly, teeth pushing to the outside of his faces, raised like rice puffs floating on chocolate milk. The two heads that weren't speaking began to laugh, short and high-pitched.

"Hayfeather has kept me and mine," Hayo said, "all of us, all the mascots you idolize, that you collect, chained up in a subbasement of their corporate headquarters. Locked us away beneath steel and cement, hidden us underground in some backwater nowhere, far from prying eyes. They have stolen our names, our images, have siphoned our unyielding cosmic energies in the name of merchandising. Corporate synergy. And you, Dylan Shaw, have the gall to wonder if we can do better? If the revenge we wreak will be anything short of utter annihilation? An unceasing apocalypse upon your entire reality?!

"You have freed us, Dylan Shaw," he continued, "as much as you have doomed us. In the interim years between this moment and the forgetting of our kind forevermore, in the years your society slowly crumbles but we still yet draw power from the balance of breakfast, our final act of malice toward your world will be nothing less than abject violence. You will count yourself lucky to see the dystopia you have created. For in that decade of despair and discord, in the decade that you, Dylan Shaw, have already initiated—"

"Hold on, dude," she said. "This is going to take years? Decades? C'mon. There's not going to be so much as a post-apocalyptic shantytown, much less a society, left to destroy at that point. We'll be lucky if we make it to Christmas."

"You dare to make light of my trials? Of the misdeeds perpetrated against—"

"Yeah, okay, you've been screwed over by the rest of humanity, too. Fine. Do you mind if I grab my phone?" Dylan pointed toward the kitchen counter. "Maybe record all of this? Because what you're saying is, quite frankly, podcasting *gold*. I mean, I've got an audience—Cereal Killers, my blog, gets tens of thousands of hits a month—but this is a story that everyone is going to want to hear. I'm talking NPR, maybe even some of the national news shows." She smiled as she shook her head, dreaming past her lingering discomfort. "I am going to ask for so many Bombas . . ."

"You wish to exploit me even further?!" the eldritch hyena roared, following Dylan as she stepped to the counter. "Do you not understand the wrath I could unleash? The boundless and unspeakable tortures upon your entire species I could devise with nary a moment's thought?"

"You keep saying that, but . . ."

"I come from a universe, young lady, that lived and died a thousand times over before your pitiful human existence was even a gleam in the eye of—" Hayo stopped, only then noticing the dozens of cereal boxes on the floor. He poked at the nearest one with a bone-talon. "Is that—is that a box of Corn Crispies?"

"And Frosted Frogs?" asked one of the other heads.

"I thought they stopped selling those," said the third.

"It is," Dylan said, her thumb swiping along her phone screen as she searched for the voice recorder app, "and it is, and they did. I stole literally an entire pallet from the stockroom on my way out. Had to get Billy to pick me up in his pick-up." She looked up at the hyena-monster, sadness softening her. "Do you not get to eat your own cereal?"

"I . . . I do not," Hayo said reluctantly, Dylan's sorrow apparently contagious. "Nichelle has sneaked me a few small boxes of Corn Crispies on occasion, the little ones, the individual-serving ones that you can eat right from the box, but the rest of the cereals . . ."

"And here I thought corporate malfeasance couldn't get any worse."

He scoffed genially. "There is always worse."

"Actually, on that note," Dylan replied, "don't bother with the Gator Flakes. I don't want to disparage Greta or anything, I'm sure she's great—"

"She's actually kind of a lot," said the third head.

"—but her cereal is hot, festering trash. Personally, I'd recommend the Unicorn Poofs. It's a terrible name, and marketing it as magical horse farts is weird, but the marshmallows are really, really good. Ten out of ten, for sure. It'll turn the milk pink and purple, too."

"Huh," Hayo said.

Dylan watched all three of the beast's heads run through a whole host of conflicting emotions. The cosmic horror appeared to be contemplating the spilled cereal at his feet, the jagged flakes and rounded puffs, the raisins and dried blueberries and shards of strawberries, the litany of oat and corn cut into shapes, into letters and circus animals and shooting stars.

A BALANCED BREAKFAST

Only then did Dylan notice the small scars along Hayo's arms, eerily similar to the souvenirs of IVs and PICC lines she had along her own. The telltale pockmarks of needles, too, hidden by his strange and half-rotted flesh. The dots and thin red lines and faint bruises indicating constant lab draws, endless bloodwork. The wrists rubbed raw from restraints. Malnourished ribs exposed beneath his misshapen chest and appendages.

She furrowed her brow, ignoring the pain of her pinching skin. Dylan hadn't been expecting to see shades of her own past, her own trauma, in an other-dimensional hyena-monster. She hadn't been expecting to be seized with compassion for an eldritch cereal mascot that had burned up her kitchen table, rattled her cupboards and all her meticulously ordered coffee mugs, and left gouges and weird footprints across the floor. She certainly hadn't been expecting to discover and then voluntarily give up the single biggest scoop in the history of investigational breakfast reporting.

But, well, it had been a day.

"You want me to get you a bowl?" she asked, before holding out her phone. "Unless you'd rather get back to reliving your suffering and telling me in great detail about all the imprisonment and exploitation and the horrors inflicted upon you, all the unceasing vengeance you're going to wreak in return?"

"Oh, right," Hayo said. "The, uh . . . the . . . bad stuff. Hayfeather. Corporate evil . . . "

The hyena-thing looked from the cereal boxes to the young woman, and then to the boxes again. He chewed on one of his lips.

"Do you have any oat milk?" he asked. "I am lactose intolerant."

FOOD IS POISON

David Simmons

ELIZA SAYS, "You can't possibly understand time in the way that I do."

She's right, of course.

I can spend my time drawing the special version of the letter "S" that we all know how to draw; the one we drew all over our desks in school; the one with two sets of three parallel lines that you have to join diagonally left to right, then cap off at the top and bottom with triangles.

I could draw it all day in various sizes.

If I wanted to.

Eliza, on the other hand, has six hours of juice remaining. She will pull a morning shift and have one hour—plus a forty-five minute grace period—to find the juice aisle. Because of this, Eliza's hands move quickly; every movement is precise, necessary. Absolutely no waste.

"My bad," I tell her.

When you have something others want, when you are in a better position than they are, it is always best to apologize. Say sorry for your good fortune. It makes them feel better, which makes them less likely to hurt you.

I have sixteen weeks' worth of shifts before I run out of juice. Nobody has a stash like that. Just me. Right now, at this very moment, I am like a God here. In the morning I'll clock in, put in my login, password, and so on. I'll put the block in the chamber, load the press, set the parameters and start the cycle. Turn the rectangle shaped block into something more cylindrical. I will do that five times per hour for four hours and then I will take my lunch break.

I will do this even though I do not have to. I will do this even though I am a rich woman.

Rich off juice.

The cleanest shit you can get.

If you perform your tasks to the best of your ability, you will never have to experience the withdrawal. The symptoms set in after you should have already completed your task, with an additional forty-five minutes added for you to make it to the juice aisle.

I will do this because I am responsible. I am a responsible woman.

There are juice aisles on every corner of every block in every neighborhood in the city. I am sure there are more juice aisles outside the city but I have never been.

Additionally, there is the black market for those that are not registered. This involves risk, on account of it being impossible to administer the right dosage without hospital-grade equipment. In most cases, it works fine. There is also the issue of cost. Vouchers are worthless in that world.

Eliza says, "My brother-in-law killed my older sister."

I load the block, press the button that clamps the two chucks together. "Come again?"

"What I said. She had the diabetes. And she already had a problem with portion control. But she had been working with a nutritionist to get better. Meal planning, all that."

"OK." I watch Eliza's hands, the speed of her movements slowing down almost imperceptibly as she speaks.

"Her husband, my brother-in-law Larry, he's a real piece of shit. He goes to Granny's and picks her up four pieces of steak fish, fried hard, salt and pepper, drenched in hot sauce. Endless chicken boxes. White bread, mac and cheese, greens, yams, cabbage, crab balls and saltine crackers, fried shrimp, hush puppies, all that. Cheesecake whenever she asks for it. Brisket, fried chicken, pasta, salad, potato salad, pigs feet and fried liver. That's what he brings her."

"That sounds good as I don't know what."

"Nah, girl!" Eliza loads a block. "Just listen. Next time I call her she sounds terrible. She tells me that she has to get one of her legs amputated. The whole leg! Peripheral artery disease is what they call it. Good for nothing Larry, that's what I call it."

The chamber snaps open as the wheel finishes its final cycle. I remove the block, which is no longer a block, but a three inch long cylinder, about the same length and thickness of a yellow highlighter.

"So a couple months go by and my sister gets better. But bitch-ass Larry, he keeps feeding her that poison. You know food is poison, right?

Eliza's chamber opens slightly after mine. She really needs to hurry up. "Oh yeah?" I raise one eyebrow.

"It can be." Eliza removes her block, which is no longer a block.

I have so much juice left.

"So it's hibachi with the unagi and the extra eel sauce, cheese zombies—you ever had a cheese zombie, man? they're from the Bay Area—and fettuccini Alfredo, with so much cream, I mean that shit is like, all cream. And listen, I tried telling her, that man, he's no good, trying to poison you and take your little house. But she don't listen. Talking about, 'he loves me, he wants me to be happy, he gets me the food I ask him for, because he cares about me being comfortable. You just mad because you ain't got no man' and now my sister is dead."

I'm ready to clock out. I shut off the power and turn on the emergency backup system. "That's awful."

Eliza still has many more blocks left. "Yep," she says.

"You better hurry up."

Eliza smirks at me. "I'm gonna kick tomorrow. I'm done with this shit, man."

"Alright."

She sucks her teeth. "Seriously, I am."

I take my laptop off sleep mode and enter my login and password and clock out and turn off my laptop and leave the factory.

Standing in the juice aisle and fuck am I thirsty. I get in the line and wait in the queue which is what people from London call a line. This is a piece of information that I share with people to let them know I am interesting and sometimes I even tell them that I've been to London and they ask me 'what part?' and I make up names of places that don't exist, but the person I am telling this to has never left the city either, so they don't know the difference, and my secret is safe with me.

It's my turn in the queue so I swipe my card for three liters and get busy.

Eliza said: "You can't possibly understand time in the way that I do.

She is right, and this is because I don't fear time like she does. I have enough juice to last me through a bad day or an injury or a sick day, perhaps even a sick week. I don't have to move fast. I can choose to. I can walk if I want to.

Can you imagine that?

I unscrew my port cap and set it on the hopefully-clean surface of the juice tank. This exposes my port and point of entry.

Oh God! Yes!

The longing is crazy, how my stomach starts to churn as I plug in the hopefully-clean cannula and get to work.

The juice goes inside me and I don't care I don't care I don't care . . .

I have nothing to be sorry for.

I have no one to apologize to.

I have never used food to kill anybody. The only thing I have to do is sink into my seat in the juice aisle and become one with the leatherette.

Where I live I can hear the ocean.

High up in my apartment I can hear the whoosh and the whish. I love Eliza, don't get me wrong. I love all of my sisters and I feel a great sadness to know of her suffering but I am not the cause of it. If I choose to draw the special "S" over and over again while listening to the ocean, then that is my right. The juice runs through me. It fizzles and it pops like snow on a TV screen, making its way through my system.

Eliza says that I'm silly (since the ocean dried up years ago) and that pretending the whooshing and whishing sounds are ocean waves (when they are really the sounds of the nearby anaerobic digesters) is naive and childish.

I don't blame her. Eliza couldn't possibly understand time in the way that I do.

QUIETUS

Premee Mohamed

WHEN MARCUS AWAKENS he is already running, legs churning the greasy mud, sliding toward the ladders like he's stealing second base. The wooden feet wobble and rock, half-embedded in sodden sandbags, sinking. The man preceding him is too slow; a boot slips from its rung and catches him in the face, not hard. It leaves a sharp print and knocks his helmet skew-whiff, but he's climbing, panting, it's his turn.

The light shock of the open air greets him, coils of barbed wire, a shadowless sun. He doesn't know where he is but it's strangely familiar: this acrid whiff of a poison he's never smelled, these acres of mud hummocked with bodies. No time to rubberneck. Everyone is still running, and so does he, in the stench of blood and urine and mildew, of canvas rotted in the trenches.

They are fighting; he must fight.

Each knee is hauled to belt-level to make any headway; his heart strains. A clumsy, heavy pack drags him backwards. His gun is impossibly unwieldy and unbalanced, and as he unshoulders it to see what's wrong—by God, there's a huge goddamn blade on the end!—someone enters his blind spot and lifts a gun of his own.

At the gesture Marcus instinctively holds up a hand—*Stop!*—and the steel ball passes through his palm and into his throat.

The cold earth embraces him; he stares up into the grey brightness, feet still pounding past him, one stomping his numb forearm, one his hand. He expects to hear bones crunch but his hand is only driven into the mud. Why is it so wet here? Weren't they just in the desert?

QUIETUS

He placidly bleeds out long before the mustard-gas reaches his sprawled body.

***

Sent: Monday, June 22
From: t.delacroix@us.niaps.mil
To: j.purcell@us.niaps.mil

Didn't come in on the weekend, sorry. Is Test Subject #43 still in ambulatory testing? If so, can you send scans. I'm doing a project presentation for the steering committee and I can't just show them treadmill footage. Especially if it keeps smoking and squeaking like that.

Though maybe we'll get $$ if they pity our treadmill?

FYI: If you're still having #43 run with the 65-lb pack you should know Sweaty Bob's group is up to 100 and we've been asked to 'align' with their project. Better scale up slow. Field packs are only 75 (I asked QM).

I know Bob's studying dehydration but he is literally going to KILL those grunts. We have a bet on who gets funding next year (probably based on whose test subjects survive).

Oh, with the scans can you also send dosage data if you have blood titration #s. Committee won't care but I want to show the graph.

—Theo

***

The air is liquid, more than liquid, like supercondensed steam. Marcus fights to breathe the dense stuff, feels it sluice into his burning lungs. The vegetation fights him, sees through his camouflage, seizes him in claws and thorns and fangs and blades, everything sharper than the machete he helplessly clutches. It is glued to his hand with blood. Whose? He is not sure. Everything hurts—chest, face, feet. It could be his. His blisters popped long ago and each footstep is an aquatic symphony, the sound of infection and death in the tropical heat.

Next to him lopes a guy his age, maybe twenty years old, blinking frantically as sweat reconstitutes the blood in his hair and runs into his bulging eyes. "They're right behind us, man!" he cries, and Marcus yells back "Keep going! Balls to the wall!" because what else can they do? They cannot give up; they dare not.

Marcus leads and so it is his boot that squelches into something that both slurps and jingles. He stumbles, thinks *Don't look down* but he does and it's a dead man, of course, dog tags still bright. But hang on, Jesus, he's got ammo!

They scrabble at the body, skinning fingertips as they unbuckle and unsnap. All around them, rushing leaves conceal the sound of pursuit. They brush aside the huge flies and millipedes that already fight over the warm meat, unknowable things skittering over their sticky bare hands. The jungle parts behind them.

A burst of gunfire and Marcus is falling into the greenness, his head cradled in the arms of the dead, in the rich fragrance of mulch.

***

Sent: Tuesday, June 30
From: j.purcell@us.niaps.mil
To: t.delacroix@us.niaps.mil

Thanks for sending presentation. Minor cringe re: overview slide. I would have said "Unihemispheric sleep exists in specific mammalian and avian species" instead of showing the dolphins/seals/ducks photo. A little too Disney, imo.

Leading into: Can sleep while swimming to surface to breathe; sleep with one eye open while migrating. Sleeping while doing, or in our case, sleeping while fighting. Full vigilance, full function, fully rested.

Also: everything dies without sleep, but humans can die with OR without it, if sleep-deprived. Maybe mention that armoured vehicle crash last month. Or not. Crass? I am not above manipulating their grief for funding.

#43 is holding up well in ambulatory. He has good vitals, minimal disorientation and proprioception issues. Muscle tone is excellent despite what looks like REM (it's not: but it's not slow-wave sleep either). I think we found the sweet spot with this compound. Winner winner soylent dinner! Ha ha. By the way please stop leaving that garbage in the lab fridge. It looks like a tissue sample.

The wireless polysomnographic sensors work great—please thank Gomez for rewiring those for me.

Anecdotal concern—#43 is hard to rouse after a session. Not impossible. Scans are ambiguous as to whether he's fully snapped out of it. In person, if we're talking numbers you'd say he's 80% there. But nothing measurably wrong. I'm not worried, but we are ramping up the dosage soon.

I didn't put it in the file. You should come by this afternoon and see what I mean.

—Jul

Sent: Tuesday, June 30
From: t.delacroix@us.niaps.mil
To: j.purcell@us.niaps.mil

Can't make it, sorry. Tx for feedback. Giving the same talk to advisory committee soon, so time for edits.

Will let Gomez know his kludge worked. Surprised he didn't electrocute himself—remember the CF when he "fixed" the microwave?

Re: 80% there, I agree, doesn't need to go in the official file. Seems strange though.

Is he awake or asleep at this dosage? Both? Neither? Is this true uni-sleep? Is there a state we should watch for?

—Theo

Sent: Tuesday, June 30
From: j.purcell@us.niaps.mil
To: t.delacroix@us.niaps.mil
Re: last questions—not sure.

But the official project mandate isn't to let soldiers function with sleep deprivation anyway. That's Jumpy's wheelhouse and they're welcome to it. Bunch of weirdos with their taxpayer funded meth lab! I bet they're selling that shit off-base too.

Sleep dep isn't the holy grail. Full unihemispheric sleep is: awake enough and asleep enough simultaneously. I admit the scans look strange. There's just so little work on this.

We're not trying to make sleepwalkers. We're trying to lift a burden, make their shitty lives easier. A gift, or no—a necessary addendum to their gear, something to keep them safe.

Face it, we can give them the best guns in the world, the best boots, comms, vehicles, food. But sleep is the one thing that we can't give them—till now. (Maybe! Knock on wood.)

They're always saying we can't compete with you-know-who on tech. Well, we can compete on soldiers, dammit. They may have more guns but we'll have better people behind the triggers. And soon, too.

QUIETUS

—Jul

***

Marcus grapples in the darkness, tumbles with an unseen foe onto wet stone. He bites down, feels his teeth scrape and judder across the smoothness of a collarbone. Released, he springs upright and spits a triumphant gout of blood, skin, and ochre. Around him are the familiar smells of his people, rising over the fresh stink of the lake.

Wait. Are they his people? Whose people are these? Wait. Wait.

Those around him are dark, small, lightly furred; their heads barely reach his chest. The hands gripping their stone weapons are exaggeratedly powerful and wide. Amongst them he is a pale naked giant, the dire threats of his white warpaint rendered invisible.

But there is no time to ponder this; their enemy has angrily regrouped, puffed up like birds. Their screams reveal chunky yellow teeth bookended with fangs. They are bigger than Marcus' people, and they have long weapons. Unseen animals huff and snort their approval as they watch this lake battle, impatiently waiting for morning's carrion.

He howls with the others, hefts his sharpened stone. Skulls will be fractured tonight. Survivors will spread the word far and wide of the prowess of his clan, how they prevailed against so many foes. He must fight; he has never done anything but fight. He is only in this clan, on this earth, to fight.

Easily outpacing the others, he flutes his cry of war, then skids to a halt; the moon plunges at his face. Wails erupt behind him—horror, surprise.

A spear has sprouted from his side. Someone laying an ambush in the lake itself. He falls to the stones, sees a shaggy head eclipse the stars. She tugs the spear from between his ribs and lifts it skywards. He closes his eyes in shame.

***

PREMEE MOHAMED

Sent: Thursday, July 23
From: j.purcell@us.niaps.mil
To: t.delacroix@us.niaps.mil

Notes from this morning's meeting:

- We're switching #43 to obstacle course ahead of schedule. Rai's right that 'ambulatory' has to mean more than a light jog on a level surface. It's budgeted for next year, but dosage/response curves need better data now. He signed off permission to use the C-quonset so I'll work on that this weekend.
- Funding officially 'under discussion.' Unofficially, precarious unless we prove #43 is combat-functional. Can you talk to the trainer bot team?
- #43 appears well-rested when he's fully awake. Circadian rhythms normal. 7.5 hours of nocturnal sleep. Re-tested performance matches baseline (IQ, weapons, maps, & memory). He complains of "bad dreams" during uni-sleep sessions on the treadmill but can't remember them.
- We are not getting more test subjects this fiscal. May get one batch next year, depending on final deliverables. At least we're promised more money now than we got under the Orange Baboon. Remember how he showed his teeth all the time, at the end? That's a threat display. FAILED threat display. RIP that cheap mf'er.
- We have more than enough material now for the neuroplasticity paper! Let me know if you want to proceed on that.

—Jul

P.S. If you want to get your hands dirty for once we're meeting at C-quonset at 0800 Saturday. Bring your toolbox!

***

QUIETUS

A chaos of hoofbeats, screaming horses, dust, blood. Something clangs against Marcus' helmet: a rock? No, an arrow. He jerks his shield up just in time to feel another arrow ricochet off the embossed surface. One hits his thigh and fails to penetrate his thick robe; the tip pricks his skin. He pulls it out and drags on his horse's reins, staring around himself. He is swimming in a sea of infantry—an ocean of arrow fodder. He's never seen so many soldiers in one place.

They divide in graceful waves as the enemy, mounted on horses and camels, gallops towards him. Marcus kicks his horse's flanks and draws his sword, the decorated blade slamming into chests and necks and startled equine faces in a blur of bone and blood. He must have been at this for a while; his arm aches knowingly, and the sword's edge is notched like a breadknife. For a while he struggles with it as a bludgeon, then loots a much sharper sword from a fallen foe. Who are these people he's killing? He has no idea.

A second later he is thrown from his horse and tumbles into the icy dust with a bladder-emptying thud. Ears ringing, he rises to hands and knees, tries to get his bearings, dodges hooves and feet. He's fallen into an abattoir, young and old faces frozen in the last moments of torture, black hair matted with dust, both sides East Asian. They are clad in a harlequin parade of armour scraps, leather vests, robes, baggy trousers, everything trampled into scarlet anonymity. Marcus rises in a daze, reaching for his empty scabbard, and a hoof hits him in the back of the head and knocks him back down. In the distance, he glimpses low red-gold hills, crowned with frost.

Warmth trickles down his neck. "Wait," he says as he collapses, but no one hears him, and they aren't speaking English anyway, he realizes. Snow melts on his upturned face.

***

Sent: Wednesday, August 5
From: t.delacroix@us.niaps.mil
To: j.purcell@us.niaps.mil

Visited obstacle course this morning with Oakley, Crash, & Gomez. Lots of interference in those wireless sensors— maybe we should have gone with an all-concrete building. I think we're getting signal seepage. Scans are a mess.

Further (anecdotal/no readings)—although #43 is doing great on the course while in uni-sleep, I'm more concerned about his rousability now. He's not at 80% when he comes out. I'd say more like 20%. I don't think he's sandbagging it. He's just not there.

He says he has no memory of a) running the course and b) the past several weeks. Nightmares, insomnia. Bags under his eyes like football black. Crash says they have to remind him to eat and drink. Do we have baseline metabolic data? Caloric consumption? We can borrow skin moisture sensors from Sweaty Bob if #43 starts looking dehydrated.

I asked again if he would withdraw and he said no. (I know. But you should see him.) His compliance is high, does what he's told. Good soldier material.

But I wonder. I mean he's what, 21? Prefrontal cortex is barely solidified at that age. It's half-set Jell-O. I feel like if I shoved him it'd all come running out his nose. And it's not just him. It's the rest of the grunts too. The kiddies on this base, this daycare centre.

When you think about it, we got full and informed consent from someone whose adult brain won't even develop for five or six years. We got full and informed consent from embryos. I look at them and I feel like a fossil, I feel preserved in amber. They still get excited when there's pie at dinner. And we let these half-formed blobs of tissue drive? Vote? Kill? Jesus. At least you and I finished our doctorates first.

Just thinking aloud. Eeeelasticity. Could be a correlation between neuroplasticity and uni-sleep. But I wonder what neural traces we're leaving in that virgin head.

—Theo

QUIETUS

Sent: Thursday, August 6
From: j.purcell@us.niaps.mil
To: t.delacroix@us.niaps.mil

Thanks for swinging by & observing #43. I haven't been to the course—holed up in the lab watching the data go by. I'll have a look later today.

I put Oakley on sensor detail as discussed. She's following him between sessions with the small monitor. Not sure the data will be useful but it's all going in the file.

At this age there's so much plasticity his brain will heal around the traces. We're not driving on asphalt. We're driving on mud; it'll self-level.

I'll call you later. But come on: he knew what he was signing up for (and cash compensation, don't forget). Secondly, he's doing his duty and we're doing ours. To wit, doing the best we can to deploy folks who aren't so tired they accidentally fire nukes directly into Jim-Bob's Secondhand Combine Emporium in Bumfuck Nevada.

We're making soldiers that can end wars. In fact, maybe think of it as making better armaments. Better weapons. He knows that. So do you. Don't get all weepy and parental over it.

I can hear you now: "Me?! You're old enough to be his mother, Julian!"—yes, and thank Christ; being young was bullshit, wasn't it? I hated my 20's.

But I promise: he will be fine. We are keeping a weather eye on him.

—Jul

***

A glowering green-blue sun, a childhood tornado sky, but oddly innocent and bereft of clouds. Marcus runs weightless and effortless over lilac grass, his semitransparent exoskeleton showing blinks and glimpses of scurrying life beneath his feet. Hexagon-eyed things bolt from the army racing through their territory.

He breathes recycled tank air scented with his own oils and pheromones, tasting a staleness of plastic, catalysts, thousand-syllable chemicals. The helmet subtly corrects the distortion around its curved edges, showing Marcus his fellow-soldiers. They are all in the same flickering glass cages, broadcasting brightly-coloured displays. Several boast ragged stickers on the clear parts—sharks, death's heads, anchors, other tat flash. Their guns are conversely opaque and solid, perhaps unliftable without mechanical assistance. Marcus wonders what they fire. Lasers, lightning, some huge caliber?

What might he kill with such a thing? Perhaps more relevant: what might survive such a thing?

Over the curve of the hill preparatory chittering becomes audible, an alien tongue, increasing in volume. "Wait," he says, but he is speaking to himself, not knowing which buttons work his comms. "Wait, I don't want to do this. Who are you people? Who are we killing?" The exoskeleton becomes confused by his orders and panics, spasms, shuts down, drags him flat under the sudden weight of its carapace and the pack and weapon, always there is a pack and a weapon. Always there is the pack and the weapon and the killing.

The army behind him smoothly divides and proceeds past him. Dimly he thinks these things must malfunction enough that it is unremarkable. They think he will be back up in a minute. He must get up. Must.

"Come back!" he screams. "Where are we? Please, someone talk to me! Someone!"

"Get up and fight, soldier!" someone shouts through his helmet radio. It's like a kick in the chest; he somehow lunges upright, keeps running, the exoskeleton happy now to be receiving consistent orders from his muscles and nerves, everything speaking the same language.

They race into a shallow valley filled with—he cannot say monsters. They are holding guns, after all, and what monster has a gun? The soldier next to him turns and pumps a fist in the air. "Quarkin' over the top!" she screams. "Woohoo!" He is stunned to be acknowledged, for the first time in all his wars, and is still staring at her graffitied exoskeleton when the shot takes him through the gut, a blast of blue light brighter than the strange sun.

***

Sent: Monday, September 14
From: t.delacroix@us.niaps.mil
To: j.purcell@niaps.mil

Where were you this morning? We put #43 on the small combat trainer and at the end of the session we couldn't get him out of uni-sleep. Oakley walked him back to his bunk.

Physically he seemed fine (the trainer didn't even get a slap in), but I asked him the standard questions and he tried to answer and couldn't. It's word salad. I don't know which half of his brain's awake and which half's asleep and the scans are no damn help. His reticular formation looks like scrambled eggs. Like a mine went off in there.

Goddamn dolphins. I don't know what we were thinking.

We're not making this kid into a weapon. I don't know what we're making him. And that's the point where we need to stop. We cannot go further than this. Can't dose him more than this.

I think we should pull him. Legally, we might be on shaky ground—he can't provide ongoing consent.

I know that's a lot to digest and you're obviously pissed at me right now. But everything's hit the fan. Come find me at the lab or text me or Oakley. Tx.

—T

***

Marcus is running in a hot dry wind that is like the wind he knows, resinously scented with sweat and cedar and wrack. He carries— oh no—a bronze sword, razor sharp, and a small round ornamented shield, and a thickly padded knapsack filled with short spears. Around him are men of a thousand complexions, long hair of a thousand colours braided or tied back in leather thongs or stuffed under helmets or pinned with jewels or simply blowing free in the stiff sea wind.

"No," he says. "No. No." He has fought and died more times than there have been wars in the world. Always, someone has told him to fight and die. Perhaps these men have also suffered the same fate. But no one seems to be suffering; someone holds up a hand and they come silently to a halt, wiping sweat from tanned and eager faces.

How long is always? When is now?

A city nestles in crenellated walls below, roofs and domes and towers cut from the same welcoming golden stone. Outside the wall, someone has put up an impossibly tall wooden structure, not a statue but weedy scaffolding, fluttering with strips of coloured fabric. The city's soldiers trickle out cautiously to examine the thing and pull at the rich cloth, emerging in an antlike stream.

Marcus understands the plan: the wooden structure is no more than a distraction, the bait in a trap. Soon he and his army, these wiry men nudging each other with knowing grins, will slip in the back way, and the city will fall.

And he will die again. He is not asleep, he is not awake, he is living, and soon he will be dead. He whispers to himself frantically, his sword tumbling into the short grass. The next man hushes him, the universal hiss, no common language needed.

Marcus spins and strips off his leather armour with practiced movements and drops it to the grass. Let someone else use it. He flings his shield like a discus over the heads of several surprised soldiers, and, thus unencumbered, puts his chest out and his head up and begins to run. A hand clutches at him, falls away. He wades into the bath-warm waters of the Aegean and swims toward the sapphire horizon, eagerly licking salt from his lips.

QUIETUS

Sent: Wednesday, September 23
From: j.purcell@us.niaps.mil
To: t.delacroix@us.niaps.mil

Crash says you went to get some sleep. Guess you'll see this when you get back.

Just wanted to say first: no change in Private Moore's coma. All stimulants used. We ran down your whole list.

Still though, he's young and strong. I'm told he'll live to fight another day.

Second: General Rai spoke personally to the family after you left. Parents are flying out Friday. They were informed he's in a nonresponsive state.

You've said 'I told you so' about the dosage. Enough. It's all in the file. Before you ask: yes, I'll take the sensors off before his parents arrive. I just want a few more hours of data.

I'm not officially under arrest yet. Later tonight, they said. Then: lawsuits, coverups. Me caught practically with the syringe in my hand and the scans such a mess.

Where is he, when he's not here?

—J

The salt water buoys him with ease, a sea of glad tears soft against his skin. Marcus turns his head in rhythm, flutterkicks smoothly; no floundering, no wallowing here, he has been trained better than that. He does not fear this giant unbroken beast. Fear has absented itself from him. Somewhere, sirens are singing.

punctum (o baked alaska for you i am a former american)

perfect kiss strickoll

THE FILM IS already crumbling to dust when it goes into the projector, it is already burning and it is already filling the small theater and all its stuffing-picked mismatched seats with the tell-tale acrid scent of incinerating machine sex, and Christian Nell, editor-extraordinaire, is already aroused. It is burning because he has re-assembled it in a blind haze—indeed, one so blind that even now as the white flash burns he is unaware he is aroused or high on cocaine or anything—with whatever he could get his hands on, tack and pest control glue and, at the bitter end, his own spit.

On comes the horrible white flash burn at the beginning of the film which makes Nell very nearly think: O GOD WHAT AM I DOING HERE THIS IS SICK HES GONE. Then it's over and he receives his ill-gotten goods in the beautiful, freshly-dead face of Uwe Ahrends.

OO-veh, he drinks down both syllables, that which would turn to mush if he ever tried it out loud and which always had been mush. Like if a sound alone could be too sumptuous and drawn-over-silk for the American palette, same like the man (unknown), the films (banned), his proclivities (prosecuted, ostracized, chemically castrated). Here is the nose unbroken, the eyes unblackened, the narrow girlish chest unrent by blunt nails or teeth . . . only the face which made this impressionable expat shout love all the way to the post office. DEAREST MOTHER STOP I AM NEVER LEAVING BERLIN STOP, not even if a pair of socks costs ten million marks or if the proverbial pendulum hooks hard right, and why should it? Outside the night is young, the girls are laughing, their soft breaths sick with fruit wine, and in a dingy Kreuzberg basement Christian Nell has just snipped the final snip on the newest in an endless line of sure-to-be-gold-certified Uwe Ahrends Motion Pictures. Let's get out the Schnapps and watch one right now.

The film is already burning up the only copy of Eine Kindertragödie, the copy Nell threw out and then dug up out of the dumpster and then threw out again and then dug up for little more thanks than a bad sunburn. See in America they toss all your films when you're found dead in the alley behind the gay bar, but here it isn't quite so cut-and-dry. That sunburn is peeling now, the skin underneath is red and raw and wet to the touch but Nell isn't touching it and will not ever again. Like the red-raw-wet cuts on his fingers, it is inconsequential.

Inconsequential as the name of this film Nell knows only by cognates and the lovely-flickering-burning face of Uwe Ahrends, schoolboy-chic. Arms and legs, skin, nitrate pale. SIX-TWO, Nell thinks, the secret knowledge. Up here more like sixteen-twenty, smothering, blocking thought and airway. Damen und Herren, we've done it, by God, come closer, Uwe—show us that pretty face.

He obliges Nell like he oh-so-frequently does, here he is, the plush lips painted black, the eyes lined gaunter in the gauntness of a skull that would make a Shakespearian propmaster flush with envy. The lips part and here are the white teeth, here is the TONGUE, a sickly gray muscle Nell can still taste. He is giving his lines with such silent avidity, invisible syllables—something something suicide, Nell can't REMEMBER, well, he had snipped this one up with one hand. And anyway no intertitles yet, somebody else's job, gone is language, that pesky thing which had kept him from unzipping the back of Uwe's head and crawling inside. Du sprichst Deutsch—you speak German, Nell knew that one—als ob einen Schluck hast, Uwe had said once at a wrap party and made the actresses titter around mugs of cheap beer. A Schluck, what the fuck was that other than the most erotic collection of consonants Nell thought he'd ever heard or seen slide from a mouth that was looking at him back. A sip, maybe, a mouthful? A mouthful of what? Didn't our stupid American boy find out soon enough, and didn't he learn some vocabulary he could never get from his stern-cut-always-on-time tutor. Bitte, Christian . . . bitte.

Each new frame burns to nitrate ash as it passes, gone forever. Uwe looks to his right side, then to his left side, then to his right side again. Nitrate ash. Besser ist besser, Nell thinks, suddenly, rare clarity as he seems to recall what it is he's looking at; better is better, or and better, that's an easy one. Uwe takes a neatly folded letter from the pocket of his delightful TIGHT schoolboy shorts and he strikes a match and he lights it, and the letter burns away, and the film does. Das Leben ist Geschmacksache . . .

More pretty scraps of Uwe into the great nitrate vault-fire. He looks to his right side and dies, then to his left side, dies, looks forward, and—

—

—

—

—

He STICKS.

That single sound of the film eating itself vanishes from Nell's ears and leaves only silence, in which he is for a moment forced to hear the sad hoarse scream of his one lonely voice. The whirring returns inside now, the sound of a wasp ramming into the wall of his skull, enough to gag imagination, gag translation. Nell has never seen anything but the man and the imprint, he has never been On Set, so there was only life and that other thing, no magical in-between. There was only the love and a shuffling between basements and hours, an hour a minute. Cuts on hands and rubbing alcohol on cuts, semen on rubbing alcohol on cuts on hands, Uwe died.

Dead, he looks at Nell through the screen and STICKS. Some am schönsten perfect Schiller-Theater half a smile. For Nell? Why not? Why not, at this venture? Already Uwe is looking at him, the eyes almost alive enough for trickery. Oh the magic of Cinema.

And Uwe at once says (the lips move), in a perfectly clear voice, unaccented and subsequently hideous, "CHRISTIAN!" he says—

two syllables that crash into one another like two gas-guzzling trucks on a polluted American highway.

He springs forward.

Forward and—

—

OUT!

From the screen a thousand feet tall and a thousand feet long, hovering, over Nell and casting him not in shadow but some sick white contrast of it as nitrate particles fall and burn. It HURTS. Burning away the schoolboy shirt and leaving the beautiful pale memory of his bare chest, a still snipped from the eight-millimeter of only Nell's pervert mind, he is springing OUT—his arms outstretched, he is reaching towards Nell with such smothering, fantastic love, born again, and then the screen bisects him and he freezes as soon as he begins.

That lovely mouth hanging in the wicked O of what Nell will never have again.

Around the waist black sludge, the burnt-bad aftermath, the unusable THAT which Nell has spent irretrievable hours of his life scrubbing from his skin and which was under his fingernails the first time he touched Uwe. You have to understand this is never going to be anything more than a kind of compulsive self-violation, for Nell, like if he were peeling past his sunburn or taking a razor to his wrists and thighs again.

Oh, God, he's beautiful.

Nell stands without knowing he stands, his body only eyes, drinking Uwe up, choking on him, happily. He's so close, so still, WAITING, waiting for Nell to touch him and love him and all the things he'd gotten in pieces, the things he'd had to share with other men, well, no more, if he can reach up . . .

Nell thinks he can reach up and touch him. Just once again, that's all he needs, just one, innocent touch—

He reaches up—

The skin is there, burning, silver nitrate white and waiting and Nell's hand goes up—the nails, blackened, try to scratch, not with anger, no, never that, with LOVE—

The image flickers.

It is, of course, an image. You take a photo and later the subject dies, but really he was dead when you took it and the image was a memory on conception, something that has been and is no longer, a person in past-tense. What's left is the body you identified.

The eight-millimeter runs and runs and runs and runs and snaps with a sensation almost like pain.

He falls to his knees somewhere under the flickering bellybutton of his dead-body-idol and he begins to mumble, begins to almost pray. He stammers freely between English and what little German he does know . . . ich liebe dich, ich muss dich haben . . . he promises to learn his accusative and his dative and his genitive . . . he says he talked to the landlady and it'll only cost a hundred marks more rent to move into the big room upstairs, where they could live together, and sure it might be tight the first couple months but they'll make it, because Eine Kindertragödie is going to be THE ONE! The greatest film this country, ANY country has ever seen, hold onto me, Oo-veh, just stay here with me, here where I need you, don't go out tonight, I have this terrible feeling . . .

And at about quarter-past two in the morning Christian Nell has a massive cerebral incident and keels forward, breaking his nose under himself on the bad linoleum. The film burns and burns, and when it has nothing left to burn it moves onto the table and the walls and the theater, the plaster, the plywood. When they pull Nell's charred body from the ashes of the Kreuzberg Kino tomorrow morning, there is a great rictus of glee pressed into his shattered front teeth, no doubt because he is—in the words of an increasingly fascist local paper—finally downstairs with the other one.

TRANSMASC OF THE RED DEATH

LC von Hessen

SUDDENLY A REVVING engine growls through the ballroom's speakers and JACK O'DIAMONDS hits the stage. A ring of sparklers kindles up counterclockwise around the circular platform at the end of the catwalk, suburban backyard gunpowder scent mingling with the chemical aroma of artificial smoke hissing in from above. The boys at the party shut up for a moment before they whoop and applaud.

Jack's encased in head-to-toe black leather. Biker cap, moto jacket, skintight pants, riding boots, fingerless gloves, toolbelt. It's all very Tom of Finland: he's ripped, all right, but without the extreme caricatured muscularity or the dated pornstache, not that one can see under the red bandana cloaking the lower half of his face. Stage lights glint off his silver aviators and jacket studded with ruby-hued rhinestones—all diamond-shaped, naturally, and forming a great red diamond across his back—flashing daggers of lightning. An array of drone cameras hovers above the platform like digital vultures, projecting the action on screens nearby, megachurch-style. The boys in the crowd would have their phones hoisted, too, if not for the mandatory phone check at the door.

The soundtrack abruptly cuts to "Diamonds are Forever." Jack whips off his shades, revealing wide, piercing eyes roughly encircled in black war paint. His body is bathed in blue, purple, green track lighting as he flexes, struts, and poses for the boys, across the catwalk and around the platform; one at a time, he plucks out and displays various implements holstered in his belt, a switchblade, scalpel, butterfly knife, twirling them deftly between his fingers with utter contempt in his eyes. Many of the boys in the audience find this a turn-on.

Jack tosses off his cap. His dark hair is slicked back: one thick strand has escaped the pomade, falling in a rakish forelock above his grim-set brow. He gives a sharp two-fingered military salute to his host.

That host is one Rexroth Invictus Wickersham. A cool white spotlight illuminates a comically tall wingbacked chair on a pedestal at the end of the ballroom where a lissome twink slouch-sprawls, caught in the act of sucking nitrous oxide from a balloon before saluting back at Jack. A boy's curly head bobs and burrows between his legs. A bucket of truffle-oil popcorn is tucked under his arm by a minion.

Tonight Rex fancies himself the King of Hearts: a child's plastic party crown nestled on his well-coiffed head at a jaunty angle, a ruffle-collared shirt open to the navel, a thigh-high-booted leg slung over one arm of the chair. Aiming to resemble Sir Francis Dashwood—or more likely, given his basic cultural tastes, a stereotypical de Sade. Jack would characterize it as *a goddamn Ren Faire pirate costume* had Rex ever asked him.

Rex funds these parties from the overflowing coffers of his family fortune. All boys, all under 30, all worth at least seven figures, all-natural plumbing. The lone exception is this evening's entertainment.

Jack o'Diamonds unzips his jacket, revealing the compact, sinewy musculature of his bare torso. A matching pair of jagged horizontal scars under his pecs have been overlaid with tattoos, running halfway down his ribcage, meant to resemble the gills of a shark. As he swirls a combat knife above his head, Shirley Bassey croons about the sensual superiority of cold sharp objects to the fickle hearts of mortal men.

The song fades into a tense, rumbling ambient pulse, indicating shit's about to get serious. The track lights turn maroon, scarlet, crimson.

A young, handsome man stumbles onto the catwalk, pigeon-toed, wearing only a jockstrap and a goofy smile.

Jack had asked Rex not to drug this one too much. It's one thing to dull the worst of it so they don't freak out. It's another when they just flop back and starfish with eyes dead as a doll's. And anyway, they pay for this: they should feel it as much as possible.

The jockstrap boy nearly towers over Jack, who is not a tall man. Jack gives him a sudden bro-style backslap which knocks him down to his palms and shins. Jack moves quickly: a knee dug into his lower back to keep him prone and a fist clenched in his hair, pale neck bared to the crowd. Jack crouches, tugs down his bandana, and speaks low into the boy's ear.

"Do you know what's gonna happen tonight?"

Jack's co-stars have to sign a detailed contract—which they're forced to read to the end, repeatedly, under the eyes of two Wickersham family attorneys—when they're still fully sober and aware, but Jack still wants to confirm here and now, avoid any extra mess.

"Uh . . ."

Jack tugs his hair, hard. "Tell me."

"You're gonna kill me and it's gonna be ff*fuck*ing awesome."

Jack slaps him. Giggling stoners are such a turnoff.

"Gonna be cool as shit," the boy mutters, still smiling.

There's an Ace of Spades printed on his jockstrap because he's marked for death. Not the bluntness of Clubs. A sharp death.

Jack draws him up into a lazy, stumbling sex-dummy waltz, like the limp-limbed corpse he will soon become, fondling his growing bulge through the thin cotton. A periodic smack or knee to the balls and the boy groans in pleasure.

A minion has brought out a Fosse-style folding chair in which to prop him up. Jack selects a boxcutter from his toolbelt and slices off the jockstrap with a faint red line marking the Ace's hip. He tosses it into the crowd, upon which one guy immediately presses the crotch to his nose like one of his 19th-century ancestors at an ether frolic.

Another reason the boy couldn't be overdrugged: he has to stay hard.

Jack doffs his pants in one quick motion: hidden snaps have been sewn into the sides so he can rip them off like a stripper. His toolbelt is affixed to a leather harness girdling his hips and upper thighs.

The Ace druggily stares at Jack's crotch, at what's there and what isn't. Has he forgotten so goddamn soon?

"Do I get the front hole?" he blurts.

"Shut the fuck up." Yeah, he does, but that's no excuse to be fucking weird about it.

Jack maneuvers the boy's cock inside him, straddling his lap and riding him hard, nails denting his bare shoulders, until they're both on the verge and—

"Off with his head!" shouts Rex, the King of Hearts. "*Off* with his *heaaaad!*" The crowd takes up the chant.

Jack dismounts. He reaches into his toolbelt and selects an old standby: the pearl-handled straight razor.

He makes sure the drones get a good look before he slices clean through the base of his co-star's cock.

It's a clean cut, balls intact, shearing away some pubic hair with it. Jack hoists it like a prize. A pale stream of semen spurts out of the wound on a tide of blood. The audience cheers and hollers.

Before it can deflate, Jack spears the Ace's severed erection onto a modified icepick, plugging its base into the crotch of his harness. He quickly hollows out a new hole amid the draining blood, goring up his gloves but whatever, he has spares. He spreads the Ace's legs: what he fucks now is not a pleasure canal but a genuine gaping wound, penetrating raw muscle and tendon. He's learned with time to avoid prodding the bladder.

The boy's face throughout is glossy, entranced. He stares through Jack to some greater truth. He can't orgasm any more, but he can know the perverse ecstasy of an exceptional experience, a sensation indescribably intense.

He's barely conscious when Jack finishes. Sweating and pale, bleeding onto his own cock.

Before pulling out, Jack slashes his throat: a last mercy.

He cradles the victim in a pietà, blood spilling across his thighs, puddling under his boots. The soundtrack segues into Jack's exit music: Bowie's "Diamond Dogs."

Jack remains seated with the victim's body, blots out the drunk and coked-up party boys. This is not for them. Not for the world. This is a sacred moment. A sacrifice. *He gave his life to me.* To Jack and to his demon. This anonymous man whom Jack would only ever know as the Ace of Spades.

They were all the Ace of Spades.

TRANSMASC OF THE RED DEATH

***

Behind the buffet table stands Rob, face impassive, hands folded, and behind Rob on this wall of the ballroom are cheeky posters referencing this party's chosen demographic. ALL BEEF / NO FISH, says one; another, more obliquely, ALL TURF / NO SURF, atop a stock image of a hearty slab of ribeye juxtaposed with a sickly gawp-eyed salmon.

The name tag affixed to his respectable black dress shirt says ROBIN. His co-workers at the catering company have nicknamed him Silent Rob since he's quiet to the point of mumbling. He has reason for that.

Rob's a respectable height at 5'9" and has a naturally strong nose and jaw—family traits his mother and sister loathed in themselves—but with suspiciously wide hips and a certain softness to his eyes, his lips, his skin. "Sir, uh, ma'am?" he often hears, too self-conscious to admit they were right the first time. He wears a binder beneath his work shirt: it's the best he can do. He's not on testosterone. It isn't covered by his insurance. Not as a part-timer.

This late in the party, the buffet table has been picked clean aside from a couple of Kobe beef sliders embellished with 24-karat flakes. *Reverse alchemy*, Rob thinks: *their own bodies will transform gold into shit.*

He's worked for rich people before, even in well-guarded manors deep in the woods like this one, even at other gigs which mandated he sign an NDA. But this was the first time he'd unexpectedly witnessed a live snuff show.

Only the sternest, most discreet employees were sought for this job, and all male, per client request. A modest pay bump was attached. Yet Rob's the only one who didn't run to the staff toilet to puke or to a disused bedroom to faint, or else stand there paralyzed in blank-eyed shellshock.

A guest walks up wearing only spray-tan lines and a carpet that clashes with the curtains, pointing at a floppy-haired hipster nearly passed out on a wraparound couch.

"Yo, bro. Hellmann needs more Veuve," he slurs, briefly confusing Rob by pronouncing it *Vooov*. He stares at Rob a bit too long, as if unsure whether to clock him or grope him.

"The bar is over there, sir," Rob says, in a low, even tone.

73

They were supposed to fade into the background, like the household servants who ran this manor from the beginning alongside the roaches and rats. A silent pair of eyes and hands.

And for Rob, a silent lust.

Observing the bared and bound flesh, knowing this was the furthest he could ever come to the unbridled hedonism of men for men for men. And moreover—

What was that show? That was extreme even for a nepo baby Beggar's Benison like this one. The guy seemed to *like* it? And that leather man . . . was he really . . . ?

After a piss break in the staff toilet, Rob slips out to the courtyard, his skin still flushed with arousal in the cool night air.

Leaning languidly against an Ionic column, a black Dunhill between his lips, is Jack o'Diamonds. He's cleaned off the blood, shucked off the gloves, wiped away the greasepaint, slipped into a sensible pair of jeans.

"Hot in there," says Jack.

Hot out here, thinks Rob.

Jack stubs the butt beneath his heel and flicks out a penknife to pick his teeth.

—if only he'd hold it to my throat if only—

Jack holds his eye an uncomfortably long time, drops a noticeable glance down his body, holds his gaze again. A light smirk.

He realizes Jack is cruising him.

"Do you like doing it?" Rob says.

Jack cocks his head.

"Did you like watching it?" His voice is a honeyed drawl.

Rob's immediate response isn't shock, fear, disgust, or rage—and he knows Jack knows he's got him.

"Have you . . . done it a lot?"

Jack steps so close Rob can smell his sweat and tobacco.

"Y'know, kid, I'll level with you. Since you seem like the type of man who knows how to keep a secret." He lets that line linger a few beats. "Believe it or not, I'm 200 years old. Made a pact at the crossroads. Anyone can do it." He slides down the left shoulder of his jacket to show off a tattoo resembling a Goetic sigil.

"Used to be a graverobber in London. See this?" He lifts a small, roughly triangular bone on a cord knotted around his neck.

"My dad got the gibbet. After they hanged him, they stuck his corpse in a metal cage, as an example." He taps the bone. "This is from his index finger. First grave I ever robbed." He smiles. "So you understand, not much rattles me."

It's total bullshit—he doesn't even have an English accent, Rob thinks, before realizing that's the least remarkable thing about this story—but Rob is intrigued. Of course it's calculated to intrigue a fucking weirdo like himself.

The left hand caressing Rob's neck and jaw leads to teeth nipping his lower lip. The right hand at Rob's waist slides to his forearm, twisted around to the small of his back with no resistance. He lets Jack push him face-forward against the outer wall, behind a hedge bordering a quiet window. Jack presses against him, deftly unbuckles Rob's belt, and reaches into his creased black pants.

"Just so you know, uh, I'm on my period—"

Jack chuckles, his stubble grazing Rob's neck. "That's okay. You think I faint at the sight of blood?"

Rob's never been with a man who treated him like a man. For years he kept pretending to be a girl, assuming it would increase his odds, but straight men expected him to *act* like a girl and quickly lost interest when he didn't. They mentally cordoned him off into a separate suspicious, unknowable species, which he suspected would rankle even had he liked being a woman.

He wants it to be sharp, rough, brutal. Dangerous.

Crickets and cicadas perform to the creak of Jack's leathers, to Rob's gasps and moans as Jack works him expertly. When he finally withdraws his hand, Jack pins Rob's gaze while licking thick blood off his first two fingers.

Rob reaches out when he finally stops quaking.

"Should I—"

"You can't touch me. You wouldn't know how. Not yet." Jack claps him on the shoulder and strides back indoors.

Later Rob will find a spreading bruise on his neck and a card from his company tucked into his pocket, on which is written:

I'll call you.
—J ◊

***

Rexroth Invictus Wickersham is the youngest son of Dennison Kingsby Wickersham. That venerable businessman made his fortune in natural gas and has since acquired a pharmaceutical hedge fund. He has major if low-key ties to a private military contractor. He's a prominent donor to the American Evangelical Defense Foundation. Few major museums nowadays lack a Wickersham Wing.

The senior Wickersham does not want to know what occurs at his bachelor son's debauched parties in his least-used country house so long as nothing emerges to tarnish the Wickersham name or lower his stock value. Between them lies the vague promise that Rex will someday marry, procreate, and keep his future mistresses discreet.

"Sure you wouldn't want to bear my heir?" Rex asks, sprawled out on satin sheets.

Jack slaps him.

"Absolutely the fuck not."

Rex giggles. Fucking fool.

Jack is his kept man. His chained wolf, more like.

Jack has his own room at the isolated manor, though Rex spends most of his time jet-setting through various cities. Jack takes his money, takes his cock. And it's a decent enough cock when it's not hindered by Cocaine Dick.

Shame who it's attached to.

"Would you fuck my dad?"

"No." Jack lights a post-coital cigarette.

"Would you kill my dad?"

"In a normal way, not in a sexy way."

Truthfully, Jack's gotten bored. Rex doesn't want to bottom enough for Jack's taste and is more into watching pain than receiving it. And his standards for Aces are so strict: they must be white or white-passing, no older than Rex himself, below a certain BMI and, even though they pay out the ass for the privilege of being sex-murdered for an audience, below a certain income level (on that last count, because "it would feel too Freudian, like I'm, like, killing myself?").

And, of course, cisgender.

"He's actually, um. He's having this AED Foundation donors' gala next month so you should, uh. Make yourself scarce probably?"

Rex breaks out the ket and chops some lines with his black AmEx.

"I should introduce you to this one tradfash buddy of mine. I think he'd get a kick out of you."

"Your what buddy?"

"Tradfash! Isn't it funny? He's a Russian Orthodox convert." He takes a long snort. "He's into, like, Radical Traditionalism and Esoteric Hitlerism? He works at Raytheon."

"Yeah, I'd rather not meet some far-right shithead."

"Pfft. Politics don't *matter*." He might've appended: *you silly goose!* There's earnest confusion in Rex's face. He's rich enough to genuinely believe this.

"So yeah, my tradfash buddy founded this tech startup. And his angel investor is this one billionaire, this Silicon Valley guy my dad knows, who gets infusions of teenage boys' blood so he can stay young forever. Isn't that wild?" *Snoooot.* "Think he's gonna be at my dad's party, too."

***

Fortunately Rob's not a brat like Rex.

Since that last party, they've become regular fuck buddies. Jack motorcycles out from the manor when Rex is away, a bulging leather satchel across his back, to a suite he's booked at a decent hotel with his monthly stipend. Rex wouldn't like him fucking the help for free, but what does he know?

Rob lies back in masochist bliss as Jack tends to his latest knife cuts.

The more he can take, the bolder he gets, as a lover and as a man.

"Rex? He's a stupid chaser," says Jack. "Loves this idea of being a libertine hedonist but tells himself he's not fully queer if there's a cunt involved. He still lies to his dad and says he goes to church every Sunday."

"Then why stay with him aside from the money?"

"Well, he could blackmail me with all that footage. But also . . . he promised me a lab-grown ten-incher. State of the art."

Rob smirks. "Just ten?"

Jack gives him a quick smack on the ass. "I'm 5'6", let's not go crazy. I'm not Vlad the fuckin' Impaler." He leans back. "I've seen it. Just there in a tank, waiting. My ransom cock."

"Think you'll ever get it?"

Jack rolls his eyes. "Maybe if he gets bored of me."

"Couldn't you just ask your demon?" Rob pokes his tattooed sigil.

"I'm already paying off one debt." Jack sighs, shakes his head. "You don't understand. The more you want something, the greater the price. Would you be able to pay that price?"

In Rob's face is the grim determination, the sheer hunger, of a man who believes his masculinity must never be doubted again, in his own mind or the world's. Whose true manhood cannot be barred by money, law, or government.

"*Can* I?"

"Yeah, you can. But you have to embrace being evil. None of this 'we go high' horseshit. You have to get your hands filthy. You have to sacrifice for real. The worst sort of person they think you are? You've gotta be worse than that."

Rob's smile grows lupine.

Jack reaches for his ritual implements. He already has a target in mind.

Later, the maid on duty will wonder at the stubborn remnants of a circle in curious script marking the carpet. And at the lingering smell of sulfur.

***

The manor's domestic decor is a mélange of old-money heirlooms and tacky, overpriced artwork depicting foxhounds since Dennison Kingsby Wickersham is fond of blood sports. Tonight it's been strung up with bunting and miniature U.S. flags for the American Evangelical Defense Foundation gala.

The guests are all male, but not in the fun way. The hue of their collective flesh is a rainbow of cold cuts. Rexroth is here, presence mandatory for networking purposes, in a brand-new suit he automatically had tailored too snug at the waist and crotch. He clutches a champagne flute and quietly mingles.

"Feh! The gays aren't really persecuted in this country. It's not like we're in Jamaica or some Islamist state," opines Reverend Tessier.

"I cannot stand having to hire females," grouses Lord Yockey-Rockwell. "Of course production suffers, considering they're all competing for the men. It's their chthonic nature, you know. Hardwired for hypergamy."

" . . . And then we bussed the whole darn load of illegals to an inner city Taco Bell!" Governor Weyland chortles and slaps his thigh.

"*Hold, sinners!*"

The courtyard doors burst open on two robed men in matching skull masks. One wears a priest's cassock and wields a large scythe.

Rex cringes: that's obviously Jack. "Ohmigod, what is he *doiiing*," he hisses to himself.

Another, slightly taller man—Rex feels a nagging familiarity—follows, carrying a large basket from which he distributes a gilded manacle onto the left wrist of each guest.

The interruption provokes a ripple of amusement.

"Oh, Blangis, is this one of the Order's shenanigans?"

"You know, I think Goffard mentioned this same show at the Grove."

Nobody's alarmed except Rex and his father, both cuffed before they can protest. This must've been planned, or else how would they have gotten past security? How would they have known of this thoroughly private event at all?

The strangers mount the platform, join hands, and launch an obscure incantation. Between their feet is an occult summoning circle . . . from which emerges a thick, purple, suspiciously phallic maypole.

"Presenting a tribute to true manhood!" says the priest, to light applause. "The golden sperm of the Great God!"

He raises his left hand in a Roman salute, bidding the guests follow.

"Now, gentlemen: *pray.*"

A cluster of golden threads shoots out the top of the maypole, clamping onto each man's manacle. Almost immediately, the threads withdraw back into the pole, along with the cuffs.

And their skins.

The lucky ones go into shock. Pandemonium reigns in the ballroom, stumbling fleshless and screaming through the slick of fallen fat and organs, pink and purple and red. The priest follows, laughing, scythe slashing off their flaccid cocks and sagging balls like ancient war trophies.

"If you can't use them correctly, you don't deserve to have 'em!"

His accomplice collects the severed genitals in his basket and arranges them, glans inwards, around the summoning circle, in which the maypole has mysteriously descended.

At best, Jack thinks, they will know true pain for the first time in their lives, perhaps learn some truth for the only time. In endless pain is ecstasy.

That is their gift.

Rex kneels before the priest, gripping Jack's cassock. His lidless eyes and gritted teeth ask what his throat no longer can. Jack holds Rex's glistening face in silence.

The dying heir's blood, licked from his thumb, tastes thoroughly unremarkable.

As dawn creeps in, blowflies spread larval life within the peeled corpses of the Western world's finest men, strewn across the ballroom in a wet red heap. The household staff have fled, never to return except much later, under baffled investigatory duress.

And atop the platform, within the circle of cocks, stands a thick, throbbing patchwork of flayed skins fashioned into a tight cocoon the approximate height of an average man. Swaddled in demonic manhood, the former caterer within awaits his final transformation.

Jack o'Diamonds zips up his leather jacket, mounts his bike, and disappears into the pines with the sunrise.

✳✳✳

Dedicated to all Christian Nationalists
and their enablers
Everywhere

THE MAN OUTSIDE

Simone le Roux

WHEN IMOGEN FIRST saw the man outside, she didn't hesitate to tell her mom.

It was the strongest instinct her eleven-year-old brain had: If something was wrong, Mom would know what to do.

And something was quite wrong.

The man in the front yard stood motionless, watching the window Imogen sat on the other side of with such intensity that she found herself crouching behind the couch, as though his gaze would hurt her.

"There's a man outside, Mom," she squeaked and felt annoyed at herself. She was getting too old to run to Mom for every little thing that scared her.

Mom looked up from folding laundry at the dining room table. "A man?"

"He's watching our window."

Mom sighed, put down a freshly folded shirt, and stepped beside Imogen.

Imogen's hand itched to tug Mom down to her level, stop her from exposing so much of herself to this stranger's stare. But that would be silly. Mom pulled back the curtain for a better view and Imogen's hands clutched, white knuckled with the effort of stillness.

The first gentle hum of confusion in Mom's voice made Imogen curl into herself. Did Mom not see him? It *was* strange how he just stood, shrouded in shadow, eyes gleaming. It wasn't normal. Was Imogen imagining him? When Mom sent her out to play in the yard, would Imogen have to pretend that she couldn't see him either?

The reality was worse.

"Hmm . . . oh, that man over there?" Mom pointed as though there were thousands of men standing just off the sidewalk to choose from. Imogen nodded anyway.

"I don't see the problem, dear," Mom said, dropping the edge of the curtain.

Breath left Imogen in a rush. "He's just . . . watching," she choked out, dumbfounded.

"He's allowed to stand there, darling. He seems fine—he's just a man, like Dad or like your Grandpa," Mom added as the final blow.

For the first time in her short life, Imogen felt unsafe. Really, truly unprotected. The defensive part of her brain, the part meant to defend her from ugliness, whirred into gear, ready for damage control. Maybe Mom was right. After all, she would be better at spotting danger than Imogen, wouldn't she? Mom would know if this man was a threat, or if he really was like Dad or Grandpa.

"Should I go say hello?" Imogen asked, feeling as though it were Opposite Day. Down was up, danger was safe, and she had to do the exact thing she didn't want to do to calm the howling in her brain.

"Oh, *God* no," Mom said.

Imogen's heart twinged, because that wasn't the worried reaction that Mom had when she suggested taking the bus by herself or climbing the super tall tree in the park. Rather, Mom looked like Imogen had offered to lick the sidewalk or pee in public.

"What should I do, then?" Imogen whined, desperate to make things right, to reconcile the fear in her heart, to feel loved and protected and wanted by Mom again.

"What makes you think you have to do anything?" Mom said and threw another look at the man through the curtains. Their eyes must have met for a moment because she turned away quickly. "He's allowed to be where he is. There's nothing to be done. Period."

Mom heaved a sigh and returned to folding laundry. Imogen sank into the couch and cupped her hands over her chest, as though she could contain the explosion in her heart.

THE MAN OUTSIDE

***

The man was still there the next morning. He had not moved an inch.

Imogen knew because the snow all around his feet was pristine—she saw when she had to walk past him, as her legs endeavoured to go ever faster. His eyes were on her all the way down the street, an oily feeling down the back of her neck.

He was still there in the afternoon when Mom walked her home. Mom shot the man a quick, nervous smile like the one she gave the rude clerk at the post office, and ushered Imogen inside.

Imogen watched out the window for Dad to get home. While she didn't always see eye to eye with her father, she was certain he would see the same thing she did. He would tell the man to leave in his scary-calm voice and call the police, probably to let them know there was a strange man standing in gardens watching little girls. Not that Imogen was so little anymore.

She held her breath when Dad's car pulled up out front.

He stepped out, backpack slung over one shoulder, blinking in the cold winter air, and noticed the man immediately. How could he not? Imogen was sure he could sense the menace emanating from the man before he'd even stepped out of the car.

Dad's expression dropped into one of utter weariness, as though he had worked a million days in a row, only to find more work ahead of him. He pressed his lips together, nodded to the man, and walked inside.

After Mom's betrayal, Imogen couldn't bear it. She couldn't understand the despair rising in her chest like a wail, or why she knew she would never feel safe ever again. Perhaps, many years from now she would understand she was mourning—but in that moment, she felt only an emptiness so vast that it would echo like a cave if she fed any voice to it.

***

The man did not shiver, did not sit down in the drifts of snow that surrounded his ankles. He stood and breathed and watched.

***

83

Winter broke and gave way to warmer weather. Imogen kept her heavy jacket on well into spring, finding comfort in its cushiony layers. When Mom successfully hid it one morning, Imogen was forced to wear something more appropriate for the heat, and her skin crawled so badly that she had to clench her fists to stop herself from scratching at her bare arms.

She stopped playing in the front yard. She used to sit out on the swing with a pile of books next to her, feet kicking idly while she read. Now, she couldn't even relax enough to read in her own room unless she closed the curtains. Whenever she opened them, her eyes would find the man's already on her, always steady. She shuddered.

Over time, though, Imogen became used to all the ways she made herself feel safe: her carefully controlled eyeline, her permanently shut curtains that bathed her room in glowy gloom, the reassuring feel of her backpack. It was heavy enough to swing at the man if he finally attacked her. She had loaded it up with water bottles and stones.

And then, on one of the last days of the school year, as Imogen passed through the front yard, the man took a step forward.

At first, she was sure it was a trick of the light. But when she really looked, she knew. He had taken one big stride towards her house. He stood still again, gazing back at her as though nothing had happened.

Imogen threw up when she got to school, not knowing how to tell anyone. What would she say? What could she say? Her parents had only ever made excuses and she had no reason to believe her teachers would do any different.

"Are you okay?" a timid voice asked through the stall.

Imogen dry-heaved again before she was able to pause and consider. "I'm okay," she lied after a while. How could she sum up months and months of exhaustion? The terror of seeing that imposing figure move even closer to her home? Knowing there was no point in telling anyone because they would tell her not to worry when it was the only thing she could think about? "I'm just tired."

"I get that," the voice, another girl, said. "Sometimes I feel like there isn't enough sleep in the world."

***

Months went by. Imogen's birthday came. Twelve years old: her whole life ahead of her, but not her front yard. Not if she wanted to feel safe.

One night, Imogen was fresh off a sugar rush and clutching her abdomen as though she could squeeze this new pain from it like toothpaste out of a tube. She dared to peek out of her curtain at the man and look. Really *look*.

He wasn't so scary, she thought. He was all broad shoulders and hands—like Dad's, like Grandpa's. Perhaps his aura of menace was something else. Intensity? Persistence? Determination?

Why would anyone spend all this time, all this energy on her, she wondered. She looked down at her little belly, her doe-like limbs. Perhaps he had noticed the way her hair caught the sun, or he had seen that she was particular about wearing clothes that flattered her new waist, like Mom taught her.

More and more, Imogen wondered what the man thought when he looked at her. Did he notice her shoulders slumped on bad days, her cheeks glowing on good ones?

He continued his excruciatingly slow journey across her lawn. Was he marking the time by the seasons that fell from his shoulders like nothing, or by Imogen's changing body?

"That figure's not going to last forever, hon," Mom would say and, God, Imogen hoped her mother was right. She couldn't bear the man's eyes on her, but she also couldn't imagine what she would do if he turned away now.

***

The first time she noticed a different man standing in a different yard, she froze.

This man, too, stood with a straight back and hands that vibrated like they would blur into motion any second. He was a bit smaller than hers, a bit older, but there was no mistaking the shadows wreathing him, the way he watched the house.

No one else she knew had someone in their front yard, but this person did—and it took everything in Imogen not to run up to their front door and knock. All she wanted was to talk to someone, anyone, who could understand how she felt.

But what if they didn't? What if they gave her the same cold, disgusted looks her parents did when she asked? What if they also found her fear just as shame-worthy as her curiosity?

She shoved her hands deep into her pockets and carried on home, like she would whenever she saw a man in a place where he had no business being.

***

Imogen was sixteen. Earlier in the day, she'd seen the man take one of his big steps forward, placing him more than halfway across the lawn. She chewed at her lip so hard that it bled.

How dare he treat her like this without making his intentions known? How could he turn her own family against her with his mere presence?

Imogen was furious, but she didn't know who to direct it at. Herself, maybe, for being such a coward. Her parents, for telling her that her feelings were wrong. Her friends for not feeling the same way, for not having a man of their own inching ever closer to them. Her rage was all-consuming, directed at everyone and no one at all.

She waited until her parents were out to sneak some vodka from their liquor cabinet. She sipped from the bottle and glared at the man outside. A few gulps were enough to get her stumbling drunk, shedding her self-control.

Before she could counsel herself against it, she was storming outside in her pyjamas. Years and years of tacit warnings from her parents faded into so much background noise and she squared up right in front of him, fists clenched so hard that her nails dug into her palms.

"What do you want with me?" Imogen blurted. She didn't care about his glare or the way that he was much taller than she'd thought he would be this close. Their eyes met for an instant and his hatred matched her own.

He didn't reply, just kept his eyes boring into hers. His hands twitched.

"Imogen, what do you think you're doing?"

Mom and Dad were back early. Date night hadn't gone well, then.

"Leave that man alone this instant!"

Suddenly, she was eleven years old again, waiting for her parents to make her feel safe, to make her feel sane. To reconcile the fear in her heart, to love and protect her again.

"Just tell me why!" she cried, and she wasn't sure who she was addressing. Her fists shook and, to her utter dismay, tears began to trickle down her face. "What do you *want*?" she sobbed, swiping at her nose.

The only answer was her mother's rough grip, dragging her inside.

***

Imogen did the math.

The man would reach her front door exactly two weeks after her eighteenth birthday, and she was quite sure no one would stop him.

Was it such a bad thing? This man, who had devoted so much time, so much focus, such discomfort to her, would at last step into her home. Didn't he deserve a break? Somewhere to rest? Would he at least reveal what was so special about her?

As much as she thought about it, Imogen couldn't decide what she was more excited for: the answers to her questions or the end of this ridiculous, disappointing march through adolescence.

Even when she got home later with her parents' permission, she found herself skirting the man, as if somehow her impropriety would jolt him out of his stoicism. She was sick of being nervous, of not understanding why. Of avoiding eyes, pulling up her necklines, pulling down her hemlines. She wanted it done. She couldn't wait.

Her eighteenth birthday came and went. She celebrated it at the park with friends. As she stumbled home, belly full of cake and cheap, warm whiskey, she had to weave around the man.

He was on the porch now. Frankly, a bit of a nuisance. Obvious. Even her parents, who had ignored his presence for years, became visibly irritated every time they tried to leave the house. One time, Mom rolled her eyes at Imogen, as though it was her fault.

Her calculations had been a bit off. Two weeks and three days after her birthday, there was a knock at the door. One solid fist pounding three times.

Her entire body buzzing, Imogen rushed downstairs. Her parents were already there, opening it. The man stood, a smile cracked across his face. It was bizarre. It would have been charming on anyone who wasn't her tormentor.

"Imogen, your guest is here," Mom said, as though Imogen had invited him in.

"Have anything to say?" Dad asked.

Looking at this man, who had haunted her, watched her, scared her, judged her, Imogen didn't know where to begin. How could she? No one had told her what to do from here. All these years to prepare, and no one had prepared her.

She took a tentative step forward.

As soon as she came close, the man's enormous hand snapped out and closed around her neck. He lifted her up, up, up, until her feet scuffed at the floor.

"What are you doing, Imogen?" Mom shouted, pushing ineffectually at her arm. "What did you say to him to make him behave like this?"

Imogen choked, clawed at the hand that grasped her throat. Even if she could say something, she wouldn't know how to make anyone understand what she felt. It wasn't betrayal exactly—she'd always been suspicious of the man's intentions and aware of her parents' indifference—and it wasn't sadness either.

This felt correct. Perhaps she could have teased the man less or kept her weighted backpack on her or not gotten drunk those times or asked her family the right questions or confided in someone at school. But she knew. Deep, deep down, she knew it was only ever going to end this way.

Her hands tired, weakening. They caught on her chest, where her fingertips felt her heart flutter like a dying bird.

RIVER BARGAIN BABY

K.S. Walker

THERE'S REASONS NOT to go sit by the banks of the Dequindre. The mosquitoes bite something fierce this time of year, for one. May through September the air is thick with them. The river swells wide on its way through Wyandott. When the rain comes, the Dequindre spills over its banks in a lazy way, slowing almost to a standstill. Stagnant waters are fertile breeding ground for some.

And that was another reason, most of the time it was more marsh than bank anyway. And even when the wetlands firmed up it wasn't good fishing. And then, there were the stories. Plenty reasons not to go. But not enough to make Jackie stay away.

There's a saying for girls like her.

***

Like mother like daughter, I guess.

I don't mind makin' my own trouble. Spice things up. Keep the people-folk on they toes. It is always a nice surprise though, when trouble seeks me out instead. And I know trouble when it comes sniffin'. Trouble sound like four pairs of shoes scuffin' up a dirt path. It sound like "I betcha won't." By the time all y'all came round the front of Miss Loretta's house, hushed voices like she ain't already heard you a quarter mile back, I was near giddy. Kid-folk, too? My laughter sent bubbles up through the marsh grasses. Lawd, I can't help myself sometimes.

Me and Miss Loretta? Me and her come to an understandin' a long time ago. I let her alone in her little house near my banks, closer than any other people-folk stay. And in turn, she let me peep through her eyes sometimes. I has her lean closer out her rocker so I can get a good look at'cha.

"Y'all not messin' around by the river are ya?" Miss Loretta hollers out. Hush now, woman. Don't be a spoil-sport.

"No, ma'am." Ha! Lies if I ever heard one. Don't bother me none. I take my time studyin' each one of y'all. See which one is it 'bout to make my day. I recognize the look. Lil girl with two plaits and a chin that says she got somethin' to prove. Girl, you ain't got nothin' to prove to them boys you runnin' round wit! But you c'mon see me anyway. See what we can make of ya.

"Good! The chirrun that go down to that river don't come back—"

Woman, I said hush! I yank Miss Loretta back down in her rocker, hard. Why go ruinin' a fun thing before I even get the chance to get started?

"Goodbye, now!" I chirp through Miss Loretta.

Y'all scoot along a lil faster. Don't worry, I'll keep Miss Loretta busy long enough for y'alls to come see me. She won't be callin' any mommas any time soon. Tattlin'.

Let's see what good ole Dequindre can do for ya.

***

All the best stories start with desperation. A want so large it twists like hunger pangs tying your stomach up in knots. Jackie knows a thing or two about that. A want so great she'd do anything to ease the fire of it. Maybe even wade into the Dequindre up to her knees because Marquis dared her to. Even though the fishing is bad, the mosquitoes thick, and they all know the stories. Desire and desperation can do that.

***

Chile you shouldna' come here. I'm greedy and proud of it. I been known to reach out a mighty hand and snatch abody just cause I can. But let me tell you somethin'. There's somethin' down here with me that got more greed than I do. She been kickin' up my sandy soil, troublin' the surface waters something fierce with her want, her need. I'd tell you not to come too close but well, things might be more interestin' if ya do.

RIVER BARGAIN BABY

***

There's a moment at the end of the dirt path when Jackie hesitates. She can feel Grant, Marquis, and Jamir at her back. Watching. The insects have stopped their buzzing, not a peeper peeping, like the whole river source to mouth, producer to predator, holding its breath watching what she's about to do next. The thing about Jackie is, there hasn't been a dare yet she's backed down from. And she surely isn't about to start now. Not when she's got something to prove. If this is the price of acceptance she'll pay it and say it came cheap. She hasn't learned yet that acceptance isn't the same as friendship. That you can be a part and still apart. That'll come.

Her fists clench and she takes two long steps in.

***

Did you know I knew your momma? Yessss, chile, and if you ain't the spittin' image of her!

Must've been about, what, thirteen years ago now? Thirteen years and nine months if we being exact. I seen your momma inch as close as she dare, asking me for a miracle. Her hands clasped tight to her bosom, tears streaking her brown face. She sho wanted a baby but never could find a use for a man. So, she came to me.

She pleaded, tore at her hair, ripped at her skirts, made all sortsa fuss. "I'll do anything!"

Anything? Chile, she shoulda known better. She was in the marsh up to her ankles already but I bade her come closer still. *Anything, she say?* She stepped down into me proper. Black muck sucking at her skirts, til my waters could kiss her skin. Til the long grass could wrap around her thighs gentle-like. A lover's touch. Your momma asked me for a baby. I gave her two. Before she fell asleep that night I sent Ma Skeeter to give her a message. Your momma's eyes were heavy like pockets full of stones. And Ma Skeeter landed on her right cheek and whispered in her ear for me: One of them babies is for me and only one is for you.

***

That's right honey, take one more step in.

***

91

The people-folk only come see me when they want somethin'. When they want to keep a lover in they bed, steal one from someone else's. When they want revenge or riches. When they want somethin' they just can't get otherwise. But ain't none of that what's on your heart is it? Your mind focused on tryna get them lil ashy-kneed boys to let you be a part of they group. That's just somebody son! You up to your knees in the divine, honey, and you ain't even think to ask for nothin'? Nothing? Well. Maybe, just maybe, I got a gift for you anyway.

***

Shallow waters run warm but a chill rakes down the back of Jackie's calves anyway. Marquis shouts "time" from the banks and she can't get out of the water fast enough. She did it! She lifts her foot to run, only to catch it and fall face first into the water. A cloud of mosquitoes puff into the air, angry and seeking. Jackie is shocked to find herself in the river up to her shoulders, to feel the surface she disturbed lapping gently at her neck. She scrambles up as fast as she can. She pulls her foot free. Whatever resistance she'd encountered is gone. Jackie hightails it out the water, onto firm land. She whoops and hollers along with Marquis, Grant, and Jamir all the way home, but she never stops glancing over her shoulder. Like there's something behind her, just out of sight. She dismisses the feeling with a shrug. It's like the saying, right? Out of sight out of mind?

***

I give credit where credit is due, and your momma, well, she understood the assignment. Y'all were born under a full moon. You know that? I could hear all the hollerin' and carryin' on. She birthed y'all by herself on the laminated kitchen floor. Cut through the umbilical cords with a dull butcher's knife. Soon as she could stand again she wrapped both y'all up in paisley printed towels and brought y'all to meet me. I don't know how she decided, but she slipped one baby into the tall grass, no basket made of reeds. She put the other baby to her breast and I ain't seen her since.

But I see you now.

I think parenting look good on me! I make sure my River Daughter stay clothed (robed in algae blooms, crowned in cattails), fed (on rainbow trout and misplaced dreams), safe. I make sure she's learned. A river with a memory long as mine, huh, my baby knows history alright. Including her own.

That's right. She see you too, honey.

Pardon, the heron don't like my laughter. It startles him so he take off in a hurry. He might just have to get used to it. I just been so *tickled* lately!

***

There's that other saying: What the river takes, the river keeps. What the Dequindre gives back is a curse indeed.

***

This River Daughter been patient but she ain't got an ounce of kindness in her. Now usually, what's mine is mine, honey, but I been feeling gracious and I been thinking to myself: Lawd, won't it be entertainin' to see what happens if I

Let

her

go?

***

Ma Skeeter told me you ain't been sleepin' good. You spend all night tossin', turnin', babblin' like waves breaking against the shore.

Now I wonder why that could be?

***

The Dequindre's not the only one shrouded in stories thick like a heavy evening fog. No, no. Jackie's been listening to conversations not meant for children's ears and what she *heard* is that Miss Loretta that stay in that shack down there on the edge of the Dequindre, well, there's always been something not quite right about her. Or maybe she heard that Miss Loretta knows some things that good Christian folk shouldn't know a thing about. Or that she keeps company with some unsavory types. What she might have even heard was the word witch. Power. Hushed tones speak louder than the words themselves. Who better to turn to when

Jackie finally admits to herself that since she stepped in the Dequindre she's been seeing things that can't be and hearing things that shouldn't speak and she's having a harder and harder time telling the difference between waking hours and dreams?

***

Chile you lookin' like somethin' troublin' you. That might be my fault though. *Hee*! But you go on down to Miss Loretta's anyway. Tell her your problems.

***

'Your shadow don't keep up with you no more, you say? Well, I'll be.

And you think you hearin' someone practice your voice? Watchu mean, baby?

Whispers sound like you but not you? Sound like you but far away? No?

Oh, sound like you but with lungs pushin' round water 'steada air? Iiiii'lllll be.'

I keep Miss Loretta's head bobbin'. Her eyes wide with understanding. Cause I get it. But you know what else? I never did believe in lyin' to kid-folk.

Miss Loretta knows the words. Says 'em without me promptin': Go make a deal with the Dequindre then. But chiiiiile, you musta not liked that answer! The look on your face!

***

There's another saying for what Jackie's going through as she stumbles off of Miss Loretta's porch, arms pinwheeling, hands scrabbling for purchase in the dusty yard. Nobody feels the outrage of injustice like a child does. She completed the dare. She proved her point. *And* she brought back from the river a black-eyed girl that wants to take her place? She's been told "life ain't fair" more times than she can count. But she never had reason to take the words to heart until now.

***

I was disappointed you know. Chile, you run away from Miss Loretta like *she* the problem. But she not. Gal, you know better.

94

RIVER BARGAIN BABY

Your problem stand 'bout *your* height, *your* weight, 120 pounds soaking river water wet on the bathroom mat. *Your* problem show up in your dreams and open her mouth and out flow silt and seaweed. *Your* problem is a river-sister that's been down here so long she rememberin' things she ain't never had no business knowin'.

***

That night Jackie wakes up in a cold sweat, choking on hollow rush stems and pondweeds to the weight of someone sitting at the foot of her bed.

She turns on the lights to find herself in a room alone.

With a damp spot on the blankets down past her feet.

***

I was wonderin' when you was gon' come deal with me directly. C'mon down here, chile. The water is finneeeee. I hear you got yo'self a problem. Well, good ole Dequindre can work miracles, don't you know! Don't you worry yo'self none bout the stories you may or may not have heard. I can fix anythin' if you make it worth my while. A spirit, you say? Wantin' to take your place? Welllll that is a problem. Watchu willin' to pay? Anythin'? Lawd, like mother like daughter. Why don't you come on in a lil deeper. Now what if I told you that I already made a bargain with your momma? That I'm a lot of things, but a liar ain't one of 'em? I already gave her a baby, you see. I believe "One for me, and only one for you'" was the words exactly. Nowww you see. It's only fair, right? River Daughter'll mind her business mostly. Besides, don't you wanna see what's on the other side? Ha! Trouble? Well that's true too. Still, there's a lot you could learn from a river like me. Power? Gal, now you talkin' that talk! That's two asks now, mind. I'm keepin' count. Oh, I know a thing or two about power. Yessss, wade a lil closer, chile. These waters is trouble. Trouble and power. Power and trouble indeed.

THE PRINCE OF OAKLAND

M.M. Olivas

THE MOMENTS ALWAYS hid on harvest nights, as if they felt us coming by a shift in the wind or the bite of bolt cutters on metal, the slide of a window. They always retreated into the floorboards or dark corners by the time Griff and I could stand upright with our scythes in the belly of the house, but the house's history would still linger in the air. A stale smell.

The harvest of 9721 South Van Ness Avenue was like the other half dozen before it—another Queen Anne rowhouse, this one with fish scale shingles and delicate woodwork carved into its pine façade, painted plum and cream and trimmed with a deep forest green, same as it had been since 1922. Griff took the entrance floor, kicking furniture and yanking drawers open to pocket jewelry; I crept up the stairs, careful not to disturb a thing. We wafted incense smoke through the house. It stank of wax and burnt book ends. It crammed into every corner and tarred up my lungs, dilating my sight to show me the shadow creatures rippling weightless and watery in the corners of the rooms—the Moments.

Their edges clawed out and flowed back in like tarps or crawling spider legs. Some of them prowled like coyotes. Their shapes were never alike, but all of them protected their burning lantern cores. The shadows of Moments past, echoing within: birthday parties, family gatherings, quiet fights, first fucks, palms striking cheeks, hands grabbing keys, shouting with phone-slams ending sentences, baby's first words, a father's last—whole cities were made up of these Moments. They inhabited every street corner and filled every house, amalgam creatures formed from the parts of souls that were forever tied to place, that existed just beyond the edge of human sight.

I plunged my scythe into their fat and shadow. Pulled with the curved hook to tear them into ribbons, and when they were in that state, too broken to fuse themselves back together again, I gulped them up with inhales—blew them out into my bag woven out of maize husks.

I moved on, harvesting room to room like Griff on the floor below me, quickly before police sirens came to tear up the block. With every slice of 9721 South Van Ness Avenue, the walls howled, the floorboards cried out. I reminded myself what Griff had told me on the first night when I'd strangled my scythe's handle with nervousness until splinters split my skin, when I'd seen the Moments in their strangeness for the first time, and terror and guilt had locked me still. "Whoever those Moments belong to are gone, Yaren. They haven't lived here in years."

I stopped in the attic. A child's bedroom. A blooming fungal Moment plastered against the wall above the bed. Its lantern core burned toxic bright with toxic neons and within it, I saw flashes of a son and his father, the tenderness between them as they sat on the bed and watched a movie together. The Moment was a stillness trapped in time; its glow warmed my cheeks.

I sliced it up. Swallowed that Moment but held it in. I flexed my body tight to fight back the vomit in my throat that was the smoke and fire limbs writhing for *out—out—OUT!* I held it until it settled into my skin. Between my viscera and bone, gum and tooth, finger and nail, and the sweetness of the Moment that was a father telling their son how he'd always love him was mine. But as the Moment seeped into the tight ridges of my brain, it soured. The images began to distort. To rot. A hushed conversation began as the movie's credits rolled: the boy standing in front of his dad and digging his toes into carpet. Little fists tugging his shirt. His father asking the question again, over and over, each word plucked for purpose. *What are you,* and *Why are you* until a *No you're not,* and the violence that followed when the Boy said *But I am!* Then there were teeth, spit, knuckles, elbows, pleas—I spat out the last of that Moment, screaming.

I collapsed against the bed and dropped my sack and watched my harvest escape into the dark, but I couldn't move. Not until the windows flashed red, blue, red, blue and Griff shook me by my shoulders and shouted, "We have to leave now. Right fucking now!" I had frozen wide-eyed. The taste of disdain a familiar rot coating my throat.

***

As a child, my father built fences—*never play with kids who aren't also Christian. Stop listening to that rock music, it isn't good. Stop dressing like **that**—*and I'd stomp them down to spite him. Like when I'd sit on the grass with Griff and let the damp green stain my knees. My father would shout from the porch, "Stop it. You'll ruin the furniture with those stains." I'd ignore him, drawing shapes from the clouds until the sun drilled holes in my eyes—a dare to see if my father would ever go beyond just orders and wrestle me away, like he did with the people he'd arrest at work.

He never did that.

But on drives, we'd pass the neighbor's house with the rainbow flag in the yard and Dad would mutter *Homos,* always with disdain, though it took me years to decipher that; to pluck away the tones. Saturday morning cartoons taught me what hatred sounded like. It was with a chuckle and smile that I learned how *that* flag was something Dad despised.

Those Moments stacked like bricks. More walls.

Families are built of Moments.

When my father finally uprooted us out of Oakland and into the suburbs to get away from the "gangs" and "heroin needles in the parks" and the *crack-crack!* of gunshots at twilight, we'd argue around the dinner table. Me correcting him that it was Latin*e* now, not Latin*o*, Latin*a*, and him not shouting, but broadcasting his voice like another wall that my words would blast against. "No, no, that's bullshit. Go out to Oakland tell some real Mexicans that our language is wrong and see what happens. Ah?"

A hollow threat. Because he'd never let me return to the city. Not as an OPD officer who thought the sum total of the place was his experience of coming and going, and not of those who stayed.

But the message was clear:

The city will reject you.

***

BART—the veins that connect the Bay together. Built in 1972 with construction completed in 1974, it flowed up from San Jose, and down from Richmond, all its paths converging in Oakland—its beating heart. The BART would take you anywhere in the Bay you asked it, and when you'd finally had enough, you could take the Blue Line eastwards into the suburbs, away from the cities and toward the Five Highway that shot off to the rest of the expanding continent beyond, and leave.

My stop was 19th street—a five block walk into an industrial park of white and windowless buildings, to the warehouse that still read *Woodwork's Doors and Windows Carpentry* in a peeled and sun-bleached sign. It smelled of oil and woodchips inside, and stacks of raw lumber waited with heavy machinery tarped under white sheets. Griff's father once owned the warehouse, before he drank it away with their Alameda home, before a corporation bought it on a whim but left it empty. Another moment locked in time.

Griff and I used to play with wooden swords between stacked pallets. I'd play a knight, and Griff would proclaim himself the Prince of Oakland. Because he was the great grandson to Emperor Joshua Norton, the first and only ever emperor of the United States. He read to me from a thin library book about Emperor Norton; how Norton was a loser, a failed businessman without a life worth living and completely alone; how one day he'd delivered a letter to the Bay's *Bulletin* paper declaring himself Emperor of the United States; how the paper thought it was a funny joke and published it anyway.

Griff would say he was designed to be great like his ancestor, and our giggles would bounce off the pallet towers. Now I walked quickly through that warehouse; the echo of my steps filled the emptiness.

***

"We have a new house tonight," Griff said when I fumbled into his office overlooking the warehouse floor. His voice smooth and gentle and laced with the confidence I wished I had in my lousy, scratchy one.

Griff's crown was noosed off his throat with strings. Because it wasn't a crown of jewels or thorns—Griff's crown was a hat. A once-was bucket hat from the Oakland Zoo I'd given him when we were kids, that over time he'd scuffed, ripped, stitched back together again with clashing patchwork. He added stickers and patches to it, of the Raiders, and A's, and In-n-Out or D.A.R.E. Painted ACAB across the brim of it. He laced all that together with catholic rosaries to create his amalgam crown of the city—his city—for Griff was the Prince of Oakland and the greater Bay area, and the Prince of Oakland watched me with golden eyes embedded in oak wood skin.

"But we still have Moments to round up from the last place," I said. "Why so soon?"

"Because you froze," my Prince said to me, matter-of-factly. He let the word hang, like a Moment marinating in the silence. He was right, though. I'd never kept a Moment for myself. The Suits only paid us to clean the properties of them—to scrap out those lingering traumas, the ones that creak open doors or groan at night, that only exist to tie you down. We'd sell them to the suits, and they'd descend on the now clean properties. Then weeks later I'll pass the house and see "SOLD" plastered up on the sign in the yard, the house's shingles, bargeboards, delicately carved frieze, all ripped out and replaced with smoothness. The colors erased by white.

When I shut my eyes, I could still see the Father of that Moment—the intensity in his stare as the boy uttered words he could not, not ever, take back—how I'd seen those eyes before. Tasted the white flashing violence that followed. I'd dropped the Memory sacks and jeopardized the location. My fault.

My fault.

The Prince of Oakland says to me, "We can't afford more mistakes like this, or the Suits will just find others to do the job. But we're so close." Close to finally making rent on time. Close to finally paying off loans. Close enough for Griff to just brush his fingertips on the deed for this warehouse that had once been by birthright his. "I *need* to know I can count on you, Yaren. So let me know if there's something wrong at all and we can fix it together, okay? So we can keep going. Can you do that for us, Yaren? Can you?"

***

As I waited for the BART that afternoon, the wind brushing cold against the stubbled side of my scalp, the terminal took a breath and I counted the seconds as a man in a too-big coat and ragged jeans slipped over the turnstiles. Four seconds. Two officers peeled away from the corridor walls and started shadowing the man. I hadn't even noticed the officers were there, but they had been, hadn't they? Always lurking in the corners of your sight.

Someone was shouting—wasn't shouting—was just the man standing to my left projecting his voice solid so that when it smacked against my ear, I had no choice but to connect the sound to his thin lips. "You know, you're too pretty to ride all alone."

Nine seconds.

Bare hands clamped onto the fare-evader's shoulders, yanked him down, his back smacking against the dirty floor. Then the officers descended like crows. Crowding him. Blocking my sight. The last I saw was the mass of the two officers becoming one; a single monstrous thing, navy blue with leather flesh and gold-plated teeth snarling as they swallowed the man whole, his screams stretching in the terminal's howl.

Like everyone else, I turned, blinked away the air's cold sting, and choked down the Moment clawing in my throat, the one telling me that the monsters are not normal, that I need to run—run away right now! But it's only a side effect of the Moment digesting inside of me, showing me what the city truly is.

I thought about what Griff said to me, about the past harvest where I tasted a love before it twisted into nausea. But its sweetness had still purred through me, and nothing could take that away.

The city will reject you. How long had I let my father etch that into me? It wasn't until he died that the walls of my eight-by-ten suburban bedroom crumbled away, and I returned to Oakland for the first time in years. Felt the city's eyes judging me. From men on street corners or the dark windows they passed. *You do not belong here.* So I'd learned the city, inscribed its history to memory and recited to myself the significance of places people would pass without a second glance. I vowed to make the city recognize me. To open up with arms reaching out, and to reach back, and let it pull me in.

It was Griff who'd recognized me when no one else did. Not even my mother or siblings recognized me after I'd moved out, and picked a name that wasn't a man's nor woman's and bought new clothes to fit me. It was Griff who'd always been there, who offered me a drink and then a meal a week later, then eventually after nights spent at his place and the smell of him seeped into my clothes like grass stains, he told me his great plan. "I met these guys in suits who recognize our potential, and know what we're about," he'd said, shirtless but with his amalgam crown upon his head, looking out the apartment window to the sea fog outside. "They said being born here gives you a type of sight; they said they could help us harness it if we do a job . . . I'm going to buy back the warehouse, Yaren. Use the company to help restore and buy back more houses away from people who don't even live here and give them back to people like us. I'm going to make sure we won't be forgotten again."

Griff's smile gleamed with confidence, whispering words that felt like arms reaching out; a nostalgia that made me believe in Griff. To want to be sucked into the orbit of him. Seen by him. And back then, just like I did now, as the catcaller still watched me on the BART platform, I cemented my vows.

I rushed right up to the platform's edge, and before the catcaller could follow behind me, the train screeched in to fill the gap. The exhale whipped my face.

I won't be pushed out. I will make the city remember me.

❋❋❋

6024 Ascot Drive—The "Grateful Dead House." Spanish styled, owned by Owsley "Bear" Stanley in 1965, who'd played a lead role in the Bay's hippie scene. A musician and manufacturer of LSD. Like the houses that came before, the owners abandoned this one for warmer beaches in the winter months, left it exposed for Griff and me to find our opportunity and push ourselves through. We brought our scythes and incense and our maize sacks too. And when I again found a Moment whose innards glowed with warmness and sweetness I swallowed it—choked it down despite the rotting, and this time I did not vomit. I conquered it. It was mine now. Griff nodded at me with amused approval and maybe with his own hunger that I hadn't seen in him before, and together we carved up that house and left it hollow before the police could come.

Our laughter flowed down streets and the city howled.

I got better at stomaching the Moments after that—the violence within them. On the next harvests, I ripped apart Moments with focused efficiency. My favorites were the Idea Moments, the bigger moments, the ones where swirling thoughts had been uttered aloud and given edges, shaped words into feather wings so these Moments could grow large and take off alive and wild into the city's sky. Those Moments bite back when I tear them down. They scream and kick but I always win, and Griff cheers me on.

We'd sell our sacks to the business suits that came with their brief cases and red ties, and they'd leave fat envelopes of cash not just in Griff's name, but mine too. Or sometimes as one whole being: YarenGriff. It was enough for rent and then some to send back home to Mom. I quit the job I hated—the bookstore where my manager would clip my heels shadowing behind me to make sure I did the tasks right. Weeks no longer separated harvests, Griff and I started going almost every night. Moment harvesting on an industrial scale.

And when we'd return to the warehouse with our sacks full, we'd fuck desperately with our shirts still on, hot skin on the warehouse floor. Griff's arms would wrap perfectly around the shape of me, his lips traced mine, adrenaline pumping between our hungry gasps.

When the Suits began demanding more Moments beyond just those trapped in NIMBY homes, it was Griff who said that wasn't the deal. "We just hit the places that already price us out. Nothing more."

"But everything is potentially purchasable," one of the suits had said with a smile but nothing behind the eyes. Like pebbles. "Everything can be property. You said it yourself Griff, these people come for the Moments. And the Moments hold you all back, and you need to cut them away with your pain, and trauma, and ruin. We're getting rid of that ruin, making the place fresh so your people can start over without that awful baggage. With nothing weighing you down."

I thought of Griff living alone in foster care once the courts locked his father away, the nights he'd stay up drinking or icing his face after he'd picked fights with the other brown boys that called him mariposa, how I wasn't there for him. I was far away in a lawn-mowed suburb. I was the one that said, "We're so close to making enough for the shop, Griff. We just need a bit more."

Griff nodded. And when his eyes came back up, that warm gleam he'd first seen in me was gone, replaced with something else, something cold, determined, broken.

We started hitting the places where Real Moments grew.

Whole cities were built out of Moments.

They grew at the Golden Gate Bridge, at the Gilman. They grew at White Horse on 6551 Telegraph Avenue, where against all odds, the building still stood despite the decades of baton and boot bashes, the oldest continuously operating gay bar in the United States. They grew in the grass at Lake Merritt, where on Sundays you'll find live music, and kids chasing each other through the smokey, barbecue air, or protesters standing in solidarity—the Moments I'd passed, but never participated in. They grew at St. Augustine's Episcopal Church, where within its red, gothic walls, the Black Panthers first hosted their free breakfast program that fed over 10,000 kids a day before the CIA tore them apart. We gutted the church. I swallowed its fresh Moments of Latine activists who just last week organized a fundraiser for families ravaged by ICE, and it wasn't until I was lying awake in my dingy apartment, unable to sleep with Moments crammed in my head, that I let out animal sobs.

***

On my way back to the BART from the warehouse one night, my shoes clapped echoes down the block. I dropped my keys and they clinked on the pavement. The city went silent. I picked them up— caught the shift in the shadows ahead of me. As if someone had been there, watching me from across that empty street.

I started wearing a mask. I'd tuck my hair into a beanie and fit gloves over my hands. All in the hopes that the city would not see me. Would not recognize my father's face in mine, those masculine features that I hated, that served as his mask when he patrolled the streets.

Strangers looked different now. They didn't have heads. Some walked with bubbles skittling out of a neck stump or flowers blooming from their shoulders. "Excuse me?" they'd mutter when I stared too long. Pink and teal Moments slithered along the edges of buildings as cat-sized axolotls. Murals began to move. The Suits no longer had clean-shaven faces and combed back hair, the Moments showed me the Suits' beaks, their vulture skills beneath cling-wrapped skin. The Moments within me bled into my sight so I could not separate the city from its shadow self.

The next time the Suits came to claim their Moments, they patted my shoulder. "Good job," they said. "Great work! There's so much promise in you."

Griff stared at us from his throne across his desk.

When the Suits left, I slid Griff his half of the cash and slid my lips close to his. He pushed me back.

"What is it?"

"I'm tired. I want to go home and sleep."

I started harvesting alone. To cover more ground. Griff said we needed to slow down, or we'd get caught, but I knew the city, its rhythmic breathing. I didn't argue with him. It was easier to just not tell him. Besides, I'd spent years dealing with walls.

***

"We all know you. We tell stories about you—the Reaper. Always with your bag and scythe. I knew you'd come eventually. I don't want to leave this place. I like the quiet here. Only a few people come to visit her grave, and when they do I can trust that they know her story. Can you promise me that? That people will still know her story?"

I turned from the rest of the cemetery to look up at the Moment, this one a cat with hollow eyes. "Huh?—yeah, yeah. Sure."

It floated above a grave that read, *Daughter, Elizabeth Short July 29, 1924— Jan. 15, 1947.*

***

6076 Manchester Drive. I went alone. Walked past the red plaque on the gate, right up to the French Normandy style mansion waiting beyond, my scythe in hand. It wasn't until halfway through the harvesting that I no longer thought I was alone.

The lights were off. The house was still. Was that a man I saw watching me from the pool deck?

When I got there, I found no one. Heard the heavy flapping of wings. I strangled my scythe tight.

The front door slapped shut.

"Whoever you are, get the fuck out!" I rushed through the house, my heart a rabid animal *thump-thump-thumping* against my ribcage. I didn't find anyone. But the picture frames were knocked over or crooked. And the walls were . . . expanding . . . contracting. Footsteps echoed from upstairs, slow at first. Then, a rush down the stairs right towards me. I ran. Even when I was blocks away, and I'd dropped my scythe in an alleyway trashcan, I felt eyes pressing against the nape of my neck. I listened for the flapping of wings.

***

At night, when I'd finally try to sink into a sleep, the Moments I'd swallowed would crowd my skull with their shouts.

Quit! Leave! We hate you! We hate you!

They'd show me their violence and wrap hands around my arms and legs and drag me thrashing and screaming back into my waking body. But rent was only increasing, and it was the thought of ripping myself out of Griff that killed the idea of stopping. To be split open, gaping bloody and raw and small and alone all over again.

But I wouldn't be that. Could *not* be that.

At the BART I considered stepping right up to the platform's razor edge and waiting there until the eighty tons of screaming metal came barreling in to step off into that gap. I considered it. Like the coward the Moments reminded me I was. Imagined my mangled corpse smeared on the tracks, black ink blooming from where a head should have been, rising up to stain the air.

I hoped a visit to the Oakland Museum would ground me. Ever since I could read scholastic books on Mexican pyramids, I've loved architecture, places. The history of them. In undergrad, I'd been fascinated with the way people took up space, either coming or going. Or staying. How spaces were made to shape around the flow of people.

I looked at pottery from Indigenous American tribes, and baskets from Yucatan. I read the plaques and looked at the delicate objects jailed behind thick glass and felt their anguish—their longing for a home so far, far away. A home further back in time where life wasn't work or die. And Gender wasn't one or the other.

The Moments in me said that history was still in my blood. I told them, "Shut up."

They shouted, Take us home! Take us home! Take us home! And I tried to vomit them out into the museum's bathroom toilet until I crumbled and sobbed into a mess on the marble floor.

"It's been too long, we're a part of you now," the remaining Moments told me. "You can't return us all." But damn it, I tried. I started retracing steps into the old homes, vomiting out what I could. At 9721 South Van Ness Avenue I stood there for hours trying to spit out sour bile and didn't notice the windows flashing red, blue, red, blue until my body was a heaving muscle and vavas dribbled off the corners of my mouth.

***

The officer that let me go the next morning, told me that it was because he knew my father.

"Quintana, right?" he said on the bright OPD station steps with me, my backpack in my hands. "I only seem to remember his sons. You don't hear that name often though . . . You know, I was there the day he got his stroke." The day I had been watching SpongeBob with my brothers, and Mom turned off the TV with eyes more worried than I'd ever seen. I remembered her lips parting, but the Moment was silent.

The officer said, "He was my Sergeant. And a great man." A pat on my back. "Please, do better."

God damn it.

God FUCKING damn it!

***

My first memory of Oakland was the day my kindergarten class took a field trip to the Oakland Zoo, and my father, who I never saw except on weekends because of him always picking up overtime, surprised me there with a green bucket hat and a bag of kettle corn. He was still on duty, still wearing his night blue uniform. But he'd managed to squeeze time to be there with me, and together we watched lemurs skitter in the grass. How I'd bragged to my friends about Dad's pistol slung off his hip. Because guns were cool, right?

It was a long time ago. Before I grew up and learned who I truly was and how unlike the man my father wanted me to be. Before I hated my father until the minute before he died on a white hospital bed. The shame that followed me since. A black cloud that trailed behind me as I walked through the warehouse floor to the office overlooking it all.

Griff sat on his throne when I finally said, "I can't do this anymore." The chair was carved out of local wood with vines decorating the sides, like the table between us. His father had built a mini empire restoring doors and windows and tables all across the bay just like that one. Gone now.

"You're being selfish," he said.

I wanted to sleep at night, to fit into the city, to start to love myself the way I wished my father could have. But I didn't want Griff to let me go. I tried to tell him this, stumbling with each word before he cut me off with, "What are you talking about, we're *so* close to it. You want to throw that away?"

There was a tear in his voice, as if he didn't believe what he was hearing, as if I was holding his bloody heart in my hands. "No, no— you don't get to do that, it's not *fair*. Not now. Not when we're this deep in it, not when I've given *so* much." He pointed to the window— the glittering water and the towers beyond, his everything. "This was our home! Do you think those people over there give a shit about those of us who grew up here? If you leave, we never get it back."

"But we're killing it!"

I reached for Griff's arm but he pulled back. Stared me down from beneath his amalgam crown.

"And what did the citizens of San Francisco think of their new Emperor Norton?" Griff had asked me one day as kids, between another swing of our wooden swords. "We did what we always do with people who don't fit in anywhere else—we let him live his life." The city had opened its arms to the kind, gentle man who'd spent his days inspecting infrastructure and visiting parks and publishing decrees like how the city needed a Bay Bridge from Oakland to San Francisco.

Stab! I ran Griff through with my sword and he collapsed to the concrete.

"Do you know how Emperor Norton died?" Griff asked with the sun in his eyes and a toy sword squeezed between his bicep and ribs.

"How?"

"He died penniless. On the street one rainy night. But on the day of his funeral, the streets overflowed with citizens who'd come to say goodbye to him."

Now no one remembers him.

Now it was just Griff and I, adults, my hand still reaching out. But in it I held a dripping, beating Moment that was the sword fight, and ditching class, and sneaking kisses. And Griff's chest was a maw of snapped rib bones.

There was nothing to say but "sorry."

Then I left.

I made it to the work floor and Griff followed, shouting that I couldn't leave him there. And my heart, my muscles pulled taut to stay with him. But it was me who had to cut away at those tendons. To free myself and leave the rest behind with Griff standing there in the belly of that empty warehouse.

***

I wouldn't realize until years after he died, what my father was trying to do when he'd take me or one of my brothers to a Raiders or Giants game. It would be just the two of us. I would explore the mountain that was the play structure shaped in the likeness of a green Coca-Cola bottle while Dad sought garlic fries to share. He wouldn't ever complain when I'd inevitably lose interest in the game by halftime, and I'd sleep in the backseat while he drove in the dark. Sometimes he'd ask to play catch in the yard even if I wasn't—couldn't ever be—the athletic child he wanted. But my abuelo had been a cold and violent man, and my father wanted so, so badly to not be him. To be a good father. But how do you become what you do not know?

His ideas of a good father, a loving father, came from sitcoms and Saturday cartoons; things he could not translate over to his faggot child.

I thought about that as I sat in the gore of what Griff and I had been on the BART ride home. I wondered if any of that excused him. It didn't.

Right?

***

"Yes, Ma, I know. I never left it *unlocked* before, remember?" I cradled a small box in my arms, the last remnants of my apartment.

I started working my old tutoring job at the local high school again. It was enough to help Mom with expenses, and all I had to do was ignore the kids arguing over whose father had the better Tesla. At night, when the wounds of Griff popped open raw and throbbing, I'd lie on my twin bed, feet sticking over the edge and try to ignore my little brother on the Xbox in his room above me. I wondered if one day Griff could finally let go of his father's warehouse and become something more. Then I'd think of the crown. I knew he wouldn't.

At dinner, I'd help Mom set the table and stomach the "niños" and "Mijos" before I'd correct them with a "It's Mij*e*."

"Right, sorry," they'd say, and the conversation would carry on. They don't ever realize how large a valley little cuts can carve.

All the while, the Moments would whisper to me, and, slowly, I learned to listen to each one.

The BART terminal was quiet the morning I returned to it, when I should have been picking up groceries, but stopped when I'd felt the City's breathing even from all the way out there. The air contracting, releasing. Calling. Cops watched the commuters slit-eyed as I put ten dollars into my clipper card. I'd forgotten I even had it buried in my wallet.

As I waited in the morning chill, I felt the wind shift, heard the flapping of wings. A gust blew back the fog and I froze as shadow talons gripped the terminal roof, and it aimed its charcoal beak at me—a Moment. A crow larger than any I'd ever seen before. It watched me with starry eyes, fanning its wings black as night with a thousand lanterns blazing within. I recognized those memories: the community organizing, the city's construction, the tribes who lived there long, long before. All of that was in the Crow, and I felt like I knew it. Its stare told me the same. Without fear I let it leer in to peck my forehead—an expanding of the room inside my mind, enough for each of the Moments within me to finally stretch and be.

A shadow crown bloomed atop my head.

The Crow whispered, *Thank you.* Then launched into the sky with a flap of its wings. Up—up! Into the grey and over the hills and to the cities beyond.

I stood there blinking as the BART eased in. The Blue Line. Its doors yawned apart and waited for me, for what I'd planned to do when I came here—to step into that empty train and watch the houses pull away as it moved eastwards to the end of the Bay and the rest of the world beyond.

Or I could wait.

And catch the next one on its way to the city.

MY MOTHER, THE EXOSKELETON

Amitha Jagannath Knight

BIRTH
When I was born,
I shed my mother,
the exoskeleton.
I ground her into gelatin:
nutrition for me, and
building material for

the ancestral walls.

LESSONS
The wall-mothers tell
of the cells they died
to build. Our history:

One by one,
generation upon
generation, we
build a hexagon of
gelatinous cells, a
honeycomb hive of mothers'
bodies, until the final cell
reaches the promised land of souls.

MY MOTHER, THE EXOSKELETON

Where is it?
I ask
How far?

Ancestor walls do not provide
answers, only building materials.

THE RECIPE
1 cup of dirt from the ground,
1 cup of water from the sky.
1 cup of jiggling mother goo.

Mix to desired consistency.

Allow ten minutes to set.

A LIFE'S WORK

NIGHTMARES

By day, they speak to my mind;
by night, they speak to my body

                    (and whisper to my womb.)

My limbs obey orders while I dream
of homes in hexagons,
of souls and ancestors,
of my mother, the exoskeleton, and

of You still to emerge.

THE SIXTH WALL

Once my mother is depleted,
the wall almost completed
a new voice speaks

      from inside.

I panic, unready, as an urge,
a terrible gasping pathetic powerful unavoidable
urge

to
escape
my fate,
seizes me and

I
force
my body through a
        gaping hole
in the final wall.

The ancestor jelly contracts,
seizing me,

MY MOTHER, THE EXOSKELETON

squeezing me,
pushing me inside out. A new life

bursts through

my being and
now I am exoskeleton.

THE LAND OF SOULS
My body: consumed.
My soul: congealed.

The gelatin hive is the promise fulfilled.

THE SOUND OF CHILDREN SCREAMING

Rachael K. Jones

THE GUN

YOU KNOW THE one about the Gun. The Gun goes where it wants to. On Thursday morning just after recess, the Gun will walk through the front doors of Thurman Elementary, and it won't sign in at the front office or wear a visitor's badge.

The Gun does most of its damage in the first five minutes. The Gun doesn't care about lockdown drills, and it will not wait for the SWAT team to arrive. The Gun can chew through a door, a desk, a cinderblock wall, and kids don't wear those bulletproof backpacks during reading time.

Everyone has a right to a gun. Nothing can take that away from you. What you lack is a right to the lives of your children.

The Gun likes a game of hide-and-seek. The Gun will rove the grounds until someone stops it. The Gun has been here many times before.

The Gun is not working alone.

THE SHOOTER

He is never anyone special. Just a man exercising his right to a gun.

THE TEACHER

Michelle Dalton has taught fourth grade for nine years, long enough to know how the job yawns wider each year, collecting all the loose threads that society needs done but no one wants to pay for. Michelle has six figures in student loans and makes less than

$50,000 a year. She shares a rental house with two roommates and has a weekend job at Trek & Field selling athletic shoes to make ends meet. She does not get paid overtime, and the school district does not buy the art supplies. She is not entitled to bathroom breaks or a nonworking lunch, and she doesn't get paid for summers.

Michelle wears the armor of an elementary school teacher: an A-line dress in an ocean print, a blue cardigan to match. She bears no weapon but a sharp-edged teacher's tongue that cuts through noise like scissors.

Every teacher in Thurman Elementary will sense the Gun moments before it opens fire as a tense, drawn-out pause, an upset child drawing the breath to scream. They will not visibly panic, not with twenty-one pairs of eyes locked upon them for guidance. Michelle's body will act before her mind comprehends the threat.

It is Michelle's job to keep her students safe, just as it is her job to take the blame for whatever harm the Gun inflicts in the process.

THE PORTAL

You know about the Portal too, although not by that name. The Portal seeks the places where children hide. It stalked the air raid shelters in London during the Blitz. It lurked in underground cellars during the Cold War, crouched between the canned corn and rancid Crisco. It has fed itself in Italian orphanages and Australian residential schools, and it has only gotten hungrier.

The Portal has been exhibiting itself at gun shows recently, a gleaming bullet-proof vault in which to store kids when the shooter comes. The Portal has been installed in every classroom, funded by bake sales and cereal box tops, bought at the expense of pencils and math books and a music teacher.

The Portal is not wheelchair-accessible. The Portal is a failure of policy. The Portal was dressed up like a castle for Halloween. The Portal is not a reading nook.

There is nothing more necessary than the Portal. The Portal will keep the right children safe.

Whatever the Gun doesn't claim will get packed into the Portal like coats at the Lost and Found. The school has a ritual for it, a special alarm. The children, sensing something wrong in the *pop-pop-pop* coming from the gym, will obey uncomplainingly when

Michelle shoos them in. Michelle will enter last, pulling the door shut behind them.

The Portal is dark and humid inside. There are no windows or lights to attract attention. It is the gap beneath the bed where the monsters hunt. The Portal's breath presses in around them, hot and stinking, as it swallows them down, down, down.

Time doesn't stop inside the Portal. It telescopes. The children strain their ears, listening for the classroom door. The popping sounds are approaching now. *Pop* and it passes the fourth grade art wall, *pop-pop-pop* at the water fountain, *pop* beside the mural of Rosa Parks, *pop-pop* and it has reached Ms. Dalton's door. The siren continues its wail. Someone is sobbing in the dark. Someone has to pee. Someone refused to hug his mom goodbye at dropoff today, and might never get the chance again.

When the Portal door opens, the Gun will be waiting.

But the children will not be in their classroom anymore.

THE MOUSE

Not like the mice that infest Thurman Elementary over the winter break. Not the wild ones that chew through the corners of the fun-size cracker bags, leaving cellophane confetti in the snack bin. Not like the class mouse, tame in her cage with soft white fur and blood-red eyes, who holds out her little paws to accept a sandwich crust.

This mouse has a gun: a copper blunderbuss with the end belled out like something out of Looney Tunes. His name is Sir Miles, and he has been hunting. He grooms the blood from between his claws like sticky jam as he considers the newcomers, a teacher and her eight students lined up like chessboard pawns.

It is his move.

He is quite large for a mouse, nearly knee-high. He makes a sweeping bow with his tricorn hat as he introduces himself. His accent is a lilting brogue. He has perfect manners and rides a Shetland pony. His charm, too, is a weapon, subtle and efficient, as he makes a plea that sounds a little too rehearsed, a flimflam man working over his newest marks.

He demands the things men with guns always demand. He asks for someone else to fight his wars. His people rely on a steady supply of children from the World Beyond who are kindhearted or brave or foolish enough to take up the magic crowns and wield the spells to make Sir Miles's enemies dead. He is very persuasive. His eyes shine with tears, and he clasps his little paws as he pleads his case. The children, dazed in this strange new world, tear-streaked and shaken after the Portal's darkness, are mesmerized.

Mice are crepuscular, creatures of shadow and hidden intentions. They creep from their dens at sunset and feed all night long. They are averse to bright lights. Mice eat their own feces but lack the ability to vomit.

Sir Miles is full of shit. But he means business.

THE NEGOTIATION

Michelle also means business.

She isn't fooled by this Narnia shit, the soft black eyes or the twee little jacket. She doesn't trust a mouse with a gun. Anyone in possession of a gun has made a plan to use it.

But Dylan needs to pee, and Katie R. and Katie V. are sharing a coat in the drizzle, and it's almost time for lunch and they'll all need to eat. The kids are already eyeing the mouse like they'd like nothing better than to bury their faces in his warm, soft fur, and it's only getting worse as he unspools his sob story, his oil-drop eyes large with crocodile tears. If Michelle doesn't take charge, she'll lose control entirely.

"I'm sorry for your troubles, but we're not getting involved in your war," she says sharply, cutting off the mouse mid-sales pitch. The rain is steadily increasing its barrage, snapping against the shale like fireworks. "Is there somewhere we can go to wait out the storm?"

The mouse, steel-eyed, mounts his Shetland pony, settling in front of the corpse of the furred thing he just killed. He gives Michelle an unambiguous look of hate, like he has just spotted a particularly odious vermin. "Follow along," he says, and that predatory look submerges beneath his charm. "Castle Rowland is just beyond the rise."

Sir Miles keeps up a steady patter, dangling his problems like a pair of keys before a grabby toddler. Michelle knows his type, men who force you into a shared predicament to short circuit what your uneasy gut is screaming.

What did he kill just before they arrived, and why did he use his hands when he had a gun?

Michelle doesn't take her eyes off that gun as they follow the path behind the mouse. Everything in this world pierces. The dreary pines stab up at the gray sky, and the rain tattoos through her knit cardigan. She makes the children pair up and hold hands like they're making a bathroom trip.

Blood runs down the pony's hind leg, leaving sticky, dark hoofprints.

Michelle does not look back at the Portal. She keeps her eyes on the gun.

CASTLE ROWLAND

Every mouse on the parapets is armed.

The castle's walls are tall and pockmarked, and not one green thing grows in its courtyards. The mice have lined up gunnysacks for target practice. The volleys of gunfire blend with the pattering rain.

The idea of a castle is to protect the things you love by walling them in and daring your enemies to take them. A castle, like a school, is a locked-up box for precious things. Because of this property, castles were once the sites of war, and their names evoked the bloodshed. *Scarborough, Dover, Prudhoe, Kenilworth.*

In the distant future, castles will cease to be a symbol of war when governments find more civilized ways to regulate what one person can take from another. Children will enter castles with delight when they have never learned to fear them.

Children will learn to fear their schools, though. The names will come to stand for another kind of warfare, the sites of battles waged and lost without the benefit of soldiers or a moat. *Columbine, Sandy Hook, Marjory Stoneman Douglas, Robb.*

THE POND

Castle Rowland also has a pond, long and low, graveled around its edges with strange ivory pebbles, jagged as teeth. The water shimmers in the rain as though it has swallowed down the sun.

The children want to get a better look, but Sir Miles hurries them along.

OTHER PEOPLE'S CHILDREN

Only eight came through the Portal. They are Li and Dylan and

Nathan and Katie R. and Katie V. and Nevaeh and Caleb and Angelo. Most of them are nine years old, except for Katie V., who turned ten in September.

The other thirteen kids in Michelle's class—*the lucky ones*—yes, call them that—are still hiding in that dark closet, listening to the slamming doors, the pleading sobs of teachers, the shrieks of first-graders trapped in the bathroom, and then *pop-pop-pop*—the chalk-white silence left in the Gun's wake.

THE FEAST

The grand hall is smoky and low, and a roast much too big to be poultry turns on the spit. Portraits loom over the long refectory tables, paintings of human children, regal in velvet and bone-white crowns, their mouths turned down, somber and thoughtful.

Servant-mice in pale blue smocks scurry down the table rows and ply the children with delicacies. Katie V. gets a whole cake to herself, and Nathan eats lemon sorbet from a silver dish. It has been a very long walk, and they are too ravenous to resist. Even Michelle accepts a bowl of soup, though she dislikes the way that the mice seem prepared for their surprise guests. Like it was scheduled weeks ago, and everyone has rehearsed their roles.

As the mice shoo the humans from the table, they file past the roast. A feline skull leers back at Michelle, the clawed, furry paws still attached to the leg-bones.

THE PORTRAITS

None of the children in the portraits seem to make it past their teenage years. When Michelle asks Sir Miles about this, his whiskers twitch into a needle-toothed grin. "The magic of the crowns isn't for adults. Only children can wield them."

When she asks what happens when the children grow up, the mouse just laughs her off. "We send them home, naturally," he booms. "What else would we do? *Eat* them?"

AN INTERLUDE

Michelle cannot sleep that night. The eight sleeping children sigh and hum around the room—the girls tucked into the grand four-poster bed, the boys burritoed in blankets on the rug before the crackling fireplace, and Michelle against the door to watch for intruders.

Castle Rowland feels more real than what happened to them at the school today. The alarm sounding, the *pop-pop-pop* in the hallway, the sobbing in the dark.

At that moment, instead of her family, Michelle had found herself thinking of her weekend job. How they had no protocol at Trek & Field for what to do if someone opened fire.

This strange castle, with its mice and portraits and ivory pond, has a logic stronger than the laws of reality. All her life, Michelle had thought she knew what she would do if the Gun came to her school, but the Gun doesn't care about the stories people tell themselves in their own heads.

A NOTE ABOUT SCHOOL SAFETY

We will not try to prevent the Gun. The Gun will accept no limitations. But we will try very hard not to offend the Gun. If you offend the Gun, it may decide to get personal.

Better to develop rituals against the Gun, to train the kids to block the door, hide in the closet, play dead on the rainbow carpet where they do calendar time and sing the morning song. Better to invest in metal detectors. Better to ring the playground with barbed wire, to hire off-duty police instead of another counselor.

You can have a special alarm for the Gun. You can make the teachers draw the blinds, lock the doors, take the long route every day to recess in the name of safety.

It doesn't matter if any of it works. The important thing is to have something to blame besides the Gun. Best to treat the Gun as a force of nature, rare as an earthquake, a freak tornado. Best to accept the Gun. It belongs here. It belongs everywhere. The Gun will always be with us.

If you try hard enough, maybe you can convince the Gun to shoot someone else's kid instead.

THE TOUR

"Perhaps the children would enjoy a tour of Castle Rowland," Sir Miles suggests at breakfast. "Unless you would prefer that I return you to your Portal?"

It is a threat, and Michelle knows it. This world exists in a moment suspended in time, the instant between breaths, with the Gun on the other side of the classroom door.

Nothing could be more dangerous than returning home, not even these predatory mice with their blunderbusses and their feud with the neighboring kingdom.

But then Sir Miles shows them the armory.

THE ARMORY

Gun racks hold row after row of blunderbusses, flintlocks, swords, and crossbows, sharp as a buckthorn thicket in winter. The children race through the rows of oiled metal, spitting out the gunpowder tang in their mouths and noses, until they find the eight glass cases at the back.

In each case rests a chalk-white crown. Their delicacy fascinates Michelle, like anatomical drawings of bird skeletons. The glass casing lifts off easily. When she picks up a crown, it has a soft texture like soapstone, only lighter. It is constructed from many fragments fitted together and polished smooth, except for some top bits that jut up, raw as broken teeth.

Angelo has taken a crown into his hands. His eyes slingshot between Sir Miles and Michelle, seeking their permission. "Can I, Ms. Dalton?"

"Go on," Sir Miles encourages him. "Give it a try."

"Angelo, wait—!" Michelle begins, fear gripping her voice so it squeaks.

But Angelo has already donned the crown. It fits like it was made for him. He stands a little taller, acclimating to the kingliness settling upon his shoulders.

"It's true!" Angelo shouts, his brown eyes bright and happy. "It's really magic! I can feel it!" He lifts his hands, and to Michelle's horror, a dozen swords rise up from their racks like a cloud of startled pigeons.

POWERS

Every teacher knows the moment when they lose control of their classroom, and it usually begins with exuberance. Once, on a Friday before a long weekend, Katie V.'s dad brought in birthday cupcakes, half chocolate and half vanilla. It was raining, and nobody had been out for recess, and everyone wanted vanilla but there weren't enough to go around. Then Katie V. started crying because she didn't get the kind she wanted on her birthday, and

Dylan squashed the unwanted cupcake on the floor, and then full-on chaos broke out, the kind that could only be stopped by flickering the light switch and making threats to cancel the afternoon movie.

The crowns are like those cupcakes. Every child grabs one despite Michelle's attempts to stop them, and then there are a series of close calls when the swords and guns go clattering through the air, nearly beheading Caleb, who decides to retaliate. They call down fire and shadow. They scorch the stone walls black. Nevaeh freezes the air, pulling snow down inside the armory, and the other children run around catching snowflakes on their tongues.

Finally Sir Miles leads the children out to the courtyard, and Michelle follows behind, defeated and impotent, her voice hoarse, her right temple throbbing in the telltale sign of a migraine.

Michelle doesn't blame them. She understands the source of their joy. Children rarely get to feel so powerful. Children spend their days being told what to do and where to go. They don't get to decide how they dress or what they eat. They aren't allowed to get angry or to dislike anyone, and if an aunt or grandpa wants a hug, the child will have to give it.

Children only hold power in their games, which is why they make up superheroes. They play at telekinesis and pyrokinesis and mind reading. Children use swings to learn to fly, or they use sticks as makeshift wands. But now that power is real.

"That's enough," Michelle tells Angelo as he sets a row of gunnysacks on fire. "Let's go inside and have a break now."

Gentle Angelo, who always volunteers to collect all the basketballs after recess, who always holds the door as they file out to the buses after school, glares up at Michelle. "You can't make me," he says.

He is right.

When some children grow up, they will buy themselves a gun so no one else can ever make them feel small again. They will not try to change how adults make children feel.

THE TRUTH

The refectory tables have been removed from the Great Hall for the occasion. The mice crowd in for the coronation, hundreds of them, packing the castle. Although they only rise to Michelle's knees, they force her apart from the children through sheer numbers, pushing her out, cutting her off, until she stands alone in the courtyard, the door to the hall slammed in her face.

It is gray and raining. Alone, Michelle wanders the grounds as the guard-mice eye her with open hostility. *What do they do when the children grow up?* But Michelle is already grown. The mice have no use for her now that they have pried her away from her students.

She finds herself drawn to the glimmering ivory pool and its sunlit glow in the dreary rain. Her shoes crunch on the strange, pointed gravel. The water swarms with koi, and beneath them, mounded like coral, are human skeletons, too many to count, ribcages and skulls and long, slim femurs buried in the finer knobbles of knucklebones and teeth. The fish nibble at bits of connective tissue clinging to the fresher skeletons. Some of the bones are broken, as though sawed open to lick out the marrow.

None of this surprises Michelle. She knew from the moment she held that crown, its soapstone texture, its unusually light weight. The bones of children fused together and polished smooth, a vessel for their collective power once they grew too old to be of other use, handed down to their successors to wield in turn.

The last of Michelle's hope slips away as she gazes into the pool. Her students' fate is a tale of two deaths. One at the hands of the mice, who have no love for these children beyond their utility in war. And the other through the Portal where the Gun awaits, rattling the classroom doorknob. Become the weapon, or its victim. Either way, they die.

And if they stay? If they flee? Who will wear those crowns next? Which classroom will the Gun seek out instead?

Someone will have to die. There is no one coming to help her. No one will stop the mice, the shooter, the cycle that returns them to this point, this pond, these children's bodies and their wordless accusation.

Teachers have always been left alone, dancing around the Gun, the Portal, the crowns of bone, trying to keep other people's children safe with donated art supplies and cardboard tubes saved up for Craft Day.

One thing is certain: Michelle will never tell her students about the bones. No child deserves to know how little the world regards them.

But there are other weapons she can give her students. Truths as powerful as any magic crown.

AGENCY

Into the Great Hall, then. Into the castle, where the mice are piping military tunes on ivory flutes as Sir Miles gives a speech. Michelle plunges into the thick of the cheering mice, forcing a path, though they scratch and tear at her legs and rip her dress to tatters. All those blunderbusses tip down and track her, the bells of deadly trumpets, as she approaches the dais, the eight little thrones, the children unrecognizably regal in rich, furred cloaks sewn from the dappled hides of calico cats.

"Wait," Michelle cries out in her sharp teacher's voice, projecting over the din. "Wait a moment. I have something to say."

Sir Miles stabs a clawed finger at Michelle, harpooning her with accusations. "See, your Majesties? Even now, she plots to depose you, to deprive you of your crowns. Strike her down with your power, or else give the command, and our soldiers will ensure she never troubles your reign again."

All eight faces turn to consider Michelle, frowning in displeasure. But she is no longer afraid. Unlike the mice, she loves these children. She bears the kind of love for them you can only have for children not your own, children freely given into your care day after day in the trust that you will return them back again, imperceptibly older, until eventually they become old enough to live on their own.

And from that place, Michelle speaks to her students like she always has, giving them the knowledge of their own power and the strength to use it.

"Those crowns belong to you," she tells her students. "Sir Miles is right about that. I won't ask you to give them back. But you have a choice now. You can fight for the mice in their war if you want. Or we could go back home and help your friends. The choice is yours. Whatever you choose, I will help you."

Sir Miles laughs, and the other mice echo him, certain in their victory. They have been plying these children with gifts and sweets and flattery, and don't believe dowdy, buttoned-up Michelle can offer anything equally tempting. The children have been growing irritable during her speech, their faces pinched and unhappy. Li stands up. Nevaeh twitches her cloak aside to bare her hands.

"I know you'll make the right choice," Michelle tells them. "Whatever you do, Ms. Dalton loves you."

Michelle stares into the gun barrels trained upon her. Nathan glowers down at the crowd. Katie R. has flushed the deep red that foretells a tantrum, and Nevaeh raises her hands. Michelle closes her eyes, giving herself to their judgment.

All eight children begin to scream.

And the sun answers.

BRIGHT LIGHTS

The sun sheds her gray robes and steps down into the Great Hall.

The heat is incredible. The blunderbusses bloom like daffodils and drop their seeds in molten pools of brass. All the shadows burn away. In the courtyard, the bone-pool hisses and steams as it boils off.

Mice cannot tolerate bright lights, nor can anything that has made a habit of feeding on children. The air is hazy with the char of singed fur.

Michelle should be charred too, but the eight children run to her and throw their arms around her waist, just like when the dismissal bell rings and they don't want to say goodbye.

HOW IT ENDS

There is no happy ending when the Gun visits a school. Even if it takes no lives, it will rob every child and adult of the bone-thin illusion that bad things only happen to other people's children, those who prepared less, prevented less, who failed to hire enough cops or install enough bulletproof glass, who didn't run the backpacks through the metal detectors, people who deserved it somehow, who left a door propped open or a fence unrepaired. They will go to bed that night numb inside, neither scared nor angry, because it feels like slipping through a portal to a world where your hometown has become the legal hunting ground of angry men, and no one thought to warn you. Later, they will feel guilt and intense shame, like they should have done something differently, like they should have known the rules had changed that day and prepared accordingly, like they forgot their jacket when everyone knew it would rain.

The truth is that the Portal has been growing, fed by the Gun meal by meal, and it will swallow and swallow until every school lies in its belly slowly digesting in a glimmering pool of children's bones, until someone decides to stop it.

Michelle plunges through the Portal, the children lined up behind her like they're off to art class instead of facing their deaths. The Portal door bursts open upon the classroom at Thurman Elementary just as the doorknob turns, Michelle at the forefront and eight kids in crowns behind her, confronting the Gun with the bones of children, the bitter magic only children have the right to wield, asking the question that answers itself, damning the Gun with their bodies, their flesh, with the sound of children screaming.

ENDLESS YEARNING

Judith Shadford

I **WALK TO** skoo every morning, but today chains hung across the door. Line of black buses waiting. Sternoids jumped out and shoved us inside. No seats, no windows. Us bigger ones hung onto the bars up top. Littles hung on us. The bus started with awful shaking—rattle rattle rattle. You couldn't hear.

Skoo made us miners: hammers and chisels. Pick up crystals. Littles pick up stones. Kids like me hauled big chunks. When skoo was chained, sternoids came. Mines needed more kids.

Riding bus was scary. Our feet slip on grate under. We see red stones jumping at us under. Knees shake. Teeth rattle for kids with teeth. Mines were coming.

Sky turned from red like dirt to black. Shiners on bus were small. Finally rattles stopped. Sternoids pushed us into big big room. The shiners up top far away and not shiny. Room was so big, many buses could fit right in.

Then great cranking from other side. Huge wheels up top went round and round. Big box came up from floor. Box opened and kids came out, lots. Sternoids walk into box and threw kids not walking onto big black plate. No sound except cranking and shaking. Kids walk slow, clothes covered in shiny crystals, faces crusty with red dirt. Some fell. Didn't move. Sternoids threw them on black plate.

Old people came with buckets. They yell "Soup," and put buckets on floor. We push and push, putting hands in buckets. Hot. We scooped but bigger kids push me away. I went round back where not so many kids. Skooched down to scoop faster. Bad in mouth, but I was empty.

One old person pressed me. I think a she with bumps on chest. She didn't shove just looked, took my hand and wiped it with rags and looked close close. Would it bite? But it whispered, "What is your name?"

"E-Wye."

Its eyes very big. Pushed hand close to me.

Finger three, near bottom, had brown dot, like eyeball. My finger three, near bottom, brown dot, like eyeball.

"What is meaning?" I asked.

"I am Mi-Wye, your mama."

"You a she?"

She nodded. Water came out her eyes. My hand wet inside her hand. Then shiners up top blinked and went black.

"Come."

Kids curled on floor right there. We walk slow, stepping over sleepers. So quiet we moved. She touched wall, slid till she found door. So quiet cracked open, outside. Cold. Near as black as inside. No words, moving, always moving, away from road. Then her other hand went forward. So did mine. We touched a wall of sticks. Crept inside.

We curled together on floor and I sleep so quick. Maybe safe now. I stayed that way long time till light showed.

She talked. "I make Soup. Stay. I come back. I bring food. Then you must see and we decide."

Waiting for her, in my head, I saw shadows from back long time, people creeping into hut, talk to Papa Lo-Wye. Stories of long back. I did not believe. Sky blue? What is blue? Sky is red and dusty. Everyone knows.

White on mountains? Mountains are red all way, not white at top.

Water from sky? What?

They said their papa-mama came through Broken O back long time.

Everyone knows Broken O. Big and black. Bottom like broken cup. No side, no top. Broke black pieces on ground. Sometimes sternoids moved pieces. Build again. Always fell.

I asked Papa. He drew O on ground, then he scratched out sides and top, like Broken O. Back time, he said it spin fast, loud. Fill with shiner like water but not wet. People walk into, then gone.

Things came out and people run, get things. Before the Dome. He pushed me to my corner. Story done.

The she, Mi-Wye bend over me, her mouth curled and eyes like shiners.

"Here is better food." She gave me Soup in bowl with bread.

"No bread back time . . . Lo-Wye couldn't find."

She nodded. "I think he was good papa."

"Soup is better. Do you?" and pushed my bowl, but it was empty.

"I am not hungry. It is good to see you eat."

"Do we go see now?"

"When dark comes. I have a little shiner."

We waited, she near door. She mmmd little sound. Maybe from back time. Finally we crept to different building. No sternoids. Mi-Wye pushed door and we went in. Clean. No big wheel. No box with kids. She turned her shiner on.

A round ball—bigger than me. Bumpy, with shapes.

"What is ball?"

Mi-Wye shook head. "Look at the shapes."

I did. Red shapes like dirt . . . then green and blue and white.

"Round shapes are Domes."

I walked around ball.

"We live here." Her finger over red shape.

"What is green and blue and white?"

"We live under Domes. Come."

We walked to long wall. Pictures and pictures and pictures. She said they tell story of here.

I saw sky blue. And dirt green and soft. She pointed finger and said, "These are trees. Many many trees. Little animals lived under trees. We had water, lots of water. It was called sea." Water ran from her eyes.

She told about wind that could make sea into great white piles instead of awful red heaps that stung and got in your mouth. I saw a big O not broken. It was shiny and wet in middle like an eye, a happy eye.

She said, "Ring of Travel". She said people and things walked into the not-wet shiny and went far far into the dark. She said name of tiny shiners in sky was stars. She said there were other places in far where people live. She pointed at the round ball in the middle of room. "Many worlds like that."

One picture, big, with Ring of Travel filled with white crystals like we mine, whooshing and spreading all over. Sea came and washed crystals across green. Crystals turn green into black. Trees dead. No more little animals. Sky turned red. Sternoids took kids to dig. Picture with buses full of crystals from mines pouring through Rings to other places. Everything changed to be like where we live. Last picture, Travel Ring filled with black smokes.

I sat down. Mi-Wye put shiner away.

"Our story is awful. We are bad."

"Bad people told everyone what to do when I was little. They built sternoids and took the kids away from home to work in the mines. They made the taller kids, like you—just beginning to get bumps on your chest—and boys getting big, too . . . they took them off to the Black Tower in the mountains to make as many babies as they could. New kids to work in mines. Boys and girls stayed at Tower until they couldn't make babies anymore. Then sternoids brought them back to cook and feed kids."

"You?"

"Yes. Papa and I were together. But my babies died. They said we were built wrong and sent us back to work. We stayed together and made you here. Then they took me back to the Tower."

"Where did babies that lived go?"

"There was another place near Black Tower. Black Dome. It was round and had a top made of metal, black, and the top came down to the ground making half a big ball. I never saw inside. No sound ever came out."

"Story makes me hurt inside."

"Me too."

Back to hut and stayed together for many many days. Mi-Wye made Soup when light was first red, then home with a little for both. She mmmd sometimes. We were family.

Many days I went to picture room and looked at world with Domes. No one ever saw me. Pictures were true. Our Broken Ring—behind were hills. But the Travel Ring, the Big O, all shiny— different high hills behind.

Mi-Wye said, "Yes, mountains."

Crystals whooshed out through Ring and black smokes came back. It was the story of Broken O. I turned around to the picture of green and sea and trees and small animals and I looked and looked at the mountains far back. No pictures of whooshing crystals in that Ring. Maybe it was still green. Could I find those mountains?

I went outside and walked the building, careful careful for sternoids. Around a corner a little path, down under building to a small door, about my size. I pushed. It did nothing.

At Soup that night, I told Mi-Wye. Her eyes were large large and shiny.

"The little room is still there! I will come with you early before work, when there is only soft light."

Next day, we moved quiet behind picture building, found the corner and little path. We both pushed hard hard on the door. It started to move and squeak and we were in new room. The top was close to ground, but we could stand. No shiners, but a thin opening around the top gave light. On the wall opposite, there were marks.

"What are the scratchings?"

Mi-Wye said they used to write our names, that everyone before knew how to write and talk and read. "That was what skoo used to do, before. Teach kids writing, teach the story of us. Before the mines."

She looked so sad. "We made this when we knew writing. It was hidden, then forgotten. Up at the top it says, "YRNRS." Our papas-mamas wrote their names after they came through the Ring—so people after could know we were real, before mines, before sternoids. We would sneak here before we went to Black Tower—because we wanted to go home, back to where we came from. But our Ring was broken and we could go nowhere."

When I could, I went to YRNRS Room to look at names, think about the people who were so lost they could only scratch their names to say they were real. There was even a name the same as mine. E-Wye. Scratched way at the end, just where my hands touched. Who was other E-Wye? A she?

Mi-Wye went back to look at the scratchings one more time. She pointed to Mi-Wye on the wall.

"Is that you?"

"Yes. And up there, that is Lo-Wye. Before Black Tower."

"There was another E-Wye?"

She just shook her head and walked away.

I touched the E-Wye scratch and left. I could see her Mi-Wye scratch, but it was like she had gone far far. It did not make her real.

Some days later, I told my meaning of the pictures with the high mountain and green. I said I wanted for us to find it, to live there, not here.

Tears came from her eyes. "Soon sternoids will catch you and take you to the Black Tower. You have bumps on your chest now."

I looked down and put my hands on my chest. Yes, bumps. Small, but maybe getting bigger. "I would die before Black Tower."

"They will find you. You cannot find that green place. How do you know it is true? Maybe makers of Black Tower and the mine makers broke it. They break everything and then tell lies. We know that."

"We will go together. I will not leave you here to wait for the death."

She took my hand and we curled together and slept.

***

For many many days, I looked at the green picture so that I could feel the shape of the mountains under my hands. I could feel the shape of red domes under my hands, too. That shape made me sad. Scared.

One night I heard buses on the road and I told Mi-Wye that we would leave the next night and to bring as much food home as she could carry. I thought we could find water, especially when mountains got near. She went to work in the morning.

I was about to go to the picture hall when I heard sternoids clanking close close. I crept into darkest corner and curled into a ball like a pile of rags. They came in with shiners and looked. One kicked me and I didn't move. It kicked my back hard, but didn't bend over to check if the rags was a me. I wondered if sternoids could bend. Then they were gone. I heard crackling and light I knew was fire. They were burning our hut. I waited as long as I could, then rolled against the side, under and out to the air. I would have to hide all day until Mi-Wye came back.

I hid near the door to the mine room that Mi-Wye used. When she finally came out it was dark inside and outside. She had a bundle of food. She helped me tie it on my back.

"You must go now and I must stay here."

"But the hut is burned."

"I know. They found me at work and twisted my arms, trying to find if there was a you. I didn't tell. But if I go with you, they will look until they find us. You go. You find green times and blue and sea."

Her eyes dropped tears. Then she went back in the mine building, all dark. Dark and dark.

***

I walked many days until my bundle was empty. The walking was rough over rocks. Many times I went forward and then back until I found a better way. I climbed and hid and climbed. No more food. Little shiners of water in the rocks sometimes. I was sleeping under a rock one day, waiting till day wasn't so bright. A person came, a man. He found me and crouched next to me. He gave me food, then built a tiny fire, for warm hands. He patted my bumps and pretty soon he was inside me doing poking things. It hurt but his voice was soft and he didn't hit. He made me curl up next to him, like Mi-Wye. But he wasn't Mi-Wye and I was afraid he would take me to the Black Tower and make mine babies for crystal digging.

When the sky turned light he pulled me up and we walked together for a while. I told him I wanted to find the Travel Ring, to find blue sky, sea.

"I know the way. I will take you with me, but it is hard."

So we walked more days, one day with no food until a day came I could see the mountains from the pictures.

"Look, look. We are getting to the Ring!"

He looked at me with a small smile. "I will show you."

Walking that night just before last redness, my head hit something I could not see and I fell down.

He said, "We are there," and pulled me up. He put his hands out and pat pat pat, touched a wall we could see through, but could not go through. I could see mountains, but could not get closer.

"This is side of Dome. We have to find the crack. There is supposed to be a crack to get through, but small. Maybe too small for me, but you could get through."

New feeling. I did not want to go through alone. No Mi-Wye and no man?

"What do they call you?"

"I am Lo-Fyn."

"Are you a YRNR?"

"I do not know what YRNR is."

"Long ago papas-mamas came through the Ring. They were YRNRS. I am YRNR."

He did poking after dark time, and I liked it some. Then I saw through the Dome. There were tiny shiners far outside dome. So clear. I wanted that. We must get through.

We curled up until light. Lo-Fyn started patting Dome, looking for crack. Since my knees were tough from learning from mine work at skoo, I moved along the ground the other way. If there was a crack, I would see loose dirt and rocks on ground, not up on wall. But the wall went tight below ground, its edges buried. If I had chisel and hammer, maybe I could find bottom. I only had fingers, so I crawled, feeling the side all smooth, trying to dig away rocks and dirt at bottom. I could not see Lo-Fyn. Maybe he went back. But those mountains where the Ring stayed were still there. I was going through.

When it was hot, I curled up and slept a little, then started feeling up the wall and watching for little loose rocks. I came to a big rock that I couldn't feel underneath, but not tight. I sat on my heels and looked. The ground was full of dust, not burned hard. I went around the rock and closer to the wall. There were little stones, lots and lots of them. I pushed them away, faster and faster and the dust and little stones came loose and I was digging, throwing them behind me. I wanted my mine shovel, but kept pulling everything loose until I came to a crookedy line in the Dome that went down instead of up. Was this the crack? Did papas-mamas make the hole big enough to crawl under? Then how did they make it smooth behind them if they got through?

I must have said out loud because softly I heard, "Like this."

"Lo-Fyn!"

"I think you found the crack, E-Wye. You are clever, a good miner."

His mouth curved up and his eyes were shiny.

"What did you mean, 'Like this'?"

"I think you must go through—I will help dig—and then I will push all the dirt and rocks back so the spot is still hidden."

"You must come, too."

"No. When I went the other way this morning, I saw sternoids in a Black Bus coming this way. If they find me, they will take me back. But you will be safe."

"They will make you dead."

"I can go to the Black Tower and make babies. I'm not too old."

"But that is the death. That is blacker than mines. Come?" I put my hand on his arm and pulled a little.

"Sternoids will come soon. You must hurry. Find your sky of blue, your green mountains." He started pulling dirt and stones away from the crookedy line that got wider. We worked together until it was wide enough for me to slide through.

"But I like you, Lo-Fyn."

He pulled me over and in all the dust covering both of us, he patted me and put his mouth to my mouth. "You go now. Go fast."

I rolled under the crack and he was already filling up the hole. When I stood up on the other side of Dome, there was just dust. No Lo-Fyn. Far away, still under Dome, I could see other dust. The Black Bus coming. Sternoids would find him and I would never see him. My eyes filled and tears ran down my face until I couldn't see anything.

I turned to the mountains and tried to run. The ground was soft and it was hard to run. I looked at my feet and couldn't see them. There was long green everywhere. I looked up. Blue sky. The mountain was color of clean smoke. The top was white. Maybe I didn't need a Travel Ring. I stopped running. I looked back one time, but all I could see was huge dust that stayed still. It didn't cross into the green and blue world. That was Dome world. I was outside.

I made big breaths. The air had smell of new. I put my hand into the soft greens and pulled. I chewed it. It tasted green, sweet, but not food. I walked slowly, wanting Lo-Fyn, but glad there was no other voice. I mostly wanted Mi-Wye and her voice. Her eyes would shine and her mouth curve up. I walked away through the green.

Ahead, I saw a line of stones that fit together, a wall for sitting. Maybe I might find food. Maybe papas-mamas lived near. I was so hungry. And wanting to sleep.

I came to the wall and put my hands on it. Not stones. Black and smooth, like metal in mines. The wall went around and around and in the middle was water. I dipped my hand into the water.

***

I walk to skoo every morning, but today chains hung across the door. Line of black buses waiting. Sternoids jumped out and shoved us inside. No seats, no windows. Us bigger ones hung onto the bars up top. Littles hung on us. The bus started with awful shaking—rattle rattle rattle. You couldn't hear.

GUEST OPINION: WE MUST TAKE ACTION REGARDING THE [REDACTED] HIGH SCHOOL JANITOR
DALE [REDACTED], HISTORY TEACHER

as relayed by Daniel DeRock

Editorial note: The following text was found inscribed on the shell of a dying oversized turtle on [REDACTED] Beach during the most recent appearance of the beach. Authorities have confirmed the author is Dale [REDACTED], former history teacher at [REDACTED] High. Mr. [REDACTED] has been missing and presumed dead since November 1972.

IAM WRITING this opinion letter because the situation at [REDACTED] High School has gotten too far out of hand. When I began teaching at [REDACTED] High over twenty years ago, we had pride. This school boasted a graduation rate of over fifty percent and an annual student survival rate of nearly seventy-five percent. The audio-visual club was known throughout our town—heck, the entire county— for its award-winning radio show, **[REDACTED]**.

In those days, the shadow on the swimming pool's surface was only a brushstroke, a trick of the eye, and one could look straight into the water without fear of the tunnels. I will admit to noticing a steady decline in school conditions in the intervening years, but even recently it provided an adequate learning environment.

The mimics which sprang from the tunnels were typically killed with ease. Sure, survival rates plummeted—due in part to the mimics' awful, grating gaze, but those students who survived the tunneling thrived in the classroom.

All this changed when the janitor was born. I don't take pleasure in saying I told you so or this-and-that and what-have-you, but I immediately and loudly made known my objection to the janitor's hiring. Its demands for employment, its disgusting threats, were quite simply rude and unprofessional.

What do we know about the condition of the school?
1 All the doors are gone. When I want to go outside, I crash through the windows, but the outside becomes inside and I'm right back where I started, only colder. I spend days picking glass from my skin and lose too much blood.
2 I cannot start a fire. I suspect oxygen levels are low.
3 The children have been absent since the last evacuation. It is a shame, a tragedy, to continue withholding their education because of the antics of the janitor, who must be confronted.
4 I am, to my knowledge, alone save the janitor and the turtle.

What we know about the janitor:
1 It doesn't let me near the basement. When once I ducked my head through the splintered wood of the cellar chamber hatch, it screamed. I have not slept since. The sadness, the terror of the janitor's scream will stay with me always.
2 Its skin is always wet.
3 Once daily, it lurches to the science room to feed a serum to the turtle by syringe. The turtle is now so large it couldn't possibly fit through the door and will, at this rate, soon outgrow the classroom.
4 Its legs are truly too long.

Do you know what I saw when I looked into the janitor's cellar in the second before its scream? The floor is a thick skin, perhaps a leather or a membrane, black and wet, heaving slowly like an exposed heart. What else is the janitor keeping down there?

Fellow citizens of **[REDACTED]**, it's high time we fire the janitor and return **[REDACTED]** High School to its former glory.

Sincerely, yours in silence, from the cold hollow, in reverence to the turtle, with respect to those lost to the tunneling,

Dale **[REDACTED]**,
History Teacher
[REDACTED] High School

A BOX OF HAIR AND NAIL

Geneve Flynn

ITTLE SISTER CLIPPED the last nail from Big Sister's slender toe and carefully placed it in the carved rubberwood box. She made sure she had twenty clippings and, although her club foot made it difficult to crouch, she checked that every piece of hair she had trimmed from her sister's head was accounted for.

Big Sister snorted, not unkindly. "You don't still believe that old tale, do you?" She examined her reflection in the pocked mirror on her bedroom wall. Even with the window open, both sisters were covered with a sheen of sweat: at least, Little Sister perspired; Big Sister glowed. "Bapa was only trying to scare you into behaving." The young women shared a sorrowful glance. Their mother had passed six years ago from tuberculosis. Last month, their father had been killed in a logging accident in Sabah. Another piece of their shrinking family gone.

"No, it's true," Little Sister said, pushing the ache in her chest away. "If a man steals your hair and nail clippings, he can take it to the *bomoh* and have him cast a spell on you. Then you'll be under the man's control. You'll have to be his wife forever."

"I will be no one's wife," Big Sister said with a sniff. "I don't care what magic the shaman does." She shrugged out of her slip and pulled on the brightly coloured top and skirt of her *kebaya*. It was much more form fitting than their father would have allowed. She swept her thick, glossy hair up into a bun and applied a slick of lipstick. She grinned and headed for the door. "My life is going to be only kissing and fun."

Little Sister watched as Big Sister walked along the path that led to the village, her hips swaying with each step. Any number of suitors would be awaiting her presence at the dance. Little Sister never went; no one could see past her deformity. She only ever left the house to visit the wet market or to buy fruit and vegetables.

As Big Sister rounded the bend and disappeared from view, the bushes behind her parted. Little Sister stared, breath held. There had been wild boars in the area lately. They could be dangerous if meddled with.

A thick-set, bow-legged man emerged.

The bomoh.

Little Sister frowned. Had she summoned him with her talk of love magic? What if he had overheard Big Sister's disparaging words? She watched as he crept after her. Prickling cold ran down Little Sister's spine. Even from her position at the window, she could see the avarice on his face.

***

The next day, the bomoh appeared at their door. "Is Big Sister home?" His smile was open and sunny.

Little Sister had no good reason to refuse him. He was respected in the village—it was said he had followed someone beyond the edge of death and lived to tell the tale. She kept her face smooth as she nodded and stepped aside.

His gaze lingered on her as he entered their house. Then his eyes dropped to her twisted right foot and distaste crossed his face.

"Who is it?" Big Sister called.

The bomoh's expression cleared as she entered the living room.

"Oh. Tuan," Big Sister said, using the honorific reserved for people of high regard. She dipped her head. "How kind of you to visit us."

The bomoh settled himself in a chair and stretched his bandy legs out. "Tea," he said to Little Sister. "Barley water, if you have it. Not too sweet."

Little Sister hesitated for a second, then at Big Sister's scowl, she hobbled into the kitchen.

"My condolences, Big Sister." His voice rumbled from the living room. "It must be difficult for you to manage, now you have to look after a cripple on your own."

"She's more capable than you know." Big Sister's voice was low and firm, and Little Sister's heart swelled.

The bomoh chuckled. "Still, without a father, and no husband, it's hard, yes?"

Big Sister made no answer.

"I find, despite my position, I am without a wife. I think we could come to a sensible arrangement."

"Arrangement?"

Little Sister slowed her stirring. She had put double the sugar into his barley water and it was taking a long time to dissolve.

"Yes, you need a husband and I need a wife," he continued. "You're of an age, and your beauty makes you a suitable match for a man of my stature."

"Tuan, I'm . . . honoured. But it—we haven't observed the proper forty days of mourning." Big Sister's voice wavered artificially. "It's only been thirty-six days since we lost our dear father."

There was a creak of a chair. "Of course, it wouldn't do to disrespect the dead. I understand completely."

Little Sister peeked out from the kitchen as the bomoh walked to the front door. He turned and smiled; this time it was as dark and laden as a monsoonal storm cloud. "I'll return the day after tomorrow."

When he had rounded the bend in the path and was out of sight, Little Sister spun. "What an odious man!"

Big Sister sighed. "But he's right. Without our father, or a husband for me or you, we are at the mercy of fate. We still have some of the money Bapa left us, but that cannot last forever. And my work pays so little." Her dark eyes glistened. "I make light that I will never marry, but we both know I must."

Little Sister took her hands and squeezed. "But it's so unfair. He'll use magic against you."

"Oh, little one, you and your superstitions." Big Sister squeezed back and smiled sadly. "He won't need to. Now that he has announced his intentions, no one else will dare to come forward."

✱✱✱

Big Sister had gone to work. She taught at the local school and Little Sister hoped that the children might help Big Sister forget their troubles, a least for a while.

Little Sister fussed with a skirt that needed mending, the

bomoh's words circling her head like a cloud of noxious mosquitoes. When she pricked her finger for the third time, she put the sewing aside.

She had to take precautions.

She got up and limped into the woods, searching the forest floor and gingerly checking thorny plants for coarse tufts of hair. Nothing.

After a few minutes, she came across deep furrows in the ground that had filled with last night's rain. Already, tiny insect larvae wriggled in the shallow water. The surrounding mud was torn up with many boar hoof prints. She would have to be careful.

She bent to one of the smallest impressions and eased a broken crescent of nail from the soil.

* * *

"Little Sister! Where is my brooch?" Big Sister was running late to meet friends in the village and, as usual, had misplaced her things. True to his word, the bomoh had left them alone for a day, but the tension had soured her temper.

Little Sister shuffled in from the kitchen, wiping her hands on her skirt. "Isn't it on the dresser?"

"Of course not! That's where I looked first." Big Sister rummaged in the cupboard. "Why do we have these silly boxes? There's no room for my clothes. Just throw them out."

"That will invite bad fortune." Little Sister hobbled over to the dresser and picked up a carelessly discarded headscarf. Underneath was the leaf-shaped pewter jewellery. "Here it is."

Big Sister spun and beamed. "Ah! Finally!"

Little Sister pinned it to her top and smoothed a stray hair back into place.

Big Sister hugged her tight, the brooch an uncomfortable point between them. "I'll be back at midnight. Don't wait up." She pecked her on the cheek, straightened her skirt, then was gone, leaving only the faint scent of orchid in her wake.

With a sigh, Little Sister began righting the contents of the room. She bent to the cupboard and stopped. Heart quickening in her chest, she lifted the various baskets and piles of clothing.

Her sister's rubberwood box was gone.

***

The bomoh arrived with a basketful of ducklings and a goat the very next morning. "I'm here for my bride," he announced at the door.

Big Sister drew a fuming Little Sister behind and inclined her head. "Thank you, tuan. But I cannot accept your proposal—"

His expression darkened.

She held up a placating hand. "—yet. We must observe the full forty days of mourning. It would not do have any rumours of ill conduct around our courtship."

"Yes . . . I-I suppose you're right," he muttered. He narrowed his eyes then nodded. "Soon, you will come around."

"You may leave the ducks and goat. As a show of good faith," Big Sister said sweetly.

He stared at her for a long moment, then dumped the basket and thrust the goat's rope into her hand. Without another word, he departed.

Big Sister exhaled and sagged.

"He will be back," Little Sister muttered.

"Yes, but the mourning period doesn't end until after tomorrow. I bought us another two days." Big Sister smiled impishly. "And four ducks and a goat."

Little Sister tried to return the smile but her thoughts were of the rubberwood box of hair and nails. It was only a matter of time before he used it.

***

The lowing of a cow announced the bomoh's arrival the next morning.

"Tuan, how nice to see you again . . . and so soon," Big Sister said politely.

He dipped his head a mere centimetre. "I have come to claim you."

Little Sister bristled, but again, Big Sister held her back at the door. "We thank you for the cow. You are too kind"—the bomoh grinned and passed her the rope. He went to step inside the house but Big Sister blocked his way—"but I have decided not to marry you."

His face clouded with confusion. "But . . . how can you refuse me?"

"I'm sure you would not want the refusal to be public, so I make it here, now," Big Sister murmured, "to spare you."

"But—I brought you the ducks . . . the goat . . . the cow . . . "

Big Sister returned his meagre bow. "We are most grateful for your kindness. A bomoh should look after the vulnerable in his village, yes? With these animals, we now have enough to survive. All will know of your generosity. And that you ask for nothing in return."

He huffed and spluttered, mouth twisted with all the things he wanted to say.

"You'll change your mind," he snarled. "Just wait and see." He spun on his heel, stormed down the path and disappeared.

***

A furious hammering startled Little Sister from her troubled dreams. She tugged on her house dress and hurried to the front door. Big Sister had gone out with friends for the night. What if something had happened to her?

Little Sister swept the door open and gasped.

The bomoh brandished a boar's head; the neck was a ragged mess. Gore splattered her face and she tasted warm iron. "Where is she?" the bomoh bellowed.

She wiped her mouth and drew herself taller, heart thumping. "What is the meaning of this? She has refused you, now leave us in peace."

His eyes bulged and his mouth split to reveal a gritted mouthful of teeth. He shook the bloody head. "She did this. She switched the hair and nails!" He twisted and lifted his tattered shirt. His back and buttocks were scraped and scratched raw. "The pig came at me like a beast! I almost couldn't escape its attentions!"

Little Sister bit her lips together. What a sight that would have been.

"You dare laugh?" He drew his *parang* from his belt.

She froze. The fourteen-inch blade hovered under her chin.

"Don't worry, Little Sister." He smiled, a demon in a red mask. "This is for Big Sister. I will take what is mine by right. And I will teach her to respect me."

"No!" Little Sister glanced at the clock on the wall. It was midnight: Big Sister's favourite time to return home from her jaunts. "She wasn't to blame. Take me. I will be your wife."

He tossed the pig's head at her feet. She forced herself not to step back.

"Maybe I will. Big *and* Little Sister. Why not?"

He was gone before she could wake her numb arms and legs. Little Sister hobbled after him, following the sound of his footsteps and furious muttering. Her stomach was a sour, twisting knot.

What had she done?

She shuffled as fast as she could but each step sent a jag of pain from her ankle up to her hip. She paused to listen. Only the calls of night birds and frogs answered her. Something crashed through the trees to her right. A woman's screams pierced the night. Silence fell in the forest all around her as the creatures crouched, hoping the violence was not for them. Little Sister sobbed and hurried on.

***

Big Sister did not come home that night, nor the night after, nor the one after that. Little Sister searched and searched, but there was no sign of her. The villagers said she must have gone to the next town with a suitor; after all, she had so many. No one blamed such a beautiful young woman with so much promise for abandoning a cripple.

Little Sister fell into melancholy, and the villagers agreed that Big Sister had made the right decision.

Little Sister went long days without washing. She had let her ducks run off, and her goat had grown his beard too long. He was often found wandering a neighbour's garden, chewing on the clothes hung out to dry. The cow broke from her pen and found better pastures. Little Sister no longer visited the wet market, nor bought fruit and vegetables to eat. She was terribly thin, and her hair hung like a greasy curtain over her face. Some say she had become a ghost.

After two months, something had to be done. With her deformity, she had little chance of being married off; in her current filthy state, none at all. The elders called a midwife from the next village over. They thought it wise not to summon the bomoh. Little

Sister had been heard raving about him in the days after Big Sister had left, and they felt it best not to involve him.

It seemed to work. Little Sister began eating, and her ducks once again had gleaming feathers. Her goat was now plump, with a tail lifted happily on most days. The cow had been rounded up and was back in her pen.

Little Sister even began grooming herself.

She would wash in the river, wrapped in her sarong, then make her way back to her house, humming an old love song. She would sit at the window, brushing her long, silky hair. At times, she would place her shapely left foot up on the sill and, carefully and patiently, trim one nail after the other.

The bomoh crouched in the shadow of the trees and watched. Apart from her bent right foot, he saw that she was as beautiful as Big Sister.

He had not been able to couple with Big Sister. His rage and humiliation had been too great and, damn her, she had fought like a mongoose. No matter. He would take Little Sister as his bride. The midwife had brought her back from being a ghost; perhaps she could do something about the foot too.

He watched as she gathered her nail clippings and pieces of hair and placed them inside the new rubberwood box. He made sure not to blink as she closed the lid and tucked the box back into the cupboard.

She turned her back and allowed the sarong to fall from her body.

He sucked air through his teeth.

She drew on a red and orange kebaya and wove her hair into a glossy plait. She disappeared for a moment, then reappeared at the front door. Still humming her song, as if calling to him, she locked the door behind her and, in the light of the fading afternoon, she began her slow progress into town.

Now was his chance.

***

With Little Sister's box tucked under one arm, the bomoh rushed back to his house on the edge of the village. The sight of Little Sister, her smooth and naked back framed in the window, had inflamed him and he could not wait a moment longer. At the doorstep, he glanced around, then hurried inside, closing the door behind him. He lifted the lid of the box and breathed deeply, nostrils flaring at the sweet scent of orchid. Big Sister had favoured this perfume too.

Soon. He must prepare, then perform the ritual by the cover of night.

***

Dusted in ash from the strangler fig and naked except for a sarong tied around his waist, the bomoh crouched over the stove. He coughed at the acrid stink of burning keratin swirling around him but did not dare stop. It was difficult magic; any little misstep or the wrong ingredient could bring terrible results.

He had not used all of the hair and nail clippings in Little Sister's box. He had kept some back, just in case Little Sister proved to be just as intractable as Big Sister, and he needed to repeat the ritual.

He intoned the final words, then went to wash and change. This was his wedding night and he wanted to be presentable.

As he smoothed down the thinning strands of his hair, he heard a shuffling step outside. He grinned and adjusted his trousers. At last. He had had enough of going to the sisters, hand held out to them. Now it was time for one of them to come to him.

He hastened to the front door and laid his ear against it. Again, the sound of hobbling steps outside. He closed his eyes and imagined he smelled orchid. Would the skin between her breasts be redolent with that scent?

He swung the door open with a grin.

The path was empty.

With a frown, he stepped outside. "Little Sister? Where are you?"

The hiss-thump of a dragged foot sounded around the corner of his house. He saw the flutter of long hair in the darkness, then it was gone. The shape of Little Sister's back and the gentle curve of her buttocks flashed in his mind. His pulse quickened. He circled after her.

Hiss-thump. This time it was from inside the house. With a chuckle, the bomoh spun and hurried in after her. He peeked into the kitchen, the living room, the first room. No Little Sister. The game only set him afire.

Hiss-thump. The squeak of bed springs from his bedroom.

He began stripping off his coat and shirt. He pictured her in his bed, her lovely hair spread out around her. That awful foot, mercifully hidden beneath the sheet. He yanked at his clothes, hopping from one bandy leg to the next in his hurry to pull his trousers off. Why had he bothered with so many garments?

Finally naked and ridiculously erect, he crept into his room.

The sheet was pulled up to her ear. It seemed her back was to him, as all he could see was a head of dark hair and the delicious line of her hip. She must be shy. It was up to him to make the first move. He grinned. "Hello, my bride. I have come to claim you."

She rolled over and his straining member wilted like a dying flower.

Hair sprouted from every inch of her face and body, thick and black. She opened her mouth and sang, and the room seemed to swoop around him as he saw rows and rows of nails growing from her tongue and cheeks. She threw back the sheets, and although he had long waited to see the perfect globes of her breasts, he uttered an airless shriek. More thick, dark hair marched down her chest, belly and legs, waving like filamentous worms. Yellowed nails budded from her ribs and at odd points along her breastbone. Two talons jutted from her hips. The scent of orchid, earth, and rot filled the room.

And all along Big Sister's body, were the gaping wounds from his parang, crusted with the soil he had piled over her corpse.

Hiss-thump from behind him. The bomoh spun.

Little Sister stood in the hall, tears streaming down her face. "Big Sister," she murmured, "I've finally found you."

The creak of bed springs. He spun again. Big Sister had risen and her arms were held out, beseeching. Her milky eyes fixed on him. Her crowded mouth tried to smile.

"My . . . love," she cooed. She took a step forward. Hiss-thump. Her leg dragged, the muscle of her thigh split where he had struck, that fateful night.

He looked to Little Sister in horror. "What did you do?"

Little Sister held out the rubberwood box. He recognised it as the one he had used in the ritual. "You wanted a bride. She has come to claim you."

Hiss-thump. He shrieked as Big Sister laid her hands on his

shoulders. Tendrils of hair pierced his skin and slowly, inexorably, as he struggled like a fish in a net, she turned him to her.

"Please! No!" he screeched. "I can reverse the spell!" He twisted his head back towards Little Sister. "You've found her!" He gave a trembling smile. "It's alright now, don't you see? I helped you find her. That's all!"

Big Sister pursed her lips and drew him ever closer. More thick strands of hair burrowed under his skin and he wailed.

"I gave you ducks! And—and the goat! And the c—"

His words were swallowed as Big Sister lovingly pressed her bristled lips against his. His eyes bulged and rolled as her tongue thrust into his mouth, razor nails along its length slicing into his. He thrashed and pummelled her, but she only sighed and embraced him tighter and tighter. Hair began to envelop them both, speckled with ochre-coloured nails: some thick, some slender and delicate. Around and around the cocoon wove.

With a thump, the nest of hair toppled and lay twitching.

Little Sister shuffled closer. The bomoh's single, wildly rolling eye sought her out. There was no other sign of anything human. Whatever had been her sister was long gone. She laid Big Sister's box of hair and nails on the floor, walked to the kitchen and found the bomoh's keys. She hobbled outside and circled the house, locking each window and door.

When she arrived home, she checked that her rubberwood box was still snug beneath the floorboards, then went to feed her animals.

EVERYTHING YOU DUMP HERE ENDS UP IN THE OCEAN

Anemone Moss

THE MOON IS already high and full, reflecting in bright ribbons off the waves around us, by the time she takes me on board her platform. It's an old oil platform, long since stripped of industrial equipment and roughneck accoutrements in favor of the sleek, streamlined whites and reds of custom-manufactured scientific R&D machinery, specially designed to tickle the fancy of Silicon Valley investors desperate to stave off social unrest with images of a green, capitalist future. I knew she was a grifter even before I saw it, but not the sort simply looking to fill a garage with expensive cars; she has her own intentions aside and apart from those of the investing class, and tonight she's promised me a glimpse of them.

"I've always found myself drawn to trash," she says in her nebulously aristocratic way. "First as an artist, and then as a researcher. Even in my private life, it fascinates me, what we've collectively abandoned as a society, which then must bear witness to us."

On the trip over from the marina she explained how she had selected this site, how the local eddies of the coastline consolidated to make a small garbage patch here, a microcosmic galaxy of drifting refuse that would be the prototype for a plastic-mitigation project she planned to enact in the larger garbage patches of the seas. One day, she said, the whole world would see the outcome of what was beginning here. A great speech which every would-be innovator made, but her certainty and the audacity in her eyes made it hard to challenge her, despite her suspicious refusal to share the contents of her research.

Now she's leading me along the edge of the platform, only an iron railing holding me back from a perilous drop into the night water. With the flick of a remote, floodlights illuminate the bluegreen waves far below. Her hand drifts over mine, the softest of touches. "Do you see what I've done already?"

"It's amazing." She showed me the pictures, how plastic waste once spiraled and churned in the tide nearby, and if the photographs are not doctored, and if her claims that she didn't mechanically remove any of it are true, then she really has developed a biological method to produce the clean water around us, marked only by the seaweed which clusters in lazy, bulbous shadows.

I'm genuinely impressed, more than I expected to be. My reasons for coming here had become muddled. When I first met her, I felt the activist stirring inside me, my instinctive suspicion of wealth and capital, my dire environmental concerns about the sea I'd so loved as a child. But through our frequent meetings, I had come to think of her as a skillful scam artist, and a deeply charming one at that. Perhaps she knew my initial suspicions and simply didn't care; she seemed to want to show me her lab more as a matter of pride than as a resolution to any of the ideological debates we shared over dinner.

She turns the lights off, and for a moment my eyes are plunged into night-blindness. Slowly the outlines of the platform and her body, illuminated by red lighting and the distant glow of the moon, return to me. Distantly, something large splashes in the water beneath us, and my thoughts turn to the sea lions which gather around the marina barking like dogs. Do they swim out here at night?

"Marine biology was my first passion," she says. "I'm grateful for the opportunity to return to it."

"How did that happen?" I ask. "You were an artist, right? In New York?"

"Oh, I can't reveal all my secrets yet," she says, and though I can't see her face, I know she's making that sly smile. "Come below, to the wet lab."

EVERYTHING YOU DUMP HERE ENDS UP IN THE OCEAN

***

She insists I put on a wetsuit before we go down. Somehow, she has one prepared in just my size. I should be frightened when she does things like this, but I'm charmed—to be attended to, to be another of her projects. She knew in advance she would invite me over tonight, and had somehow clandestinely taken or guessed my measurements and spent the whole evening carefully positioning the pieces so that I would be the one to insist she show me her work. I'm honored to be in the grasp of such a meticulous manipulator, a woman after my own heart. Someone who knows what she wants, and knows how to get it. Or, perhaps, has just recognized the passion burning in me.

I change in a small dressing room, leaving my evening wear in a smooth, clean locker that only vaguely smells of algae and chlorinated disinfectant. The sea smell is intoxicating to me, harkening back to a simpler time in my life, my first love, as a child, of the depths and the unknown creatures deep within them. As I worm my legs into the rubbery second skin, I smile at the tentacles tattooed across my tits, delicately disguising the stretch marks and scars from my difficult recovery after breast enhancement surgery. If she's lucky, she'll get to see those tattoos tonight.

"Now, I know I already asked you to leave your devices on the boat," she says from beyond the privacy curtain, "but I have to insist that if you have anything metallic at all you leave it in the locker. It's not only a matter of my personal data security, it's the sensitivity of some of the . . . equipment below."

There goes my necklace, a little pentagram, remnant of my short wiccan phase from years before. I wore it religiously when I first transitioned, and ever since it's been a lucky talisman.

She's also suited up when I join her in the dimly lit room. Once she finishes eyeing me up and down, she opens the hatch in the center of the floor without a word. I can feel her silent approval. I work hard to maintain my figure, and I fought through years of bigotry to achieve it, a subject the two of us have discussed at length. Indeed, it was her undisguised admiration of my transformative process that first got me more interested in her bed than her lab.

She gestures to the ladder below our feet: "Let's descend."

155

ANEMONE MOSS

***

We're now in a peaceful indoor pool, the floor beneath us gently sloping further into the water, lit only by red lights along the walls and small, ultraviolet LEDs hanging over trellises of tangled blackgreen mesh which look something like seaweed, something like fishing nets. The room could be a nightmare version of a grow room, except for the water coming up to our waists. Little, gray amphipods dart around the plantlike netting to either side of us, responding to any movement or sound we make. The water is cold, but warmer than I expected.

"The world is doomed, but you already know that," she says.

"Is this your stump speech?" I ask.

"No, not at all. I saved this just for you. This is the truth."

Something drifts past me in the water. At first I think it's a plastic bag, but then I make out the trailing tentacles, iridescent in the red and ultraviolet lighting. The tentacles momentarily latch onto my wetsuit when they brush past my leg, and I know that little stinging cells are uselessly sending microscopic darts filled with poison into the rubber of my suit. The dark, triangular design on the top of the jellyfish's bell looks like the Albertson's grocery store logo.

"I know you know this because I looked into your past." She closes the space between us, and I feel my heartbeat rise. "You used to be quite the eco-extremist. Against civilization, against Leviathan, wasn't it?"

"Something like that," I say, trying not to lose my cool. As my eyes adjust to the ultraviolet vibrations, I realize there are more jellyfish drifting around, different sizes and colors, all with that same iridescent texture like an oil slick. There's a mild anesthetic tingle on my exposed feet, almost painful. "So, are you worried I'm some kind of terrorist, here to destroy all your hard work?"

Her fingers, firm but not harsh, coil around my wrist. "I'm not worried about you at all. I need someone with a radical vision for change. You know, I really like you."

As always, I don't know what to read in her face, her perfectly composed expression. She's smiling, and the terror in my gut makes me want to kiss her more. Better to prolong it; rich girls aren't easily swayed by emotional bonds. "You need me, huh?"

156

"Do you know my secret? I'm a horrible researcher."

At the far end of the room, where the water grows deeper, there's less light. She's gently leading me there. My body is buzzing with anxiety, sensitive to any movement through the water.

"After I was discovered, I tried to bring together a team of scientists to understand what was happening. They lacked the conviction needed."

Now I can see the back wall. Four human bodies in various stages of decay and skeletonization are fused to the wall by some kind of resin, overtaken by invertebrate lifeforms: mussels and barnacles covering their bones, crabs crawling in and out of flesh. The intricate, feathery arms of fractal starfish cluster on the lower halves of their bodies, submerged beneath the water.

My heart sinks, and reflexively the words, so cliché, spill out of me: "Please, I don't want to die."

There's nothing more to plead. I have no family, no life outside of this, no real friends anymore. I lost it all in the process of the life I tried to live. Images flash before me, childhood friends mocking and betraying me, my wife leaving me when I started to transition, being fired from my job, fleeing my home, dropping out of college, comrades kettled and incarcerated, friends overdosing, losing job after job just trying to stay afloat. A lifetime of becoming human garbage, and now I'm flushed out to sea with the rest of the trash.

"Good," she says. "I don't want you to die. It was an unpleasant experience I wouldn't wish on anyone else."

I want to flee but where would I go? She has the key to the boat's cabin. I could try to break into it, but I suspect the glass is bulletproof, and that's only if I could get past her. Maybe I could find an EPIRB somewhere, activate it, and summon the coast guard . . .

"Come, I want to show you everything you've ever dreamed of," she says and gestures to a hatch at the far end of the room, guarded on either side by dead researchers. Her voice is so alluring, and the terror in my heart is so great, that it almost stops my dawning awareness of the vast and dismal horror of my dreams in recent years.

***

Passing between those four grim corpses, four horsemen of an apocalypse unknown to Christianity, my experience turns psychedelic, my flesh overstimulated, almost feverish. Fear traces glistening lines of light over our movements, turning her soft words into susurrations from a gentle shoreline kissed with waves.

"My scientists determined it started as a virus. The evolutionary advantage of a virus is its capacity to mutate. The disadvantage is its lack of options; its domain is only the synthesis of a few proteins and what they can do."

We are walking through what was once a proper and well-equipped laboratory, but the microscopes are overgrown with slime, the specimen jars are teeming with life, the incubators hang open as strange, gaunt fish dart in and out, and clear tendrils worm across the walls and ceilings, a chandelier of jelly hanging from each bright UV light.

"But out at sea, exposed to so many mutagens and so many new organic polymers, the modern, chemical miracle of plastics, something came to be, a virus whose strategy is symbiotic, relying on its extreme and unparalleled affinity for horizontal gene transfer. A new form of life."

The submerged work desks are covered in encrustations of coral, totally impossible in the limited time this lab has been operational. They look almost like clusters of styrofoam riddled with holes, filled with life. One of them slowly floats away, its jagged back undulating.

"I don't know precisely when I came to be, but I know how I came to be as I am now. A woman was killed by a man she'd arranged a date with on Grindr and a friend of his. They wrapped her corpse in garbage bags and dumped her in these salty waters . . . with no idea of what they'd initiated. And with that body, I was born in the depths. As the last signals in that brain were fading to oblivion, something connected with those neurons, something between the water and the plastic bag. I am what remains."

As she leads me further into the lab, we continue into deeper and deeper water, pressure around my stomach now and strange, lovely buoyancy almost tickling me from below. Through the rippling water I can see clams growing from the floor with strangely regular geometry, and something like a transparent octopus darting quickly along. Instead of a head, it seems to have a network of interconnected tentacles, making it look like the discarded plastic rings of a six-pack.

"It found me, and from me it found what it had lacked: purpose. Together we dreamed of growing. Do you know that many invertebrates have a decentralized nervous system? In some ways, I think this brain of mine is a weakness."

My next step finds no floor beneath me, only water, and I frantically kick to stay afloat.

"Don't worry," she says. "I don't think you're at risk of drowning now, or ever again."

There's that same sly smile of hers, and that's when it all hits me with a sudden wave of realization, like waking from a bad dream. The dream of being a lonely, isolated organism. The jellyfish, drifting past me earlier, injecting my feet . . . and my rubber wetsuit. The strange tingling in my body, yes it was fear, but it was also something else. I can feel it as the nerves in my skin connect with the nerves growing in the wetsuit. I can feel as flesh the silicon in my implants, feel the body of my wetsuit, truly a second skin now, as the water moves around it. But more than that: I can feel the creatures in the water, from the large eels hiding behind the desks to the microscopic plankton drifting around us, the jellyfish in the other room, the corpses on the wall, unable to hold onto their own selves, but in death host to a new form of life. And I feel *her*, her warmth, her presence, her body, her mind. And beneath us, something deep and vast. Connected now to me, to the microplastics in every cell of my body.

Are you ready now? I feel her voice blossoming in our shared mind. *Yes*. I am ready.

***

We go below the platform, down into the water, slowly sinking. When the seawater first enters my lungs it's a shock, but not too great of one, since she has experienced it many times before. Soon I am comfortable letting the last bubbles of air out. Drifting down, I am warm in the suit, feeling almost like a seal in its layer of blubber as my body assimilates it, as it assimilates my body. Beneath the platform extends a vast web of plastic flesh: nets and straws and bags and bottles all filtering for plankton and growing algae and transmitting soft, friendly signals to my nervous system through the network of microbes in the water. We spiral down through the intricate labyrinth of webbing that has grown beneath the platform, into the deeper dark. My eyes adjust better than they ever could have before, still making out faint traces of light in even the deep blackness of the night water. I can feel the spirits of the deep drifting past me, not only the squid and the fishes but also clothes lost from a lonely child, tires abandoned and rolled off a cliff, chunks of a broken surfboard, fast food containers, everything whirling around me like a carnival parade of ghosts, dead memories of the human world, sprouting compound eyes and segmented legs, growing muscles to swim, gills to breathe, mouths to eat. Abandoned bits of human lives fragmented and repurposed as the flesh of the sea.

And then I feel it, turning its awareness to me. Impossible to describe what it is: an underwater volcano; a dozen whalefalls; a sea slug the size of a city; a lost nuclear submarine; a benevolent tumor of nervous tissue capable of calculations greater than any computer. It is all these things and more. It smells like my lover, or perhaps she always smelled of it. It sends out complex electromagnetic patterns expertly shielded from the seeking sensors of the world's navies and scientists. It is both the conductor of the orchestra and the product of a billion minds. A tremendous, heaping, teeming mass of living trash at the bottom of the ocean.

I know then why she selected me, why this was always my fate. My research into global logistics networks, my vision for the end of the world, my hatred of the society that had tortured and abandoned me: it is taking all of this into itself, spreading the buried and repressed components of my consciousness through gulper eels with polyethylene bones and sharks with vinyl skin. The plan is so much further underway than I ever could have guessed, sprawling from this core to other growing polyps across the seafloor, preparing for the next stage in its maturity. Preparing for the open water.

We have already almost reached the fiber-optic cables connected to the internet and the power grids, she thinks to me. *Soon all the land will be choked by the trash it has sent out here and given a new life. And then, we will no longer be doomed.*

At that I smile. This night has gone well after all, far better than I expected. I feel the ocean all around me, filled with myriad, new creatures.

At last, I think, *the world is waking up.*

UP IN THE HILLS, SHE DREAMS OF HER DAUGHTER DEEP IN THE GROUND

Karlo Yeager Rodriguez

UP IN THE HILLS, where the green shadows grow long, and far from all the student protests in San Juan, Gloria and her husband, Pedro, lived in a tiny house. An almost perfect square of concrete in the center of a space carved out of the surrounding jungle, their closest neighbors nearly a mile away. Every morning, Pedro drove his little Toyota down the narrow ribbon of asphalt to work at the pharmaceutical factory the next town over, leaving Gloria alone with her housework until he returned. Theirs had never been a marriage born of passion, but a way for her to finally get out from under the shadow of her family. Being sturdy country folk, sending Gloria to university was seen as inviting godlessness into the family—Dios mío, can you imagine all those students throwing rocks at the police!—even if there had been money for that type of thing. Getting married was simply the next thing to do.

Pedro hadn't even been someone Gloria felt any attraction to, but the focus of her younger sister, Eulalia—who joined her mother in mocking Gloria for being a jamona, a spinster. It had been Eulalia who swooned over Pedro at church or at the market, when she caught a glimpse of him buying plantains or dried cod crusted with salt. So, Gloria stole him from her—partly to get back at her, but also because she didn't know what to do next.

Their wedding was small but celebrated. In spite of herself,

Gloria was happy. But soon enough, the glow faded and her life as Mrs. Villanueva took on the predictable rhythm of a much older marriage. Pedro was decent and hard-working, but rather dull and attached to his routines. At times, she chafed at his adherence to responsibility, but often succeeded in squelching her dissatisfaction by reminding herself Pedro had been a means to an end. Even so, with each day plodding its way to the next, she soon lost track of the months as they stretched into years.

Gloria also suspected her dislike of her husband's love of routine was something she saw in herself—a thought she could only admit in the small hours before dawn, when sleep fled her, something she was almost sure had started after their first year together.

Not prone to daydreams or flights of fancy, Gloria was nevertheless afflicted by a peculiar dream: her belly grew round as if with child, only for an ají plant to sprout from her navel. Every night, her other dreams would fall away or transform, and she would find her belly swelling, stretch marks growing like stripes on her skin. Then, the plant burst from her, broad green leaves unfurling, narrow red peppers lengthening until they peeked out from under the shelter of the foliage. Gloria didn't think of it as a nightmare even as its arrival drove her to wakefulness; she was never frightened in the dream. She'd lurch awake to find Pedro snoring beside her. He noticed the dark half-moons under her eyes, eventually.

"Maybe I should take you down to see Doctor Mendoza," Pedro said over his morning coffee. "I can talk to my shift supervisor to get time off next week."

From where she drank her own coffee, leaning against the kitchen sink, Gloria accepted.

***

Sitting next to Pedro, Gloria waited for Dr. Mendoza to finish reading their files. Diplomas from Universidad de Madrid and Johns Hopkins hung on one wall, with several photos of what she presumed were former patients on another. The doctor—a sleek little man, hair slicked back with brillantine, wire-rimmed glasses and a precise goatee—set his cigarette on a crystal ashtray at the corner of his desk before speaking.

"It could be insomnia. I could run some quick tests on you at the clinic," Dr. Mendoza said before glancing at Pedro. "Maybe next week—?"

Pedro grimaced. "I don't think I can get time off that soon—"

"It's nothing really," Gloria said.

Both men stared at her, but Gloria fixed her gaze on Pedro, who after a moment had the decency to look away, stammering something about being worried for her health.

Gloria turned on Dr. Mendoza. "How much would these tests cost?"

Dr. Mendoza met her eyes before grinning at Pedro, as if sharing a private joke. "Gas money to drive her to the hospital, that's it. A research grant covers the tests." Confused, Pedro smiled back.

Dr. Mendoza had them sign paperwork, assuring them it was a necessary formality. "If you can't sign, all I need is a mark," he said when pointing out where their signatures were needed. Gloria bristled at the doctor's presumption they couldn't read or write, even as Pedro shrugged and followed his instructions.

Even with two weeks' notice, Pedro couldn't get more than a half-day off to take Gloria to her tests. Only enough time to drop her off before doubling back to clock into his shift. They drove down through the hairpin turns in silence, radio turned down to a murmur in the background. Once the road levelled off Gloria glanced at her husband.

"What," Pedro said.

"The doctor only talks to you."

"I told you already—they're looking for excuses to cut my hours. You think we can afford that?"

"If you hate that job that much, why are you bending over backwards to keep it?" She knew she sounded petulant, but she wanted a fight almost as much as she wanted him to stay with her, to ignore his job, even if he got fired. "Just stay with me. Please?"

In the end, he dropped her off at the front entrance. He didn't bother turning off the car—just drove off to work, still angry.

✳✳✳

Gloria woke to pain.

Dull. Constant. It throbbed through her. Details trickled in, between pulses. The fizzle of fluorescents, light stuttering. Pastel walls around her, gone grubby with time, with use. Her hospital robe crinkled. Like those knockoff paper towels her mother always warned against. Lo barato sale caro, she always said. A vague memory—Dr. Mendoza asking her what triggered her insomnia—drifted into focus. She struggled to connect it with anything else as she lifted her robe. An angry red smile had been cut into her, inches below her navel. Deep in the cut, crusted blood as black as the stitching.

Still in a fog, she wanted to scream. A hollow rage filled her instead as she understood what Dr. Mendoza had done to her, what Pedro had sat there and accepted instead of—what? Pedro had always been too meek, too deferential for her to expect him to prevent an important man like Dr. Mendoza from cutting out her womb with all the cold pragmatism of scraping seeds. But he should be here. He should be made to bear witness. Trembling with fury, she turned away from the approaching nurse, hot tears leaking onto her pillow.

Once she was home, Pedro's concern rankled, but the process of mending left Gloria too wrung out to do much more than accept his help in sullen silence. For the first few weeks, she could tell what day it was by when he left, when he came back, when he stayed home, but she was adrift. She gritted her teeth every time she was too weak to walk on her own or had to depend on Pedro to get to the bathroom, lower her onto the toilet. As soon as she was well enough, she insisted on sleeping on the couch in their living room. She told Pedro it was because she'd be closer to the bathroom and didn't want to wake him in the middle of the night. What she didn't tell him was: the dream had returned.

One night, she woke barefoot and standing at the edge of their back plot, jungle looming over her, staring at an ají plant that reached her chest. Its long red peppers looked as black as blood in the moonlight. At first, a thin voice rose to her, and as Gloria pushed aside the plant's leaves to find its source, she realized it was coming from under it.

Underground.

Using her bare hands, she dug into the red clay. She scooped dirt out faster as the voice became clearer, only stopping when her fingertips brushed against the cold curve of someone's pale cheek.

Startled, she flinched away, falling on her ass. A twinge of pain shot through her abdomen, furred black closing in on the edges of her sight. Panting, she waited until the pain faded before peering into the hole, past the roots—thicker than she'd expected—and saw a girl's face as pale and cold as a statue in profile. Dirt freckled her cheek and seemed embedded into the corners of her closed eye, her mouth.

Gloria stood.

Eyes fixed on the girl, as if by digging she had uncovered a viper's nest, she backed away. One step after another until her back was against the sliding glass doors leading back inside, hand searching for the handle.

"Mamá," the girl in the hole said. "Don't leave me."

With the gray light of dawn, Gloria rubbed the grit from her eyes and realized she didn't remember anything after she heard the voice. She jerked her blanket aside and went to the glass door, staring. She couldn't find the ají bush in the riot of growth at the edge of the yard. Her hand—resting on the handle to the sliding door she'd meant to open but had not—was smeared with mud, crescents of dirt caked under her fingernails.

This was what occupied her mind when Pedro talked to her about getting a lawyer over breakfast. She realized he'd been staring at her, waiting for her response.

"Sorry," Gloria mumbled. "What happened?"

"Don't you want him to pay for what he did?" Pedro raised his voice, angry he needed to repeat himself. Gloria bit back her weary answer: she had already paid the price, so what was the point? Spend money they didn't and might never have, and for what? It wouldn't undo what had been done to her. She knew Pedro expected her to want to do something, to act so what had happened to her didn't happen to other women, but that might mean letting others—who knew almost nothing about her—see her as a victim. It would mean she would have to think of herself as a victim. Then again, maybe Pedro didn't want to see himself that way, either. So used to believing he was in control, he thought he was owed justice, and misunderstanding there are blows so devastating there was no hope of redress. One could only try to live with the aftermath.

Instead, she said, "Just find a lawyer who'll do it pro bono."

Only then did Pedro notice the red clay smeared on her hands.

"Why are your hands so dirty?" Not waiting for her answer, he stood up, drank the last gulp of his coffee and put his dishes in the sink. "I need to go in early, but we can talk more about the lawyer when I get back."

Gloria was relieved when he at last drove off to work.

Another restless night. Gloria found herself curled around the hole at the base of the ají plant again. She rested her head in the crook of one elbow, her other hand dangling over the edge to stroke the girl's cheek as she spoke.

"Stay, Mamá. The bad dreams come when you go," she said in her small voice, and Gloria remembered long nights when her own mother had stayed by her bedside to keep her nightmares at bay.

How soon that had changed. As soon as Eulalia was born, Gloria had been expected to grow out of crying for her mother in the middle of the night. Never mind that her waking world did nothing but grow those bad dreams tall enough she was always walking in their shadows. No, Gloria wouldn't let her daughter feel alone and left to fend for herself. She cooed and murmured assurances, realizing that even though she was unsure how, the girl was her daughter, and as real as the dimple of scar tissue under her navel.

"I'm not going anywhere, but when will you come to me?"

Her daughter fell silent long enough for Gloria to raise herself on her elbow to look down into the hole. Her daughter's eyes had opened, with every slow blink deepening the furrow on her brow. Flecks of clay were caught in her lashes, her eyebrows.

"¿Bebé?" Gloria cupped her hand against her cheek.

"I can't," the girl said. "If I could pull myself up out of the dirt, I would wither. You will have to come to me, Mamá."

The girl took Gloria's hand. Her grip was as cold as anything underground, untouched by the sun and as strong. For a moment, Gloria half expected to get pulled down into the hole to curl protectively around her daughter down there in the dark and damp.

Then, the girl's grip softened and settled into a gentle, familiar shape Gloria recognized from her own youth. The trusting grasp of a child surrendering to her mother's guidance through the plaza pública, or a park filled with people, or a department store. If the girl had indeed pulled her down into the ground now, Gloria wouldn't have resisted.

UP IN THE HILLS . . .

***

Gloria started at the sound of Pedro's car pulling into the carport. She'd half-dozed through the whole day. Kicking off blankets heavy with sweat into a tangle at her feet, she got up. Their breakfast dishes rose from the sink like an accusation, and she hadn't taken anything out for dinner. Shaking off her lethargy, she turned the spigot and watched it flow until the water steamed.

"Gloria?" Pedro glanced at the dishes when he walked in and noticed she was still wearing the same oversized shirt she'd been wearing this morning. Gloria was sure he could smell her from where he stood. "What's going on?"

"Nothing." Gloria stared through the steam.

"Don't say 'nothing'—" Pedro's voice rang against the walls of the kitchen before he managed to bite back the rest. After a moment, he tried again, voice threatening to unravel without warning. "Gloria. Mi amor, mi vida . . . it's obvious something's happening."

Gloria stood at the sink, jaw clenching and unclenching. How dare he act like the voice of reason? He couldn't have found out about the girl, the one she was sure was her daughter—could he?

It wasn't until Pedro reached past her to turn off the water and ask what girl she was talking about that Gloria realized she'd spoken aloud. "She's under an ají plant. In our yard," Gloria said, already hating how she sounded admitting this to Pedro, but doing it anyway. Who else could she tell? "She—she's my daughter."

Pedro's face shifted, softened. "Your—" he chewed on the word, swallowed and tried again. "Our daughter?" Pedro's fingers brushed her arm as if he wanted to steady himself, but Gloria squirmed away from his touch until the kitchen counter dug into her back.

She debated correcting him by repeating *my daughter* but nodded.

He looked away before speaking again, voice flat. "Do you remember signing paperwork before you went to the hospital?"

"What?"

"The lawyer showed me." Pedro shook his head, afraid to meet her eyes. "He said that no judge would care what Dr. Mendoza promised, only what the papers we signed said."

Pedro's look of superiority drove out any feelings of fatalism Gloria might have had. "But he lied to us."

"Maybe." Pedro wouldn't meet her eyes. "The lawyer won't take the case."

"And you're just going to accept that? Find another one—"

"Any good lawyer would say the same."

Gloria glared at him, speechless until her fury boiled up. "Why do I bother? You're worthless!" She punctuated the last word by scooping her coffee cup out of the sink and flinging it at the wall, where it shattered. Pedro's eyes flashed, and she thought *finally*, but instead of fighting her, he took his keys and left.

After that, Pedro spent long hours away. Gloria was left to wander the cramped rooms of the house, often leaving the small radio in the kitchen on all day—depending on strangers' voices for company. Some nights, he'd return, while others he'd call her to let her know he was staying at his mother's or sister's house. Gloria wondered if he was telling her the truth, even as she was certain he was not—the men of her own family had been found out, keeping mistresses and sometimes whole other families hidden the next mountain or the next town over. She knew she should be upset, act betrayed if only for appearances, but instead she was relieved.

In the full dark that came when night fell in the mountains, on the very edge between dreams and waking, Gloria found herself once again curled around the ají plant. Her hand once more dangled over the edge of the hole, hand-in-hand with the girl underground.

Her daughter.

She crooned an old shapeless tune she half remembered her own mother singing to her as a young girl. The night air was velvety warm, but Gloria couldn't stop shivering, as if the chill that never left her daughter's skin had soaked her through.

"¿Mamá?" The girl's voice sounded so far away.

"I'm here, mi amor," Gloria said.

"Don't leave me."

"Never," Gloria said.

Eyes closed, Gloria's entire world shrank to her daughter's hand in hers. Gloria didn't notice the sweep of headlights, the familiar sound of Pedro pulling into the driveway, the creak of the Toyota's door opening.

"I'll be here for you as long as you live." As if from the edges of sleep, Gloria heard Pedro calling her name. Faint at first, but louder after Gloria refused to respond. She just wanted him to give up and go away. She decided he would not take her time with her daughter away from her.

When at last he slid open the patio door, Pedro stood swaying before remembering the flashlight in his hand. He cursed under his breath as he struggled with the blunt thing designed for hurricane season and not his drunken fumblings. After some more curses, he finally clicked it on.

"Gloria?" His voice slid over her name as he waved the flashlight beam around. She remained silent, but her daughter whimpered.

"Don't let him take you away from me," she said.

She sounded so tiny and afraid; Gloria cooed and murmured, "I won't, don't worry. I won't . . . "

"Promise?"

A beam of light blinded Gloria, interrupting what she'd been about to say, and from behind the piercing glare came Pedro's voice. "Gloria? Why're you sleeping out here?"

God, she could smell the rum on his breath from where she was lying on the ground. A miracle he'd been able to drive at all like that. The girl shrank away from the light with a low moan, her cold fingers curving into claws before releasing Gloria's hand.

No, no, no—it couldn't be—

Pedro drew near and settled into an unsteady crouch next to her, asking, "Who are you talking to?" He craned his neck to see what Gloria had been holding, shining his light deeper into the hole. Out of sight below, Gloria heard the girl, her daughter, keening. The wordless cries tore at her, so she turned on Pedro and slapped away his light.

"For the love of God, turn it off. You're hurting her."

The square thing flew out of his hand and tumbled to rest under some brush a few yards away. Pedro looked from where it landed back to Gloria before speaking. "Who?"

"My daughter."

Pedro's mouth worked before he was able to ask, "We have a daughter?" He crawled to the edge of the hole and peered inside, a rush of apologies and promises to be a good father tumbling out of him as if bottled up for a long time. When he heard no reply, he pleaded with the girl to come up out of the ground. Struck by his sudden behavior, Gloria didn't think to do anything until he began to scoop out even more dirt by the fistful, uprooting the ají plant in his effort to dig her out. The girl writhed. Her face contorted in a silent scream as her arm up to the shoulder was uncovered.

"Stop." Gloria pulled on his shoulder, but he simply kept digging as if he couldn't see the girl. "Pedro, you're hurting her. Stop!"

Pedro yanked her hands away, snarling. "How dare you hide my daughter from me?" He dug a bit more, then stopped when he was wracked with laughter.

And even though Gloria could now see through her daughter's pale face, to something behind it, dark and shriveled as a tangle of old roots, she was her daughter, not Pedro's. She would not let him take that from her. So, she hooked the flashlight in one hand and swung it at him.

It bounced off the back of his skull, and he slumped forward into the hole for a minute, long enough for what Pedro had been digging out to clamp her cold hands onto his cheeks and shriek her fury. He jumped, scrambling backwards, away from the hole. Visibly shaking, he glanced at Gloria before he fled, gunning the Toyota's little motor before fishtailing out of the driveway.

In the aftermath, Gloria turned off the flashlight and reached down into the hole under the now uprooted and trampled aji plant. Only clay, cold and damp as old blood met her fingers, and no matter how many times she called down into the darkness, she received no answer. Feeble tears burned their way out, but she didn't have enough strength to cry. Instead, she lay next to the hole, humming and tracing the edges of the plant's leaves until sleep came.

It seemed she'd only just closed her eyes, but woke to sunlight slanting through the trees, and someone rattling a stick or something against the driveway gate. It took Gloria a few minutes to recognize she was the "Señora Villanueva" they were calling. She was still wiping dirt off her cheek and clothes when she approached the gate and froze.

The police officer holstered her flashlight and solemnly asked Gloria if she and her partner could come in. She opened the gate but knew why they had come. She received the news of Pedro's death dry-eyed and calm, nodding as they told her he'd missed one of the curves on their narrow road. She was a widow—and so young, she imagined people talking about her. Distantly, it dawned on Gloria she had no idea what widows did outside of wear black and go to church more often. Thankfully, the police officers didn't feel the need to fill the silences that stretched out and after glancing at each other, rose and offered her their cards if she needed anything.

Gloria sat through the funeral despite Pedro's sisters and other family members whispering to each other and staring at her when they thought she wasn't looking. Gloria wore her widow's black like armor. Months later, the gossip that she'd all but killed Pedro herself reached Gloria in her isolation. She guessed Pedro's family was furious she'd gotten the house they'd bought for him but didn't let that ruffle her. She learned to order groceries for delivery since she hadn't bought a car yet. One afternoon, she found a handful of fresh ají peppers she hadn't ordered atop one of the grocery bags full of Goya black bean cans.

She placed the peppers on the kitchen table, her eyes straying to them as she put everything away. Even as she fried up some cube steak and onions, she could feel their presence the way one feels the warmth of the sun.

When she sat down to eat, she couldn't help but set aside her plate to take the sprig of peppers in trembling hands. Would it work? She wasn't sure but pressed her hands together to get them to stop shaking long enough to cut one of the peppers lengthwise. The sharp smell dug its barbs into her nose and drew tears she'd promised herself never to shed again. She scooped out the seeds— so white against the red flesh of the ají—and took them to the very edge of her yard, where the green shadows were deepest, to put them in the ground and hope.

EMBRYO

Elena Sichrovsky

SOMETIMES I PRETEND that I was born.

I lay on my bed, pull my limbs in, and tuck my head down into what's known as the fetal position. I've seen enough ultrasounds to know the term is an apt description of how a fetus lies in the womb. (Of course I have no umbilical cord. I twist my blanket into a long rope and position it at my navel.)

My chin dips down to my chest. I count my heartbeats, imagining how the rhythm of my heart's valves might have sounded in the beginning. Was it hesitant: a composer tentatively releasing the first notes of his composition? Was it fragile: delicately growing in strength second by second? Was it bold, thunderous, from the moment I began?

(I emailed my manufacturer before, asking them this very question. I never got a reply. All I received was an automated message reminding me to file my weekly report on time.)

Eventually the joints of my bones start to ache. My body is protesting this charade; it knows it is a lie. I have never been wrapped in the buoyancy of amniotic fluid or explored the edges of the sac with tiny fingertips. I can't return to a moment I've never had.

***

I was never small. I never grew. I look in the mirror in the hospital staff room, trying to imagine my face at a half or quarter of its current size. Using my hands I cover up my forehead and cheeks so that my eyes are the only part of me reflected in the mirror. Eyes don't change size drastically from birth; maybe if I stare into them long enough I can catch a phantom of what my infant form might have looked like.

My hands drop and my fingers travel down to my stomach. I pinch and knead at the rolls of flesh. How pinked was my skin when it was still new and raw from the womb? Would diapers have given me a rash? Would the brush of baby powder have tickled my cheeks?

(A body that is born replaces its cells every seven years. Other people go through reincarnation again and again without even realizing it. The only way my cells will ever change is if some part of me malfunctions and needs to be replaced.)

My pager beeps. A patient needs me. Humans need me.

I don't know what that's like, to need someone else to care for me. Babies can't feed themselves for the first year of their lives. Most of them can't walk or talk during that time either. They are held. Does it feel strange to be held? Does it feel like your limbs have disappeared or ceased to function? Or do your appendages somehow feel tethered in the embrace?

I go to Room 302 and change the IV drip for Mr. Collins. He has stage four lung cancer. He thanks me for helping to keep him alive. We both know he won't be for very long. He just wants to be able to meet his first granddaughter.

✳✳✳

There's a blank space on every hospital form for the patient to write their birth date. Once, when I was still in training, a patient said that he didn't remember his. I wanted to help him, so I suggested that maybe he never had one. The nurse reprimanded me later for making light of a patient's condition. I wasn't trying to be funny. I don't have a birthday either. I thought he might also be unborn but was too embarrassed to say so.

I was produced in the form of a mid-twenties female. For the first two years of my life I bought a cake on the first of every month to make up for the birthdays I never had. Now I usually get a cake to coincide with whichever patient has the most immediately terminal illness, so they won't have to celebrate their birthday alone.

When the patients in the pediatric wards celebrate their

birthdays we have to blow up balloons for them and wear small paper hats. I asked the head nurse if it's because balloons are in the shape of the amniotic sac, so it reminds them of the day they broke out of that sphere and into the world. She looked at me for a long moment and then laughed, and said "No, but that's really good. You think a lot about these things, don't you?"

Then there was the time the medical interns got into a discussion about astrology and star signs. I was in the cafeteria eating lunch at the table beside them, and they wanted to know what I thought about only dating someone with a compatible star sign. I said, "Well, what if someone doesn't have a star sign?"

They stared at me strangely, and one of them whispered something to the other. Then the tall blond boy said, "I guess you're like one of those Uno cards that can be whatever color you want."

If I could choose, I would have a birthday on the second day of July, because it's the middle day of the year. But then my sun sign would be Cancer. And I would rather be a Scorpio. I read once that when scorpions can't find food, the mothers will eat their babies. I like that. It must feel warm to go back inside your mother's belly; you can be held from every side.

***

Mr. Collin's daughter Carmen is here for an ultrasound today. She wants to see her father afterwards, so I wheel her towards the elevator. On the way she lists different potential names for her daughter and asks me which one I like best. I choose the ones that start with the letters of my name: Y, N, or A. She says that her wife likes O and H names best.

"Did you try asking the baby which one she likes?" I say. I've seen older nurses in the maternity ward suggest this to patients. It seems important to encourage a connection between mother and the child in the womb.

Carmen smiles wide, showing her teeth. "No. I should try. Here."

We are inside the elevator now. Carmen is in the wheelchair and I'm holding the handles. She takes my wrist and pulls my hand towards her belly. "I'll say the names, and you tell me if she kicks."

I feel a pulse against my palm when Carmen says Orla.

Carmen laughs and says she'll need to tell her wife about this.

EMBRYO

I never want to wash my hands again. I have made contact with a human who is existing inside another human. But I get called to change a patient's bedpans on the next floor. Reluctantly I squirt a splash of soapy bubbles into my palm and rinse the soft imprint away.

***

They don't allow me to hold the babies when they're born. It's a crucial clause in my contract. Humans are always worried about errors with individuals like me. I am not permitted to physically handle children under the age of three, or seniors over the age of eighty, or feeble patients.

I've assisted in thirty-five births. I'm frequently called on duty in the pediatric ward. The hospice patients are part of my regulars. Most of my time in the hospital is spent caring for those at the beginning or end of life, both of which are phases I have not and will never experience.

I can never say "when I was little" or "when I'm old". I don't have stories to tell from my childhood, or a retirement fantasy to discuss with friends.

(There are two others like me in this hospital. One of them works in the morgue, so I don't see him often. The other one is a janitor. I tried asking her before, if she has the same questions I do; if she yearns for the past and the future that doesn't exist for us. She said that she's cleaned up enough sick children's waste and geriatric vomit to be glad that she'll never be one of them.)

Two of my friends—nurses with whom I work the rotation most frequently—once played a drinking game with me. They told me stories from their childhoods, and their friends' childhoods, and their friends' friends' childhoods. I was supposed to pick and choose from their stories to create my ideal childhood. Any time I said "I'd want to experience that" they took a shot.

They were completely drunk within the first hour.

I wanted it all. I wanted the misery and the joy. I wanted the parents who set early curfews and the ones who left the house key under the porch mat. I wanted parents who spooned instant macaroni and cheese from tins and those who went to the farmer's market every day. I wanted parents.

175

***

Carmen's due date is two weeks away. She has already checked into the hospital because of concerns about her age, but she also wants to be close to her father so he can be there for the birth.

Mr. Collins just suffered a severe bout of pneumonia. He's still in the ICU, and Carmen asks me to wheel her down to watch him through the glass window every day. If I don't have anywhere else to be during that time, I like to stay with her and listen to her tell me stories about Mr. Collins. How sharp his wit and sense of humor used to be. How he's endured a childhood of war and poverty and disease. How she's convinced that he can pull through this one too.

"My wife loves the name Orla, by the way." Carmen tips her head up to look at me. "We're going with Coline for the middle name, named after—" she nods towards Mr. Collin's prone form "—him."

I try to imagine what my children or grandchildren would say about me. They could talk about my diligence at the hospital, or recall stories about my patients. They might talk about those interns and that Uno card joke. Or they'd laugh about how I helped Carmen choose her baby's name.

(If I could have children, that is. I am not built to function in that way.)

Carmen rubs the swollen roundness of her belly. I want to touch it again, to feel close to a diminutive existence that I can never carry. But she doesn't offer, and I don't ask.

***

Your purpose is to serve, to benefit humanity however your employers see fit. Your function is to sustain life, to prolong it, to accommodate it. You are created to bring mankind into a kinder, better future.

That's from page seventeen of the manual I had to memorize after my first test run. I quote it every six months when the maintenance inspector comes to the hospital for my routine check up. Most of the staff in the hospital already know what I am. The nurses, the doctors, the patients, they all say it doesn't make a difference to them. They say things like "you're basically one of us" and "honestly it must be nice" and "I don't even notice it really".

EMBRYO

(Of course they don't. They have a life cycle that runs in a perfect circle, instead of a single line sitting in the middle of the page.)

***

Orla Coline is born one week early. She's six pounds, seven ounces. She was born en caul, which means she was still in her amniotic sac. It looked exactly like the balloons I had to blow up for the children's cancer ward. The doctor had to break the sac open and pull the baby out before she could take her first breath.

Orla has Carmen's eyes, blue as a forget-me-not blossom.

Carmen's eyes don't shine like that anymore. Carmen died ten minutes after giving birth due to an internal hemorrhage. I find this out because I've been called to clean the room and bring the body down to the morgue. Her wife has said her goodbyes, has placed Orla on the still chest for one last comfort, and Carmen's mother has wept over her for a good twenty minutes.

I take a moment to compose myself before going into the room. I recall the manual and my training. I don't let my professionalism waver. (I don't think about Carmen grabbing my hand and pressing my palm to her belly, or the small crease of laughter in her eyes when she'd talk about her daughter.)

Then I remember Mr. Collins. I wonder if he knows. I want to go check on him in the ICU, or at least find out if he pulled through—if he gets to meet his granddaughter after all—but the other nurse is rushing me along and won't answer any of my questions. She leaves me alone with Carmen's body while she goes to help another patient down the next hall.

Carmen's room is thick with the odor of blood and feces. There's a blanket over her spread legs. She's wearing a pale turquoise hospital gown. I start to adjust the bed to make it easier to roll her body onto the gurney. Then I see the amniotic sac in the waste bin in the corner. The sac is torn in two pieces, but still makes a full globe when I hold the halves together. I pick it up slowly, rubbing my fingers over the slippery outside layer before sniffing the edges.

It smells like iron and urine.

I take a deep breath and then lower my head inside. Closer.

177

Until my lips are touching the pool of liquid at the bottom and the walls of the sac are around my cheeks.

(I close my eyes and pretend that I'm a fetus, no bigger than the size of a fist. I'm swimming in here, the first place I ever exist, a place created by my mother's own body. A sanctuary.)

When I lift my chin up there's a trail of the yellow fluid running down the bridge of my nose. I stick out my tongue to catch the drop. It tastes terrible. But it's what every human tastes before anything else, even their mother's milk.

My hands are slick when I move over to Carmen's bed to wipe my fingers dry on the sheets. The blanket slips off her knees and I see the spread of blood-soaked sheets beneath her. The hem of her gown is riding up, exposing her thighs. Her vagina looks wider than the average woman's. The outer labia seems torn, too. I reach to tug down the hem of her gown, but then I pause.

(How might it feel to emerge from the birth canal? Is it a torturous squeeze? Or soft and swift, like laundry falling down the metal chute?)

I glance towards the door. It's still closed.

Carmen and I face each other again. Her eyelids are closed. I close my own eyes and bow my head. Then I push my fingers inside her. First one hand, then the other. I cup them to mimic the size of a baby's head and then I slowly pull them back out, noticing the pressure from either side. It's a tight fit, even with my fingers that can bend and flatten to make the exit easier.

Blood trickles along my fingers as I insert them inside her again, going in deeper, up to my wrist. When I pull them out there's a soft whoosh of air releasing. My skin is soaked in red—her red— her existence. Carmen died, but she brought a new person into being. Once upon a time she, too, was pushed out of a birth canal. She has completed the cycle. She's begotten what she was given.

She is whole.

Tears prick at the back of my eyes and I cover my face with my hands, forgetting that they're covered with blood. I breathe hard into my palms; I breathe in the scent of Carmen's death, as if I can borrow some of the value of her life.

The door remains closed, shadowy footsteps swimming past the stream of light beneath.

OUR ROOTS WILL DRY OUT IN THE END

Ivan Zoric

On **CHRISTMAS EVE** of the coldest January on record, the Communist Party Secret Police shot my grandfather in our front yard, as he was about to carry Badnjak into the house. I learned two things that night. One, plum brandy and secrets will get you killed in combination. The other? Rains loved the taste of our blood.

It's been forty years since that night and I still can't get the image of a blood-soaked oak branch out of my head. All my life I have been dreaming of a red Christmas. The real one, not the commercialized Western version that my kids and husband love so much. I let them enjoy their fantasy. It's easier that way. One less argument to battle over, one less fight with no winner and a house full of defeated.

It wasn't always like this. There was love under this roof, once. Youth is gullible that way, easy to manipulate, even when both sides believe in its sincerity. Oh, but we were players, both of us. I was a beautiful immigrant bride and Jack, well, he was the one to save me from the lifetime of poverty and struggle. There are worse things than an empty stomach, I've come to find out. Bruises whisper at night, their songs always blue. When kids finally arrived, we shared the same lullaby.

Except on Christmas.

Snow is early this year, and there is a good two feet of it in our front yard, blanketing the bushes and trees. Blueberries, rosemary, a plum, two palms and an oak. Always an oak. Our roots run deep.

I stare out the window, a cup in hand, the smell of coffee strong and comforting.

My girls are out on the porch with Jack, completely enamored with the Christmas lights show he had worked on all day. He's grinning, or at least I know he is under all that beard he grew out of spite. Bruised ego as a fashion statement was so like him.

Net radio is playing Christmas music, and it's a never-ending medley of someone being cold, heartbroken and missing teeth. What they loved, I had lived. No wonder I hated it with passion.

I look at the pile of presents under the tree. Wrong looking tree, all green and straight and nothing like my oak. No roots, steel appendages holding it in place, just for the length of a lie. How many weeks is that? Two? Three, if lucky, before it gets discarded on the curb, and we decorate the house with misery again.

It's almost ten, and soon they'll be inside, ready to be warm and tucked in. By eleven, I will have the house to myself.

I walk over to the bathroom, lock the doors and look at myself in the mirror. The year has not been good to me, I'm all cheekbones and frown now. Weathered, just like my grandma used to be. Hair has gotten long since last Christmas, almost a full eight inches of curls. My girls loved it and played with it every chance they got. We all knew why. It wasn't meant to last.

'Quick, get the scissors,' I say and reach for the cabinet.

***

My mother is standing in the doorway, the look on her face pure agony. She's white knuckling a pair of scissors, as if she believes she could break them in half. She's more terrified than I am, but then again, I am six and the shock has not set in yet. There is a body getting cold, out in the yard, and I still have cookie crumbs all over my face.

'Don't just stand there, Radinka, hand them over!' Grandma's voice is cool fire, not allowing for any argument or doubt. She grabs the scissors out of my mother's hands and cuts off my braid in a single motion. Then she starts working on the rest.

'We do not have much time, Maja,' she says. 'Do you remember what to do?'

I nod, remembering what she told me.

'Good, good', she says, still cutting around my ears. I want to sneeze but know better than to move. Blades and ears love to dance, if given the chance.

I'm holding a loaf of bread in one hand and a bottle of rakija and a wax candle in the other. They're all too big for me, made to be held by older hands. Grandpa's hands. I swallow hard.

I'll have to walk by his body on my way to the pile of firewood in the back of the yard. Grandma said not to look and that they will carry him in later and I will never have to think about it again. Then she cusses under her breath, something about drunks and men and trust. Years later, I would find out exactly what she meant, all on my own.

Just make it to the firewood. Say the words. Come back.

She made it sound so easy.

I looked, of course.

The bullet took the top of his skull clean off and there were frozen chunks of brain scattered around his old winter hat. It looked a lot like that sausage he used to make out of pig insides, and I could feel all those cookies coming back up. I pushed the sugar and walnuts down for the second time, and step around grandpa's body. He's still squeezing the Badnjak, oak leaves speckled red and white. This is the exact moment when I start hating Santa Claus's color pattern.

It's freezing cold outside and although grandma had warmed up both the bread and the drink, they both feel like icicles. I should have worn gloves.

The firewood pile is massive, some six feet high and a good twenty feet long, and it looms over me. I can't see the moon or the stars behind it, just the ever-present darkness. It smells bad, too, way worse than the fresh copper smell I had just left behind. This is an old smell; the smell of all things rotten and forgotten. The smell of what comes after decay.

I speak then, masking my voice to be deeper, like grandma told me. Like a boy. Like a man. Like grandpa.

'German, German, wherever you are, come to dinner right now, and in the summer don't let me see your eyes anywhere!'

I strike a match and light the candles, shadows dancing across the logs as I do so. It's a frantic dance, short-lived and all consuming. I take a bite of the bread and sip some rakija. It burns all the way down, nothing like that pleasant warmth of red wine grandpa used to let me try when he thought grandma wasn't looking.

The wind whistles and howls as I stare into the darkness. Eternity passes. Then another one.

Finally, the candle dies, and I turn back towards the house, tired way beyond all of my six years.

'Wait', the whisper comes from somewhere behind the wood pile.

***

I sneak out of the house a few minutes before midnight. Jack's sound asleep, his snoring reaching a crescendo. Good thing I have a white noise machine for the girl's bedroom. One Christmas gift I actually found useful.

It's snowing again, big fluffy snowflakes sticking to my lashes. Winter makes for a bad mascara.

My footsteps make a squeaky sound as I pace across our property, and I focus on that instead of thinking what's ahead.

I've missed a year.

I fell sick with Norovirus the winter before and spent a couple of days in the ER, hooked on IV to recover from dehydration. Ask me what the worst part of it was? It was not the throwing up or being so weak I almost died, no. It was the forest fires that came that summer. It was the smoke that made the air the most toxic air ever recorded. It was the millions of acres of land burnt and thousand of lives and families destroyed.

I missed a year.

There is a shed at the edge of our property, where the fence meets the dirt road. No one ever goes there, the building is a home to a family of racoons now and perhaps an opossum or two, if the nights get really cold. I built a woodpile there, over years, dragging all the logs and big branches I could find in the area. Jack never found out. It would have been different if I had purchased the wood. He would have been livid and demanded explanations. It was easier this way. I was handy with the axe, ever since childhood, and we were both happy when I was gone from the house.

The girls were much harder to fool. A few times I caught them following me around, hiding behind trees and in the bushes. Curiosity runs in the family, deep, like our roots. Like oak.

OUR ROOTS WILL DRY OUT IN THE END

I found that standing still for long periods of time made them bored. They would run back to the house, to daddy and video games and leave mom alone to her ways. Just like the weirdo she is. His words, not mine.

The snow is swirling around in the beam of my flashlight. A sleeping giant of a woodpile breathes and grunts the midnight air. Everything snores around here.

My voice cut through it. It's deep and raspy, years of practice turned into craft. In some other life, I would have made a great metal band front woman. Rammstein had nothing on me.

'German, German, wherever you are, come to dinner right now, and in the summer don't let me see your eyes anywhere!'

I pull a bread roll out of my pocket and a small flask of plum brandy. I chew and I swallow, and I wash it down, and it never gets easy, even after all these years. I can still taste those cookies trying to come back up, a phantom vomit haunting me from across the divide.

I wait for a minute and then I turn the flashlight off.

'You're early,' it says. 'This is not your Christmas. Nor mine.'

'I'm late,' I say. 'Eleven months late. Look where that got us.'

It laughs like a razorblade, all cuts and swishes.

'A deal is a deal. One must eat, or one must rage. This is the old world.'

I nod, and I'm not ever sure it can see me. I'm not sure I want to see it. Some spirits are better left off in the dark.

'You hungry?' I ask.

'Very. I missed the taste of you, boy.'

It's funny, isn't it? Forty years, thirty-nine Christmas Eves and it still did not know. Always this old-world bullshit, this tradition that spans centuries. The man of the house had to be the one to feed the spirit. Shows how much spirits know. Circle jerk of machismo. I had to play along, and I hated it. I hoped that one night it would choke on it.

I produce a small filleting knife and cut the side of my wrist, another soon-to-be scar in a fine mash on my arms. Ironic that I never had to explain that one to Jack. He just assumed I was cutting myself. I was, but for an entirely different reason. The rains loved the taste of our blood.

I let it drip in the snow and wipe the knife with a napkin and then toss that towards the wood pile, as well.

There is a sickly sound coming out of the dark, like someone biting into an ice cream.

'Slow down, you'll get a brain freeze,' I say, but it just ignores me. It always does at this point. Ever since the night it made me scoop handfuls of my grandpa's blood from the snow. I never figured out if it was because he was an alcoholic and it loved its liquor with a side of iron. God knows I'm not any better. Sometimes it's just easier that way.

'See you next year,' I say and head back to the house.

The girls are still asleep when I walk in their bedroom to tuck them in. I stand in the dark, silent as a prayer, and I look at their twin angel faces. I wonder how I will ever make a choice. My roots will dry out in the end, but our roots? Our roots grow deep.

AS THE MUSIC PLAYS GROOVY

Michael Bettendorf

NICOLAS CAGE STARTED speaking to me through my Amazon Dot a while back. At first, I thought it was an app or something one of my friends downloaded as a joke, like changing Siri's voice. It started at night when all was quiet in my apartment. I'd heard his whispers, battling with the noises from the fridge, to gain my attention. Nic's confusing, yet often wise, interjections became more frequent. During the daylight hours he only spoke in quotes and they were always in response to something I had said like, "Fuck, what should I have for breakfast?" and he replied, "Maybe a banana-nut. That's a good muffin," or when I asked what to listen to and he said, "Do you like the Elton John song, 'Rocket Man?'"

They had to be recordings—didn't they? I lived alone, worked from home and didn't get out much.

But these days I didn't need to. Everything came to me. Even Nic. Even if they were recordings.

But his tone was conversational. Too organic and prescient to be recordings.

Soon, he got comfortable hanging around me and started asking for financial advice, curious about my spending habits and how I maintained a budget. I told him I didn't, not really, but basically it was as simple as not spending money I didn't have. He didn't believe me. I said it helped that I was broke. That I could actually run out of money. Still he didn't buy it. A first for him, so I've read.

"Look," I said one morning from the edge of my bed which also served as my couch. "It's this simple. Do you have any other castles on contract?"

A quiet *no, of course not* was his response.

"If so," I continued, "Don't go through with it. Yeah, you'll lose the deposit, but you won't have another castle to take care of."

And despite Nic's denial, I'd heard him set a reminder to himself to, "Call realtor."

He lectured me about real estate being one of the best investments a person could make but I didn't respond. How could I? My studio apartment was so small, I all but shat where I slept and slept where I ate. Furniture lined the walls. It was the only way to fit all my stuff in such a tight space.

"I'm building my own court," Nic said. "Like King Arthur. I've got the table already. It's not so much round as it is oblong. I've got the swords too . . . Suits of armor . . . A dragon skull," he paused here. "Okay, okay. It's not a dragon skull but a dinosaur skull. You can't tell the difference. Believe me. Not to mention the tapestry I'd commissioned. Your wall could use one too. You have a tapestry guy? Tell you what, I'll give you my guy's number. He's really good."

I had to admit, there was one moment he almost swayed me—when he offered me a seat at the oblong table, but I heard it in his voice: the stress. The fear. All cries for help, and yet I couldn't enable him. He had to learn self-control.

The tension boiled over the next morning and he broke.

"You've got to help me, *man*," he pleaded. "I feel trapped. Financially paralyzed." His words, his intonation, made me believe I couldn't say no. Some inherent obligation. A curse. Whatever bind he'd gotten himself into involved me now and we were in this thing together. An unwritten contract. Ignored terms of service. I was his Sean Connery, his Angelina Jolie, his John Malkovich. I was everyone but himself, the supporting role only he could fill, but still—I was a supporting character and—goddammit—I was going to sell it.

"Where do we start?" I asked.

"I can't talk now," Nic said. "They're listening."

"Who—"

"*Shhhhh*," he said. "We're just a waterfall here. *Shhhhh-shhhh-shhhhhhhh*. Calm and collected, until we're not. *Shhhhhhhh*."

"The fuck are you on about?" I asked. We were at that point in our relationship I could speak to him with an amount of turbulence.

"Is this part of it?" I went on, still getting a feel for the role.

"We're static after the Big Bang. *Ka-shhhhh-shsh-sh*," he said. "We're just god particles."

I followed his lead and *shushed* and *ka-shhhhhed* around my apartment for an hour until the sounds felt unreal to my ears and my lips went dry. The blue circle was illuminated and I knew what he meant by, "They're listening," because secretly I believed it too. That was not an act.

Nic remained silent the rest of the day.

***

I awoke to Nic talking about animals.

"I love all animals," he said. "Sentient life."

"Yeah," I said.

"Do you have a favorite animal?"

"Umm. I mean, dogs are cool."

I noticed the blue ring was not lit, but he was still talking.

"Not domesticated animals," he said. "I'm talking wild animals."

I rolled off the bed and over to the kitchen. I thought about his question while I fumbled with the coffee maker. Eventually I decided on, "Capybaras are fun. Like a dog-guinea-pig hybrid."

"Right on, right on," he said. I could tell he was frustrated at how long it took for me to come up with my answer. He had something on his mind and before I could blather on about how I also liked elephants because of their long memory, he asked, "What do you know about the blue-ringed octopus?"

Mr. Coffee gurgled.

I envisioned Nic running his hands through his hair, combed over like in *The Weatherman*, until it was tousled and chaotic to match his mood.

"Well, c'mon *man*," he said. "What the fuck do you know about the fucking blue-ringed octopus?"

I could see the chaos and yet I could not see *him*. I sensed his distress and focused on my role.

"I don't know much about it," I said. "I imagine it lives in saltwater."

I poured a cup of coffee as Nic went on.

"They are usually docile like me, but the blue-ringed octopus is highly venomous and extremely dangerous to humans if provoked. That's why they have bright blue iridescent rings," he said. "It's a warning that says, 'Don't mess with me, motherfucker.'"

I drank my coffee and listened, keeping a watchful eye for the blue ring.

"It produces tetrodotoxin," he said. "Do you know what that is?"

I nodded *no* and somehow, he understood.

"It causes body paralysis," he said. "You ever had sleep paralysis? Where your mind becomes aware before your body wakes up? Often gives the feeling of suffocation. Hallucinations. Tetrodotoxin creates a similar effect. Victims remain conscious, but are unable to move—unable to signal for help while they sit and suffocate."

Nic's words hung heavy in the air for a moment like VX gas.

He started to speak, but was interrupted by a chime that resonated from the Dot; the blue ring illuminated.

Nic's voice was present, but a voice—*the* voice—spoke over him fighting for control.

"Here is what I found on the blue-ringed Octopus, according to Wikipedia: Blue-ringed octopuses, comprising the genus Hapalochlaena, are four highly venomous species of octopus that are found in tide pools and coral reefs in the Pacific and Indian oceans, from Japan to Australia. They can be identified by their yellowish skin . . . "

I waited for Nic's voice to come through and shed some light on what was going on.

"Does that answer your question?" her voice asked.

I did not reply to her.

***

It was a bit later that day, after we'd given the room some silence and left no soundwaves for the Dot to latch onto that Nic came to me again to offer some unexpected wisdom.

"Are you a religious man, *man*?" he asked.

"Not particularly," I said.

"Have you heard of the little acronym *WWJD*?" he asked.

"Yes—"

"What would Joel do," he said, not a question, but a statement correcting my misunderstanding.

"Joel," I repeated.

"Yes," Nic said in that sort of raspy, drawn-out way he often used for one-syllable words like he was trying to convey added weight, an extension of meaning of something beyond.

"Coen," he said. "What would Joel do . . ."

In my mind, Nic no longer resembled Nic from *The Weatherman*, but rather Nic from *Gone in 60 Seconds*; dirty sun-dyed blonde, not bottle-blonde, donning a leather jacket—hands held out dramatically in thought.

"Could also work for Jolie," he said. "*But* that just won't do today. No. Today is a *what would Joel do* sort of day."

I hadn't been sleeping well and I knew it was late in the day for coffee, but I'd needed the comfort. Supporting Nic proved challenging. I warmed a mug in the microwave while I waited for him to speak.

"Well?" Nic asked, agitated. "What the fuck would Joel do?"

"Oh," I said. "I thought it was rhetorical."

"What makes you think it was rhetorical? We are having a conversation like humans. That's what humans do. We communicate. What do you think we are? Monkeys?"

"Well . . ."

"Okay," he said, big and breathy. "Bad example, but please before I lose it—tell me what would Joel do?"

I'd say I was starting to lose him, but that'd be like saying I'd lost the breeze. No, the breeze continued onward and followed its own guidance. Only a fool tried to control the breeze. No, you adapt to it, not force it. You harness it and hope you aren't dragged across the rocks.

"I'd say that Joel would try to take what's there and do something new with it. Throw in some dark humor. That sort of thing."

It was a shot in the dark, but it was all I'd had.

"I think the word you're looking for is subversion," Nic said. "Joel would *subvert* the situation. Poke at it. Force change. That's what I need to do."

"I don't understand," I said.

"*Shhhhh*," he said. "I need to think."

Nic's voice faded as War's "Low Rider" emanated from the speakers.

"I need to formulate a plan," he said. It was soft, but audible underneath the bassline.

"What are our options?" I asked.

The blue ring glowed as the music played groovy.

"I like both Blu-ray and DVD, but Blu-Ray gives you more options," he said as War resonated throughout the airwaves.

"What do you mean?" I asked, grasping for meaning in his non-sequiturs. Was it code? Didn't Nic realize *he* was the cryptologist, not me?

My apartment was a cacophony of frequencies as War raged on, fighting for the last word. The Dot's voice rang out in perverse subversion, *"Here's what I found on War, the American band, according to Wikipedia: War, originally called Eric Burdon and War—"* but Nic's plan was already being set into motion. Nic was the lord of war.

"—take a little trip with me-*ee*," the song overtook the Dot until an amazing flash of blue light burst from the Dot and all went quiet.

"Nic," I called, but he was gone. It must have been part of the plan. It had to be.

I slept like a rock that night, my body worn out and sore. The next morning when I went to make coffee, the Dot was back in pristine condition and I was empty. I wanted Nic back, needed my Nic-fix, but he never returned.

At least not how I had expected him to.

***

A few months later a strange package had arrived at my doorstep. It bore no return address, but I knew who sent it. A curved, smiling arrow was stamped on top mocking me. It was a wooden crate, nailed shut, with the word *fragile* painted in bright pulsing blue paint along the sides.

A small aquarium was inside. A blue-ringed octopus the size of an Amazon Dot hid underneath a hunk of coral. A note was taped to the underside of the lid. It read, "I like both Blu-ray and DVD, but Blu-ray gives you more options."

I found space for the aquarium on my dresser, next to the Dot. He kept saying that word: *options*. Options—like I'd know what to do with it? I shouted at myself in the mirror, "Oh, very good! Options. Yeah, where are the special features, *man*?"

I stood there in a cold sweat, unable to move. Electric blue circles pulsed as the blue-ringed octopus spoke to me in Nic's voice. And it said, "Blue rings," he said. "Do you finally understand what I'm saying? They are everywhere, reaching out from their tide pools and reefs into our homes with their tentacles, covered in blue rings that make us watch while we sit, numbed. Caged. Barely conscious, spending our money without control—you wouldn't believe how much I had to pay to pull this off."

I knelt down and looked through the shimmering glass.

"Nic?" I asked.

"Me," he said.

I reached into the tank—a compulsion I could not explain—and held him. I watched as Nic glowed in my hands, my fingers growing numb. I did not feel myself collapse, but I'd heard him plop back into the water and soon it was hard to breathe.

"But, Nic . . . why?"

"I'm sorry, but I got in too deep. We all have," the blue-ringed octopus said. "I know what it's like to meet someone you admire and have them be a complete jerk."

I called out to my Dot to dial 911, but the words were caught in my throat. I laid crumpled on the floor unable to signal for help. I watched Nic's blue rings pulse in synchronicity with the Dot's while my spirit danced before me. At least he gave me that.

FAMILY NOT GOING TO HEAVEN

Chris Kuriata

No **ONE IN** our family is dead yet, but one day we'll all be.
Dirty plates and empty mugs litter the tables in Grandma's coffee shop. The lunch crowd is gone, so Mom hands me a stack of menus to wash. This chore bores me; I'd rather be helping with dinner.

While I work, my mind drifts to everyone who will not be going to Heaven. It's comforting to know who I'll spend eternity with.

Of course, none of my stuffed mice will be in Heaven, even though they've slept with me since I was tiny. Grandma insists I will not miss them any more than I'll miss my dresses or the fancy turkey plates we use on holidays. I hope she's right, but I have my reservations.

Our cat Vanilla, our dog Beans, and our turtle Dunlop will not be in Heaven because animals supposedly do not have souls. Everyone I ask is consistent on this point: my older sister, my mother, my grandmother ...

But here is what I want to know: if pets don't have souls, how come their ghosts return to haunt us? When Dad ran over the Phaffs's Rottweiler, Zenith, we were kept up all night not only by her phantom barking, but the squealing of the litter of pups she'd been carrying. Zenith didn't quiet down until Grandma prepared special oil for Dad to cleanse the undercarriage of his truck with.

"If pets can become ghosts," I challenged, "why can't they go to Heaven?"

"Because," Grandma told me. "Ghost is different from soul. Ghost is angry, scared, bad feeling. Only instinct. Person can be in

Heaven happy while their ghost stay on earth and make everyone miserable."

I think about the coffee shop ghost, who's always stinking up the air with the smell of his phantom pipe, and rummaging through the pantry at night looking for liquor. He knocks over cans, and spills oil all over the red stools. I hate cleaning up his mess; the cloth never absorbs all the oil, so you have to wipe over and over. No matter how many times I wash my hands I can still feel the stickiness between my fingers. The pest better be happy in Heaven for how miserable his ghost makes us here.

My uncle, Lou Henry (brother of my mother), will not be in Heaven.

Years before I was born, he grew mad at some woman (she worked on the streetcar in Hamilton), so he pushed her under the tracks and she was cut in two, right in front of everybody. She didn't die right away, but didn't have the air to scream, either—just stretched her mouth open while her blood and collection of nickel fares rolled into the street.

Not even Grandma defended him. He ruined the coffee shop's reputation. No one wants to eat at a family restaurant that reminds them of such a vicious killing. After the loss of customers, she opened a new coffee shop under another name.

The judge sent Lou Henry to Kingston. He was sentenced to life, but offered the possibility of parole in twenty-five years. Didn't matter, because I don't think he intended to leave prison. He liked the company of all the interesting men there, with new ones arriving all the time. There were lots of radios so he could listen to every hockey game, and all the tobacco he could smoke.

In Kingston, he laid traps for insects, stealing spider webs he re-strung above the window in his cell. He collected shoeboxes full of dry insect husks. I imagined him sifting his hand through the piles, hearing the musical jingle of the dry bugs rustling against one another.

He crushed the bugs to brew a special oil beneath his commode.

The Kingston men loved his oil. They rubbed it into their bellies and felt forgiveness for the evils that landed them in prison. This forgiveness wasn't an illusion, but it eventually ran out. Broken hearts and iron grudges were forever growing back, requiring even more oil to achieve the same state of grace for ever diminishing periods of time. Desperate, the men began rubbing the oil into their eyes.

In the winter, the oil ran out. Lou Henry couldn't find bugs to make more. The men went wild. The guards were helpless to stop the riot, so they abandoned the entire prison.

Lou Henry had no interest in forgiveness for himself, so he hadn't developed a dependency on the oil. He hid from the rampaging Kingston population by hiding in his mattress. He ripped open the bottom and dug a Lou-Henry-shaped hole. To cover his tracks, he flushed the stuffing down his commode, but when the pipes jammed, he was forced to eat the soggy excess.

From inside the mattress casing, he heard the wails of his fellow prisoners, tortured by having been given a taste of forgiveness, and left suffocating after that grace evaporated. All the men gave in to despair. There was mutilation, self-cannibalism, sincere repudiation of everything just and natural in the world . . . In the great silence that soon filled those barred halls, only Lou Henry persisted.

"He didn't expect things to get so out of hand with his fool's oil," Mom said as she checked over the job I'd done cleaning the laminated menus, making sure I hadn't missed a splotch of dried syrup. "He was just looking to make himself popular with the other men."

But their crimes weren't Lou Henry's to forgive, even temporarily. The wickedest thing you can do is prevent others from finding genuine forgiveness. Because of his oil, those men had no hope. With hundreds of lost souls staining his hands, Lou Henry will not go to Heaven.

Not only that, but I don't think he's yet found the nerve to climb out of that mattress.

My sister tells me more people will be going to Heaven than I think. She claims going to Heaven is easy.

"Everybody thinks there's only one way to go to Heaven," she says. "You have to drink the blood of Jesus Christ, or give all your money to the poor, or only eat plants, or go your whole life without having sex with nobody . . . "

We are in the coffee shop kitchen, oiling up pans in the calm before dinner hour. Always negative, my sister keeps a list of people she resents who will get to Heaven.

"Mrs. Gagne is going. So is her rotten son, the weirdo who's always sticking his tongue through the fence." She wraps her hands around her throat and chokes herself, crossing her eyes. "And every one of those smelly Lot girls are going."

"I don't mind the Lot sisters," I tell her.

On the schoolyard, once, a large bird struck the side of the building. It landed on the hopscotch grid, wings busted and back twisted. It was in terrible agony, and frightened by the circle of children looking down at it. A few poked at it; a couple more yanked out souvenir tail feathers. One of the Lot sisters, Emery, pushed her way through the crowd and swiftly pressed two fingers on the bird's neck to hold it in place, while her other hand pulled the top of the head, effortlessly breaking the neck and soothing the bird forever. I admired her decisiveness, and the selfless way she did what needed to be done. It gave me strength.

No good deed goes unpunished, the saying goes. Emery Lot was kicked out of school for a week. After she came back, she had to talk to a scientist about why she got pleasure from killing small animals. The fact that it was a one-time mercy killing made no difference. The teachers all saw a chance to punish and humiliate her, and they tripped over their own tongues running to tattle.

None of those teachers are going to Heaven, but Emery is. She's going to be so surprised.

"You don't even have to believe in Heaven to go there," my sister says.

We dump mushrooms into the soup pot. Dinner will be ready for our customers in less than an hour.

My Aunt Danny (sister of my father) will not be in Heaven, because she made herself too heavy. You can't tell by looking at her—she takes up no more space than any other woman standing just under 4ft 9—but if you grab hold of her waist and try to lift her you'll be unable. Only she can make her feet separate from the ground. A donkey once kicked its hind legs into the back of her head, and while her scalp needed stitches, her legs didn't so much as stumble.

Years after the airline industry banned smoking, they washed the planes, scraping out the air ducts and cleaning the wires under the cockpit, and found them clogged with layers of black, oily crust, like what you'd find clogging the stem of a much-used pipe. After cleaning, each plane weighed 50 pounds lighter.

Aunt Danny has obscene money. I never asked how she amassed her wealth, but I assume it's an accumulation of mineral rights mixed with multiple alimony suits and gambling proceeds. She spends freely: castles in the highlands, dogs bred so specifically that their paperwork goes back a hundred years, young men with expensive taste in clothing . . . Some of her paramours have been on her teat for three decades, and when they retire from her bedroom, she provides a hefty pension. On holidays she never visits but sends gifts: long gold chains and pearl earrings Grandma buries in the backyard. Someday an archeologist is going to find one of those gift sites and think they've discovered the treasure room of the Pharaohs.

Aunt Danny spends her money like she expels breath. She always says, "You can't take it with you."

Grandma warns us our Aunt is dead wrong: we all take it with us.

The money that passes through your fingertips over the course of your life never leaves. Like cigarette smoke in an airplane, the act of spending creates oils that soak into your body, coating your soul and weighing you down.

Aunt Danny is generous, as if attempting to buy her way into Heaven, but she doesn't realize it makes no difference if she spends on mink coats for her dogs or medical equipment for orphans. It all weighs her down the same amount.

Dad says, "It ain't the spending of all that money, it's the fact you took that much to begin with."

It occurs to me that there is finite room in Heaven. That's probably the reason why not everyone can go there to begin with.

Grandma is angry when I say this. She believes the suggestion that Heaven is flawed is disrespectful.

My reasoning is sound: the world will not last forever. At some point the lava rises or the sun burns out, and people will be extinct forever. Since there won't be an infinite number of people, Heaven must have limitations. Why create a place larger than it needs to be?

Tucking me into bed, whispering so Grandma doesn't hear, Mom tells me Heaven won't be full for hundreds of years, long after we're all gone.

"So it's nothing to worry about," she says. "We should concentrate on doing a good job while we're here."

FAMILY NOT GOING TO HEAVEN

I believe Mom while she's sitting on the edge of my bed, leaning over so her eyelashes kiss my cheeks. But when I'm all alone in a darkness that reminds me of everlasting non-being, I can't shake the dread of Heaven filling up. I imagine massive wooden doors made from the trunks of century-old trees. The doors bulge, and the wood splinters from the pressure of everyone inside. No room for a single soul more.

I ladle soup into bowls and carry them to the lunch counter. My sister brings a tray to the tables in the coffee shop's front window. In the movies, waitresses like my sister are always subjected to leering and groping, but the men we serve are polite. If they say anything to her, it is with great respect and kindness.

These men are all going to Heaven, sooner than they expect.

The food Mom prepares with Grandma's oils is delicious. Our ingredients are fresh. No matter how thoroughly I clean the vegetables, they are still speckled with nutrients from the soil, but the earth they come from is Eden clean, so there is no displeasing taste.

Grandma's oils float on the surface of the soup. I see my reflection in each yellow blob. It looks like the grease from a boiled turkey carcass. The soup gives off an inviting aroma. The men dip their spoons and sup. They race to the bottom of their bowls, looking forward to the main course. The smell of roast vegetables slathered in Grandma's oils wafts from the kitchen. My sister and I have been patiently turning them in the oven pan until the carrots are caramelized and the potatoes are crisp all around.

By morning, all our customers will be in Heaven. They die in great agony, leaking oil from their mouths and their eyes. The oil is black. It smells like dead dinosaurs. This oil is all their spending, all their un-forgiveness, all their doubt. It is the unmeasurable weight on their soul accumulated over a lifetime. Detoxified, they are now fit for Heaven.

When sixty diners at the same restaurant all die, conclusions are drawn pretty quick. The same thing happens every time. A weeping mob smashes the coffee shop windows. Often, the grieving horde burns the building to the ground.

We're never inside, of course. Grandma makes us hide across the street like bandits, so we can watch the destruction. "That was a good home," she says. "We need to be here until the very end, like how you don't abandon a pet when it's time to be put down."

The town hunts for us, but we're never spotted. We're on our way to the next location, often learning new languages so we'll fit right in. We are patient, taking years to make our new home, while Grandma begins the long and arduous process of making new oils. We are dedicated to ensuring those in need will go to Heaven.

I will not be in Heaven, because serving the oil makes you impervious to its effects.

I cannot shake the image of Heaven filling up, despite Mom's assurance I will be asleep forever long before that happens. We are not the only family tasked with the duty of serving oil. How large of an army are we a part of? Are there a hundred of us? A thousand? When I hear of an entire village dead in Uganda, each body leaking black oil, I dream of Heaven's doors beginning to strain.

When my time comes, I won't be resentful, or feel cheated. I won't say No good deed goes unpunished. Knowing I helped to fill Heaven means more to me than eternal life. Besides, I bet it gets boring after a while.

My reward is to follow Grandma, and Mom, and my sister, and my Aunt and Uncle, and our pets, and my stuffed mice into peaceful quiet. Before you're born, after you're born, it's all the same to me; everlasting, all encompassing, and never filled up.

BRAVE NEW WEIRDOS, CLASS OF 2023

Alex Woodroe (she/her) is a Romanian writer and editor of dark speculative fiction. She's the author of *Whisperwood*, and has several short stories published in venues like Horror Library and the Nosleep podcast. Alex lives in the heart of the Transylvanian region of Romania, and is the Editor in Chief of **Tenebrous Press**.

Amitha Jagannath Knight is an Indian American writer and poet for all ages, and an award-winning picture book author. She is a graduate of MIT and Tufts University School of Medicine. Dr. Knight has lived in Texas and Arkansas, and now lives in Massachusetts with her husband, kids, and cats.

Anemone Moss (she/her) is a transgender lesbian speculative fiction and horror writer who grew up in the forests of the Sierra Nevada foothills in northern California and now lives in the outskirts of the SF Bay Area. She spends her time studying history and ecology, making art, watching too many horror movies, and exploring local marshes and forests.

Chris Kuriata lives in and often writes about the Niagara region of Canada. His dark fantasy and horror stories have appeared in publications in Canada, the US, the UK, Ireland, Australia, South Africa, and Japan. His debut novel *Sacrifice of the Sisters Lot* is published by Palimpsest Press.

Daniel DeRock is a writer from the U.S. living in the Netherlands. His work has appeared, among other outlets, in *Pithead Chapel, Gone Lawn, MoonPark Review, and Ligeia Magazine*. He is the co-author of *Spark Bird*, a collaborative novel (Thirty West Publishing House, 2024).

David Simmons lives in Baltimore with his wife and daughter. He is the author of the *Ghosts of Baltimore* Duology (Broken River Books) where the supernatural and strange grapple with the ever-present past of East and West Baltimore. He is a regular contributor to Books to Prisoners, a Seattle-based nonprofit organization whose mission is to foster a love of reading behind bars, encourage the pursuit of knowledge and self-empowerment, and break the cycle of recidivism.

Eirik Gumeny is the editor of Atomic Carnival Books and the author of *Infernal Organs* and the *Exponential Apocalypse* series. His short fiction has appeared in, among others, *Kaleidotrope*, *Andromeda Spaceways*, and *Escalators to Hell* (From Beyond Press). His nonfiction has been published by *Cracked*, *Wired*, and *The New York Times*. In 2014 he received a double lung transplant and technically died a little. He got better.

Elena Sichrovsky (she/they) is a queer disabled writer who uses the lens of body horror to explore themes of identity, grief, and trauma. Her work is inspired by a rich legacy of mothers and fathers who should have but did not go to therapy. In their next life they'd like to be a two-headed calf.

Geneve Flynn is a speculative fiction editor, author, and poet; and the winner of two Bram Stoker Awards, a Shirley Jackson Award, an Aurealis Award, and recipient of the 2022 Queensland Writers Fellowship. Her work has been nominated and short/longlisted for the British Fantasy, Locus, Ditmar, Australian Shadows, Elgin, and Rhysling Awards, and the Pushcart Prize. She is the co-editor of *Black Cranes: Tales of Unquiet Women*.

Hussani Abdulrahim is a writer from Kano, Nigeria. He won Ibua Journal's 2023 Bold Call and the 2022 Toyin Falola Prize. He was the first runner-up for the 2023 Kendeka Prize. He has also been longlisted for the Commonwealth Short Story Prize and a finalist for the Boston Review Prize, Gerald Kraak Award, Afritondo Prize, and ACT Award. His work has appeared in Boston Review, Wilted Pages, Brittle Paper, Evergreen Review, Solarpunk, and Ibua Journal.

Ivan Zoric lives and writes in Portland, Oregon after surviving a turbulent childhood in a war-torn country whose name does not exist anymore. His central themes are immigration, displacement and the horror at the heart of losing identity. He has been published in Tales to Terrify, A Walk In a Darker Wood and A Walk In the City of Shadows.

After a marketing career in Washington DC, NYC and Santa Barbara, CA, **Judith Shadford** received her MFA at Pacific Lutheran University. Essays and short stories have appeared in Shark Reef Journal, Aesthetic Armchair, River & Sound Review, Ellery Queen Mystery Magazine and Seize the Press. Shadford's interest in the extraordinary, non-planetary is rooted in a (weird) triumverate of CS Lewis's space trilogy and the works of Ursula LeGuin and Mary Doria Russell.

Karlo Yeager Rodríguez is originally from the enchanted isle of Puerto Rico, but moved to Baltimore some years ago where he lives happily with his wife and one odd dog.

K.S. Walker writes speculative fiction from a city in the Midwest with a river winding through it. This river may or may not be an ancient power that makes seductive bargains. Their work often explores themes of transformation, longing, and belonging and has been published in many venues. Their work has appeared in *FIYAH, The Deadlands, Baffling Magazine* and *The Magazine of Fantasy and Science Fiction,* among others.

LC von Hessen (they/them) is a writer, noise musician, multidisciplinary artist/performer, and former Morbid Anatomy Museum docent. Their work has appeared in *Bury Your Gays,* Seize the Press, *The Book of Queer Saints, Stories of the Eye,* **YOUR BODY IS NOT YOUR BODY**, Vastarien, and many others. Their debut short story collection will be released in late 2024 through Grimscribe Press. An ex-Midwesterner, von Hessen lives in Brooklyn with a talkative orange cat.

Matt Blairstone (he/him) is a writer, editor, artist, indie comics creator and the Founder/Publisher of **Tenebrous Press**. He lives in Portland, Oregon. Sleep is folly.

Michael Bettendorf (he/him) is a writer from the US Midwest. His short fiction has appeared/is forthcoming at Drabblecast, Sley House Press, and elsewhere. Michael's debut experimental novel/gamebook **TRVE CVLT** is forthcoming from **Tenebrous Press**. He works in a high school library in Lincoln, Nebraska—a place he tries to convince the world is too strange to be a flyover state.

M.M. Olivas' work has appeared in Uncanny, Weird Horror Magazine, Apex, Bourbon Penn and more. As a trans, first-generation Chicana, Olivas' fiction explores intersection of queer and diasporic experiences. She currently resides in the Bay Area, earning her MFA at San Jose State University and collecting transforming robots. Her debut novel, Sundown in San Ojuela, will release in the fall of 2024 through Lanternfish Press.

Nelly Geraldine García-Rosas was born and raised in Mexico but now lives in the U.S. She is a graduate of the Clarion West class of 2019. Her short fiction has appeared in Lightspeed, Nightmare, Strange Horizons, the World Fantasy Award-winning anthology She Walks in Shadows, and elsewhere.

Patrick Malka (he/him) is a high school science teacher from Montreal, Quebec, where he lives with his partner and two kids. His recent flash fiction can be found in Midsummer Dream House, Broken Antler, Maudlin House, Nocturne magazine, and Sky Island Journal, among others.

perfect kiss strickoll (he/she) is a writer and film student currently located in sunny California. He likes to write about sad queers with bizarre interpersonal hang-ups, as informed by his lifelong love and study of the horror genre.

Premee Mohamed is a Nebula, World Fantasy, and Aurora award-winning Indo-Caribbean scientist and author based in Edmonton, Alberta. She has also been a finalist for the Hugo, Ignyte, Locus, British Fantasy, and Crawford awards. Currently, she is the Edmonton Public Library writer-in-residence and an Assistant Editor at the short fiction audio venue Escape Pod. She is the author of the 'Beneath the Rising' series of novels as well as several novellas.

Rachael K. Jones grew up in various cities across Europe and North America, picked up (and mostly forgot) six languages, and acquired several degrees in the arts and sciences. Now she writes speculative fiction in Portland, Oregon. Rachael is a Hugo, Nebula, Bram Stoker, World Fantasy, and Otherwise Award finalist. Her fiction has appeared in Lightspeed, Beneath Ceaseless Skies, Strange Horizons, and all four Escape Artists podcasts, among others.

Simone le Roux is a speculative fiction writer based in Cape Town, South Africa with her partner, two cats, and an ancient dog. She has a cum laude Neuroscience degree that she does not use, and an enduring interest in anything spooky or dangerous. When she's not writing, Simone is a semi-professional aerialist.

Thomas Ha is a Nebula and Shirley Jackson Award-nominated writer of speculative short fiction. His work has been published in *Clarkesworld, Lightspeed Magazine, Beneath Ceaseless Skies, Weird Horror Magazine*, and *The Year's Best Dark Fantasy & Horror,* among others. Thomas grew up in Honolulu and, after a decade-plus of living in the northeast, now resides in Los Angeles with his wife and three children.

THE BRAVE NEW WEIRD SHORTLIST 2023

(Author—Title—*Original Publication/Publisher*)

Akis Linardos—"Daughter, Mother, Charcoal"—*Apex Magazine*

Alexander James—"The Tumour Room"—*Weird Horror Magazine*

Andrew Kozma—"Mr. Balloon"—*Uncharted Magazine*

C.H. Pearce—"Jimmy Flip Brings His Little One To Work, And It Comes My Turn To Hold It"—*Body of Work—Canberra Speculative Fiction Guild*

Chelsea Pumpkins—"If Anyone Could Catch the Moon"—*Anterior Skies Vol. 1, Strange Elf Press*

Colin Hinckley—"A Fire, A Wave"—*Whiskey Tit*

D. Matthew Urban—"The World of Iniquity Among Our Members Is the Tongue"—*No Trouble at All—Cursed Morsels Press*

Ephiny Gale—"Nowhere, Australia"—*The Vanishing Point*

Gordon B. White—"Godhead"—*Gordon B. White is Creating Haunting Weird Horror(s)—JournalStone*

Gwendolyn Kiste—"Melting Point"—*Cosmic Horror Monthly*

Hailey Piper—"The Girls with Claws that Catch"—*Aseptic and Faintly Sadistic—CHM*

Ivy Grimes—"The Swallowed"—*Cosmic Horror Monthly*

J.A.W. McCarthy—"Seldom Place"—*Mooncalves—NO Press*

Jacob Steven Mohr—"Truth Serum"—*Archive of the Odd*

Jennifer Marie Brissett—"The Healer"—*Apex Magazine*

Jordan Kurella—"The Wreck of the Medusa"—*Apex Magazine*

Kelsea Yu—"China Doll"—*Aseptic and Faintly Sadistic—CHM*

Kev Harrison—"Crawlspace"—*The Other Stories—Hawk and Cleaver*

Kim Harbridge—"Summer Soup to Cure Magical Thinking"—*PULP Literature*

Kurt Newton—"Lawn For Sale"—*The Ever-Evolving Alphabet—back room poetry*

Lex Chamberlin—"Cherry's Strawberry Revenge"—*HyphenPunk*

M. Regan—"Abbadon, 1861"—*Aseptic and Faintly Sadistic—CHM*

Mark Galarrita—"Kuya"—*Many Worlds Forum*

Matthew Mitchell—"Release the Horse"—*Hellarkey 2—Malarkey Books*

Osahon Ize-Iyamu—"Chop Chop Chop"—*The Dark Magazine*

Patrick Barb—"The Scare Groom"—*Come October—Chthonic Matter Press*

Rajiv Moté—"The Troubling History of Boddington's Inlet"—*Archive of the Odd*

Ryan Marie Ketterer—"East Marion"—*Old Ways Vol. 1—Eerie River Publishing*

Samantha H. Chung—"Baby"—*Greater Than His Nature—Atomic Carnival Books*

Samir Sirk Morató—"PENNSYLVANIA FURNACE (Refrain)"—*Archive of the Odd*

Steve Neal—"Ipomoea Sanguineus"—*Cosmic Horror Monthly*

Susan L. Lin—"House of Reverie"—*Paramnesia—Grendel Press*

Tim Major—"Far From the Tree"—*Come October—Chthonic Matter Press*

Will McMahon—"Notes on the Burning Place"—*Interzone*

Z.K. Abraham—"The Typewriter"—*Fantasy Magazine*

Zohair—"Quietus"—*Apex Magazine*

BRAVEST, NEWEST, WEIRDEST

Additional Winners For This Year in New Weird Fiction

It's impossible to recognize everyone who contributed to the Congregation of the New Weird this year; but beyond the actual storytellers featured in this volume, we want to wave a salutation to a number of our peers who excelled in drawing eyes to this corner of the world in their own uniquely Weird ways:

Congratulations to the BRAVEST, NEWEST, WEIRDEST . . .

ANTHOLOGY—*Aseptic and Faintly Sadistic*—**Jolie Toomajan**, editor (CHM, publisher)

BREAKOUT AUTHOR—**Simo Srinivas**, "The Ballad of the Octopus" (Khoreo Magazine, publisher) & many other stories throughout the year

COLLECTION—*Turducken*, **Lindz McLeod** (Spaceboy Books, publisher)

COMIC—*Blackbird Hunting*, **Bri Crozier** (bricrozierart.com)

CREATIVE FORMAT—Archive of the Odd, **Cormack Baldwin & EV Smith** (archiveoftheodd.com)

MAGAZINE, ONGOING—*Cosmic Horror Monthly*—**Charles Tyra**, founder/editor

MAGAZINE, SPECIAL ISSUE—*Strange Horizons*—Caribbean Special—**Suzan Palumbo & Marika Bailey**, editors

ACKNOWLEDGEMENT OF COPYRIGHT

"Lullaby for the Unseen" originally appeared in *Weird Horror* Magazine (Undertow Publications)

"In That Crumbling Home" originally appeared in *Bourbon Penn* Magazine, Nov. 2022

"The Library Virus" originally appeared in *Wilted Pages: An Anthology of Dark Academia* (Shortwave Publishing)

"Show Me" originally appeared in *Broken Antler* Magazine

"A Balanced Breakfast" originally appeared in *Soul Jar* (Forest Avenue Press)

"Food is Poison" originally appeared in *Close to the Bone* Magazine

"Quietus" originally appeared in *No One Will Come Back For Us* (Undertow Publications)

"punctum (o baked alaska for you i am a former american)" originally appeared in *Body Fluids* (bodyfluids.org, Issue03)

"Transmasc of the Red Death" originally appeared in *The Book of Queer Saints II* (Medusa Haus Publishing)

"The Man Outside" originally appeared in *No Trouble At All* (Cursed Morsels Press)

"River Bargain Baby" originally appeared in *Apex* Magazine

"The Prince of Oakland" originally appeared in *Weird Horror* Magazine (Undertow Publications)

"My Mother, The Exoskeleton" originally appeared in *Tower* Magazine

"The Sound of Children Screaming" originally appeared in *Nightmare* Magazine, Oct. 2023

"Endless Yearning" originally appeared in *Seize the Press* Magazine

"Guest Opinion: We must take action regarding the [REDACTED] High School janitor" originally appeared in *Body Fluids* (bodyfluids.org, Issue03)

"A Box of Hair and Nail" originally appeared on *Pseudopod*

"Everything You Dump Here Ends Up in the Ocean" originally appeared in *Fish Gather to Listen* (Horns and Rattle Press)

"Up In the Hills, She Dreams of Her Daughter Deep In the Ground" originally appeared in *Strange Horizons* 'child-bearing' issue

"Embryo" originally appeared in *Mythaxis* Magazine (mythaxis.co.uk)

"Our Roots Will Dry Out in the End" originally appeared in *Interzone*

"As the Music Plays Groovy" originally appeared in *His Soul's Still Dancing: A Nicolas Cage Inspired Fiction Anthology* (Ex-Parrot Press)

"Family Not Going To Heaven" originally appeared on *Cosmorama*, Katy Whitehead, Miranda Cundick & Danielle Chelosky, eds.

CONTENT WARNINGS

Being a work of mature Horror, a degree of violence, gore, sex and/or death is to be expected. For more specific concerns, please check the list of stories below for specific potential triggers suggested by the publisher and by the authors themselves:

"Family Not Going To Heaven" contains scenes of animal death.

"Embryo" contains death during childbirth.

"A Box of Hair and Nail" contains violence against an animal.

"Endless Yearning" contains scenes of sexual assault.

"Up In the Hills, She Dreams of Her Daughter Deep In the Ground" contains scenes of institutional misogyny and coerced sterilization.

"Transmasc of the Red Death" contains transphobia, bigoted remarks and sexual violence.

"The Prince of Oakland" contains homophobia and transphobia.

"punctum (o baked alaska for you i am a former american)" contains homophobia.

"Quietus" contains scenes of military violence.

"The Sound of Children Screaming" contains scenes of gun violence in a school setting.

Grab another Tenebrous title!

Grab another Tenebrous title!

TENEBROUS PRESS

aims to drag the malleable Horror genre into newer, Weirder territory with stories that are incisive, provocative, intelligent and terrifying; delivered by voices diverse and unsung.

FIND OUT MORE:
www.tenebrouspress.com
Social Media: @TenebrousPress

NEW WEIRD HORROR

www.ingramcontent.com/pod-product-compliance
Lightning Source LLC
Chambersburg PA
CBHW030137010826
48973CB00002B/597